STUDY SCORES
OF HISTORICAL STYLES

STUDY SCORES
OF HISTORICAL STYLES
Volume II

Harry B. Lincoln
*State University
of New York
at Binghamton*

Stephen Bonta
Hamilton College

PRENTICE-HALL   Englewood Cliffs, NJ 07632

MT
6.5
S88
v.2

Library of Congress Cataloging-in-Publication Data

LINCOLN, HARRY B.
  Study scores of historical styles.

  Includes bibliographies, discographies,
and indexes.
    1. Music appreciation. Music collections.
  2. Musical analysis. Music collections.
  I. Bonta, Stephen. II.–Title.
MT6.5.L56–1986   85-752003
ISBN   0-13-858911-9 (v. 1)
ISBN   0-13-858853-8 (v.2)

Editorial/production supervision and
  interior design by Martha Masterson
Cover design by 20/20 Services, Inc.
Manufacturing buyer: Raymond Keating
Page layout by Debra Lopes

ISBN 0-13-858853-8 01

PRENTICE-HALL INTERNATIONAL (UK) LIMITED, *London*
PRENTICE-HALL OF AUSTRALIA PTY. LIMITED, *Sydney*
PRENTICE-HALL CANADA INC., *Toronto*
PRENTICE-HALL HISPANOAMERICANA, S.A., *Mexico*
PRENTICE-HALL OF INDIA PRIVATE LIMITED, *New Delhi*
PRENTICE-HALL OF JAPAN, INC., *Tokyo*
PRENTICE-HALL OF SOUTHEAST ASIA PTE. LTD., *Singapore*
EDITORA PRENTICE-HALL DO BRASIL, LTDA., *Rio de Janeiro*

To Betty and Lois

CONTENTS

Song

Choral Music

Chamber Music

PREFACE

The present anthology, though designed primarily for students in music history courses, may, by its nature, prove suitable for those in some introductory courses as well. Our purpose—deriving from the original meaning of the term anthology: a gathering of flowers—has been to assemble a collection of pieces from the Western tradition, each of which is generally recognized to be of superior musical value, is readily available on recordings, and is representative in a variety of ways of the time in which it was composed.

Our purpose has further been to furnish each piece with a commentary so that instructors might, if they chose, turn students loose with any piece with the assurance that they would have the wherewithal to learn something about it. To this end important musical terms are printed in boldface at their first appearance and there defined; the index serves as a glossary since it indicates both where these terms have been defined, and where else in the text they have been used.

It should be said, though, that the commentaries are not intended to be exhaustive in nature, to replace a standard music history text. Rather their purpose is to introduce students to a variety of aspects of the history of music (including some of the problems with which any student of music history must deal), to suggest avenues of approach in analysis that might prove fruitful if applied to other pieces from the Western tradition regardless of date, and to furnish some historical background that may increase the student's understanding of the piece. The emphasis in each of the above areas varies from piece to piece, so that instructors will surely have things to say about any piece, if they choose. For example, though a number of commentaries contain remarks concerned with performance practice, an area that is increasingly recognized to be of utmost importance, much has been left unsaid. And there is always more that one can say by way of analytical observations, or on theoretical and historical matters, for any piece.

Any gathering, whether of flowers, or of anything else, is bound to be discriminatory, to be exclusive—in short, to reflect both the propensities and biases of the gatherers and the possible availability of representative examples. Since some repertories are not represented here, and others only barely so, the editors can only hope that their judgment as to which pieces to include and which to exclude, and their success in finding suitable examples that meet the three criteria they have outlined above, will meet with widespread approval.

Only complete pieces—or complete sections of larger works—are included here. Each commentary concludes with a citation of the source for the piece, and a discography—save for those pieces for which a variety of recordings are readily available.

The authors acknowledge with thanks the kind hospitality of the staff of the Guernsey Public Library in Norwich, NY.

Harry B. Lincoln
Distinguished Service Professor of Music
State University of New York at Binghamton

Stephen Bonta
Margaret Bundy Scott Professor of Music
Hamilton College

=86=

SONATA

Domenico Scarlatti (1685–1757)
Sonatas, K. 394–395 (L. 275, 65)

Had Domenico Scarlatti died at the age of thirty-four he would be remembered today as a minor Roman church and opera composer who lived in the shadow of his illustrious father, the Neapolitan composer, Alessandro Scarlatti (see vol. 1, no. 75). But from 1719 when he left Italy for Portugal for employment in the royal court and chapel at Lisbon, his career as one of the great keyboard composers began. In Lisbon he taught the King's daughter, Maria Barbara, a talented harpsichordist. Upon her marriage to Crown Prince Fernando of Spain, Scarlatti moved with her to Madrid, where he lived his last twenty-eight years. During that period he composed for Maria Barbara a corpus of some 500 keyboard sonatas upon which his fame rests today.

Although no autographs of Scarlatti's sonatas survive, they are preserved in various manuscripts, including two complete sets by the same copyist that are found today in archives in Parma and Venice. Our example is drawn from one of these sources rather than from a modern printed edition, to illustrate the clarity of a good manuscript and to show the materials used by an editor in preparing a modern edition. A strong case has been made that the arrangement of the sonatas in these sources suggests that they are intended to be grouped in pairs, usually according to key relationships. In a few cases, in fact, there is thematic affinity between two pieces in a pair. Though such pairing of sonatas is still not universally accepted, it is useful to examine what is regarded as a pair, the first in E minor and the second in E major.

Each sonata is in binary form. Scarlatti's imaginative and varied treatment of this form, the vast range of his thematic and harmonic ideas, and his expectations by way of keyboard technique all contribute to making the sonatas an important part of today's keyboard repertoire. We will begin with the second sonata, which is similar in its handling of binary form to the Baroque dance suite (see vol. I, no. 85). The two strains of the binary form are delineated by double bars and repeat signs. In the first strain there is a clear movement to the dominant. The second strain begins on the dominant with thematic material that is very similar to the opening, and returns to the tonic at the close.

The first sonata, however, appears not to follow this conventional form. It is true that the first strain moves from tonic to dominant; but the second begins with new material that is totally out of character with what has been heard thus far. Another such change of character follows with repeated fifths in the left hand that are coupled with repeated notes and mordents in the right. Familiar material returns at measure 114; it parallels (but now in the tonic) the material that closed the first strain (mm. 39–63). Such musical rhyme, common in binary form, is the one structural characteristic that is common to all Scarlatti sonatas.

The appeal of these works to listener and performer alike comes from their amazing range of harmonic and melodic color. They appear to reflect the composer's infatuation with the sights and sounds that surrounded him in Portugal and Spain. The drone of bagpipes, strumming of guitar or mandolin, sounds of trumpet fanfares and hunting calls and bells—all these are incorporated into a binary form in a manner that gives color to the music without overly disturbing our expectations of order. But this is not program music. Unlike his French contemporaries, Scarlatti never supplies titles for his works. Still, certain passages, such as the arpeggios at the opening of the second strain in the first sonata, or the parallel fifths in the left hand beginning at measure 76 in the same sonata, make one wonder.

Scarlatti's music is a favorite of harpsichordists, not only for its intrinsic musical values but also for Scarlatti's superb handling of the instument. By its nature the harpsichord is incapable of producing either accent or crescendo. Through the use of such ornaments as the mordent, Scarlatti, in effect, creates accents. By the same token he, in effect, creates crescendos by gradually increasing the number of voices. Notice, for example, the shift from two to three to four voices in the first sonata (mm. 14–15) to close a long phrase.

Finally we should mention two other characteristics of Scarlatti's music that contribute to his fame: his harmonic freedom and his expansion of keyboard techinque. One is hard pressed to find freer harmonic treatment in his day than that encountered in measures 64 through 91 in the first sonata. We assume the notation of accidentals is Scarlatti's own. It argues against his use of meantone temperament, common at the time, since three enharmonic equivalents are encountered in the passage: A-flat and G-sharp; D-flat and C-sharp; G-flat and F-sharp. The demands on the keyboard player include crossing of the hands, rapid arpeggios, wide leaps, and intricate passage work. When we listen to his music we are apt to forget that he was born in the same year as J.S. Bach.

The letters *K* and *L* in the title refer to numbers assigned to these sonatas by two different catalogers, Ralph Kirkpatrick and Alessandro Longo, respectively. Both men also edited modern editions of Scarlatti's sonatas, and Kirkpatrick was for many years a concert harpsichordist and wrote the best study to date on Scarlatti.

Source: *Complete Keyboard Works,* ed. Ralph Kirkpatrick (New York: Johnson Reprint), vol. XIV.

Recording: Columbia SL221, Domenico Scarlatti: *Sixty Sonatas*; Odyssey 32260012, *Vol. 2, Scarlatti Sonatas.*

Sonatas   **Scarlatti**

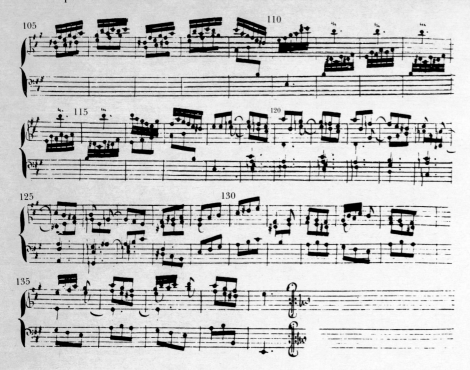

═══87═══

FANTASIA

Carl Philipp Emanuel Bach (1714–1788)
Fantasia I in F

Carl Philipp Emanuel, son of Johann Sebastian Bach, had a university education in law as well as training as a musician. In addition to being a fine performer on the clavichord, his favorite instrument, he was much interested in the aesthetics and psychology of music, especially as it relates to the performer. He combined these skills and interests in his great treatise, *Essay on the True Art of Playing Keyboard Instruments,* a primary source for information on performance practice in his day as well as for the aesthetics of the *Empfindsamer Stil,* a style associated with northern German composers in the mid-eighteenth century. The aim of this style—rendered in English as sensitive style, sensibility style, or sentimental style—was to touch the heart and to move the affections. It was characterized by rapid changes in mood, often accompanied by sudden and unusual modulations, and rhythms and melodies that tended to copy the patterns of emotional speech. One contemporary writer referred to the style as speaking emotively without using words.

Throughout his lifetime C.P.E. Bach wrote a wide variety of sonatas, fantasias, rondos, and other keyboard pieces that display an amazing range of expression. He is one of the important links between the Baroque and Classical styles, and an important predecessor of Haydn and Beethoven. Some of his keyboard writing even presages that of Chopin and other Romantic composers. Although he is most often cited for his contributions to the development of sonata form, it is his compositions in the *Empfindsamer Stil,* especially the fantasias, that mark his importance in music history.

The Fantasia I in F major comes from the fifth of a series of six volumes of keyboard music known as the *Sechs Clavier-Sonaten für Kenner und Liebhaber* ("Six Keyboard Sonatas for Connoisseurs and Amateurs"), and was published in 1785. These collections contain fantasias and rondos in addition to sonatas. Bach wrote these pieces primarily for the fortepiano, the immediate predecessor of the modern piano, and the instrument for which much music of the classical period was written. The fortepiano differs from the modern piano in having a wooden rather than a cast-iron frame, which means that string tensions were a good deal lower and the sound was not so loud and brilliant; its action was also much lighter.

A basic tenet of Bach's philosophy is that a performer cannot move others unless he himself is moved. This, of course, is the central purpose of the *Empfindsamer Stil.* That Bach practiced what he preached is clear from a description of his playing by the English historian Dr. Charles Burney, who visited Bach in 1772. Burney writes: "After the evening meal, Bach played with little interruption until eleven o'clock at night. During that time he grew so animated and possessed, that he not only played, but looked like one inspired. His eyes were fixed, his underlip fell, and drops of effervescence distilled from his countenance. He said that if he were to be set to work frequently, in this manner, he should grow young again."

The fantasia here illustrates many characteristics of Bach's use of *Empfindsamer Stil.* Much of the piece is unmeasured, and there are sudden changes in dynamics, hesitations, constant disruptions, and swift changes in rhythm and phrasing. The piece strikes one as the writing down of a per-former's improvisation. Indeed, the skill of improvising, highly prized by Bach and his contemporaries, is the subject of one chapter in his book.

Source: Carl Philipp Emanuel Bach, *Die sechs Sammlungen von Sonaten, freien Fantasien und Rondos für Kenner und Liebhaber*, ed. Carl Krebs (Leipzig: Breitkopf und Härtel, 1895, reprint edition, ed. Lothar Hoffmann-Erbrecht, 1953), vol. 5, pp. 24–27.

Recording: Spectrum SR 146, *C.P.E. Bach, The Complete Keyboard Fantasias.*

Fantasia

CPE Bach

88

PIANO SONATA

Ludwig van Beethoven (1770–1827)
Piano Sonata in C, op. 111

In the early Classical period the piano sonata, like the string quartet, was intended primarily for music-making by amateurs. The level of its technical demands was thus tailored to the purpose. Although Beethoven's earliest piano sonatas and quartets fall within this tradition, many of his later works in both genres were clearly designed to be heard rather than to be played, suggesting an increasingly important role for the professional. Not only do they make greater technical demands, they also have many effects—primarily rhythmic—that are obscured for the performer simply because he not only hears what is happening but also sees the notation, and hence such silent phenomena as barlines. The present sonata has numerous passages that bear this out.

The last of Beethoven's thirty-two piano sonatas, the present work was dedicated to Archduke Rudolph, son of the Hapsburg emperor Leopold II, a longtime friend of Beethoven and for many years his student in both piano and composition. It was composed during 1821 and 1822. For Beethoven the piano sonata was perhaps the most congenial genre for experimentation since he himself was a virtuoso pianist, known not only for his technique and power but also for the sensitivity and intensity of expression in his playing. His experiments with the form of the sonata are apparent throughout his career. Emulating Haydn and Mozart at the outset, he wrote three-movement sonatas. Subsequently he produced several with four movements, others again with three, and some—like the present work—with only two.

The two movements here embody three of Beethoven's preoccupations in what is generally referred to as his late style: sonata principle and fugue in the first, theme and variations in the second. Later views as to Beethoven's expressive purpose in both movements have been many, most of them arising from the concept of thesis and antithesis: worldly and otherworldly, resistance and submission, real and mystical, animation and response, complexity and simplicity, angry revolt and mystical awareness, and—perhaps the most controversial by today's standards—masculine and feminine. Whatever Beethoven's intent, the order of tempos and relative lengths of the movements are striking: a short first movement that opens with a slow, "majestic" introduction leading to a "fiery and passionate" allegro; and a much longer second movement, a "very simple and singing" adagio.

The first-movement introduction, dominated by the dotted rhythms we associate with the French overture, is filled with examples of the subtlety of Beethoven's late style, and thus with ambiguities of various kinds. The first three pitches in the top voice hint at the opening of the principal theme in the following allegro since they are identical, although the order is different. Beethoven's manner of defining the tonic here is characteristic of many late works: Instead of being boldly stated at the outset, as would have been the case in sonatas by Haydn and Mozart, it emerges only towards the end of the first phrase (m. 2), at the dynamic low point, and is followed immediately by a dominant chord that closes the phrase with a flourish. Thus the ambiguity inherent in the opening diminished-seventh chord is only gradually removed. A similar subtlety is apparent in his initial definition of meter. (We speak here of meter as an aural rather than a visual phenomenon, evident solely through beats, accents, and the resultant groupings, rather than through time signatures and barlines.) Accents and harmonic rhythm at the outset present a clear pattern of alternating quintuple and triple meter, with the first downbeat falling on the second beat of measure 1, the next on the third beat of measure 2. It is only in measures 6 through 10 that the four-beat pattern implicit in his time signature emerges, albeit with the accent falling (as we see, but can we hear it?) on the second beat. Ironically, just as the meter becomes clear, the sense of tonic blurs. Hindsight from the standpoint of measure 10 tells us that we have gone nowhere tonally, that the bass has merely traced an octave, moving upward by semitone. But how tension rises as we undergo the tonal uncertainties in this passage! Just as tonal matters are again set right with a clear arrival on the dominant (m. 11), Beethoven introduces a new ambiguity, concerned now with rhythm and the placement of the beat. The sforzandos on even-numbered eighth notes inevitably come to be heard as the beat, especially since each is reinforced by dissonant appoggiaturas. By the next measure, however, the beat has shifted back to its earlier position.

In the ensuing allegro, which uses the conventions of sonata form (see discussion in no. 90), another sort of emergence is encountered—that of a theme. Beginning as an upward, four-note flourish to the tonic (mm. 17–18), the principal theme next grows to six notes, ending on a fermata (mm. 19–20), and finally extends to a rounded statement sixteen notes long (mm. 20–22). Sounding much like a fugue subject, this final form will be used as such in the development (mm. 76–90), after having served in the bridge (mm. 35–47) and the closing section (mm. 58–64). The tightly constructed exposition, devoted almost singlemindedly to the principal theme, is unusual in that Beethoven turns to the submediant for the second key area (mm. 50–69). The new material stated here reappears in the tonic during the recapitulation, but in a much expanded treatment (mm. 116–146). Also noteworthy in the exposition is Beethoven's exploitation of the extremes of the keyboard for new kinds of sonorities. In two instances, the two hands lie a full five octaves apart (mm. 65, 142). Other new sonorities arise from passages where a part is doubled at the interval of two octaves (mm. 67–69, 143–146), or of three (m. 91). The development, organized as a fugue, grows organically and imperceptibly into the recapitulation, which arrives all but unannounced (mm. 90–91), but is immediately restated in its original form, in octaves (mm. 92–93). The movement closes with a short coda, based again upon the principal theme (mm. 146–158).

The second movement, a theme and variations, employs a rhythmic scheme common to the form in the classical period: Successive variations are built on progressively shorter note values, creating in effect a rhythmic crescendo. This example is unique, however, in that it progresses not by the customary powers of two—half notes, quarters, eighths, etc.—but rather by threes, in a rather complex fashion. (The reader may wish to test the appropriateness of Beethoven's successive time signatures and notation to his intent as expressed in the tempo indication *L'istesso tempo*.) Following the practice of earlier Classical composers in variation sets, he uses for his theme a binary form that is thoroughly anchored in C major in the first strain, moves to the relative minor at the beginning of the second, and returns to the tonic at its close. The simple melody of the theme is retained and progressively embellished by shorter note values throughout the first three variations. In the first variation (mm. 17–32), rhythmic displacements in the left hand—downbeats here almost invariably arrive early—contribute to the gradual intensification of movement. However, at roughly the same spot in this and the following two variations (mm. 28, 44, and 61), just as the return of the tonic is imminent, Beethoven introduces some sort of rhythmic ambiguity, coordinated with a crescendo and delayed resolution of the dominant, that momentarily obscures the meter. In addition, in each case the dominant arrives a bit earlier than it did in the original theme.

In the fourth variation (mm. 64–96), the rapid progression in rhythmic activity is abruptly replaced by an almost complete suspension of movement. The main tension here results from the accentual conflict between the hands. Subtle appoggiaturas on what appear to be offbeat figures in the right hand (mm. 66, 67, and 69) give a sense of beat that is occasionally contradicted by changes in the left hand (mm. 70–71). Now the repetitions of each strain (mm. 72–80, 89–96) are themselves varied, and play off a high, almost unworldly sonority against the darker sonority of each intitial statement. A break in the binary structure (mm. 97–105), the customary gesture signaling the end in Classical variation sets, leads one to believe that the close is imminent. The final signal of this, a cadential trill on D, turns out to be deceptive, and serves instead as an agent for opening out the piece in a new and unexpected direction through a modulation to E-flat. Instead of resolving downward to C as originally expected, this trill now resolves upward to E-flat (m. 118). During this passage much of the melody of the first strain is restated. The closing notes of this strain, used in a sequence, lead back to the tonic for a final variation (mm. 130–146) in which the original melody, now without repetitions, is clearly present. This is followed by a true coda that opens by developing the descending motive that begins the theme (mm. 146–160) and incorporates a final restatement of the first strain (mm. 161–169). (The reader may find it a challenge to determine the meter of the final three measures.)

Source: Beethoven, *Werke* (n.d., reprinted by Kalmus), vol. 22, pp. 129–148.

Recordings: Numerous available.

Piano Sonata in C   **Beethoven**

ARIETTA.
Adagio molto semplice e cantabile.

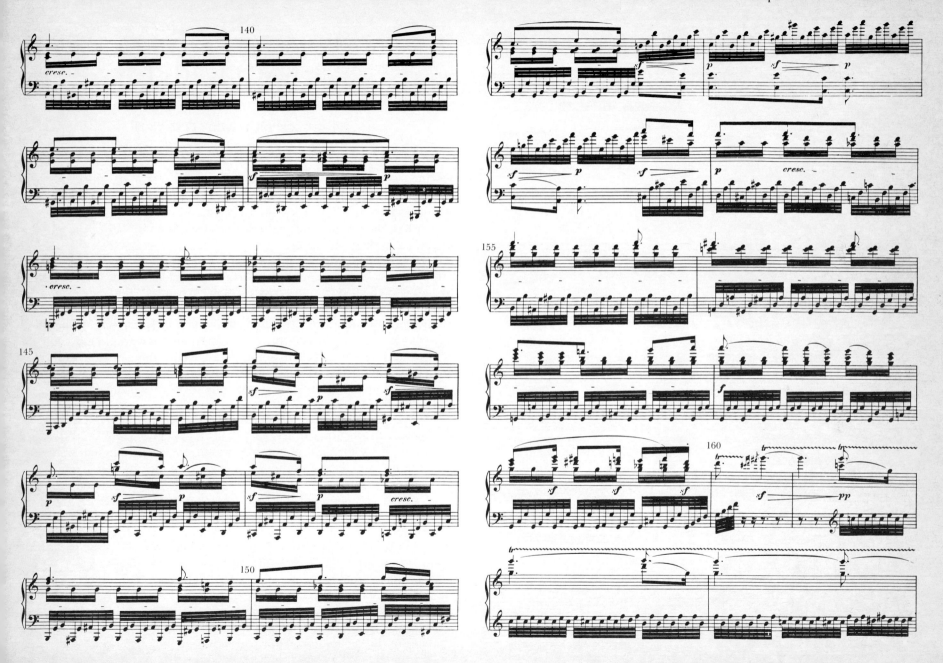

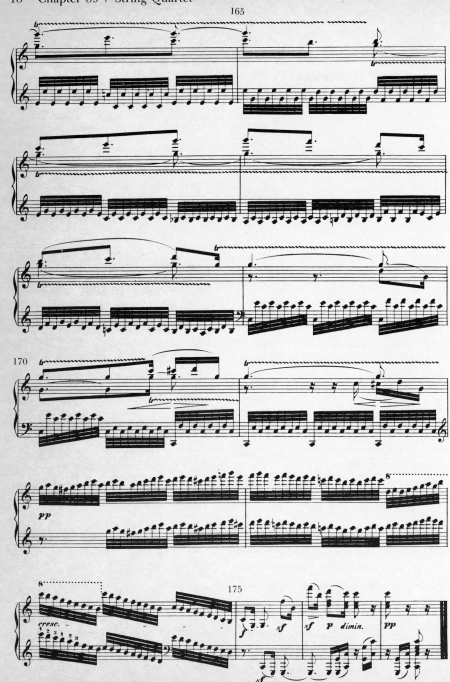

STRING QUARTET

Franz Joseph Haydn (1732–1809)
Quartet in C major, op. 33, no. 3, movement 1

Haydn is generally recognized today as the central figure in the creation of the Viennese Classical style. His proving grounds for stylistic experimentation were primarily the string quartet and symphony, in both of which he established the premises of the style, including the number of movements in each and their character.

The present work is taken from one of the set of six quartets Haydn offered to his Viennese publisher, Artaria, in October 1781. They were the first quartets he had composed in ten years. When soliciting patrons for the quartets, Haydn noted that they were written in a new and special way. Many scholars today argue that his comment is more than merely the usual hyperbole employed in sales promotion, although few would agree on exactly what is new about them. Some see a new prominence of humor, others a new kind of texture in which motives move easily and almost imperceptibly from primary thematic roles to subordinate roles as accompaniment.

Given here is the first movement of the third quartet in the set, known during the nineteenth century as "The Bird" because many heard twitterings in its profusion of grace notes. As was his custom with first movements, Haydn employed the conventions of sonata form (see discussion in no. 90). The connection with its origins in binary form is particularly clear here since Haydn has specified that both parts are to be repeated: exposition and development/recapitulation. As is customary, the coda here lies outside the convention and follows the final repeat.

In a sense the movement is monothematic since the principal theme (mm. 1–6) reappears at the beginning of the second key area (m. 27), now in a subsidiary role in the second violin; and again, in diminution, in the closing section of the exposition (m. 43). In the first two instances we have examples of the change of role that material can undergo, moving from a leading to a supporting function. Another example of this shift in role occurs in the closing section. When the eighth-note motive heard in the first violin (mm. 44–45) moves into the viola and cello (mm. 46–47), it changes roles simply because the first violin goes on to complete the phrase. A similar course of events occurs in the repetition of this phrase (mm. 48–56).

Charles Rosen has commented on the rhythmic subtlety of the principal theme. Six measures long, it is constructed in such a way as to reinforce the indicated crescendo. Initially the first violin increases rhythmic activity from whole notes to halves; the entrance of the cello carries the process a step further by moving in quarter notes. Moreover, the potential decrease in energy brought about by a descending line in the first violin is counteracted by the rising line in the cello. Both initial statements of the theme are furthermore incomplete; in each case the first violin ends on a weak beat on the dominant. The same situation holds for all subsequent statements of this theme save the last, at the very end of the coda (mm. 162–167).

It is left to the reader to determine the relationship between the material in the development and that in the exposition. But the way Haydn handles the return to the recapitulation, so characteristic of his wit, deserves brief comment. Almost all signs in measures 84 through 87 are of the imminent appearance of the recapitulation: the all but nonexistent melodic activity, a pedal on the dominant, slow harmonic rhythm, and a decrescendo. Clearly, what follows is hardly the recapitulation. When it finally does arrive (m. 108), it comes as a complete surprise, out of left field. The key is E minor, and the context leads one to expect the closing theme from the exposition. Only as the theme unfolds does the harmony veer back to the tonic.

Source: Haydn, Quartet op. 33, no. 3. Used by permission of Belwin Mills Publishing Corp.

Recordings: Numerous available.

Quartet in C major   **Haydn**

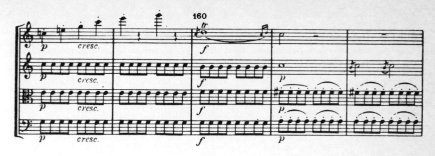

90

SYMPHONY

Franz Joseph Haydn (1732–1809)
Symphony no. 85 in B-flat major (*La Reine*)

As early as the 1760s Haydn's music was well known in Paris, even though at the time he was working in relative isolation as *Kapellmeister* at Esterháza, a giant country estate east of Vienna. It is no surprise, therefore, that he received a commission in about 1784 from le Comte d'Ogny, a backer of one of the Parisian concert societies then flourishing, Le concert de la loge Olympique, to write six symphonies for the society. It is also no surprise that the works should have been so well received by the French aristocrats

who attended the concerts. In fact, when it was first performed in 1787, Symphony no. 85 was the favorite of the French queen, Marie Antoinette, and was subsequently published in Paris with the subtitle "La Reine de France."

Some consider this symphony to be among the finest Haydn ever wrote, noteworthy not only for its brilliance, elegance, and wit, but also for the inventiveness and expansiveness in the handling of its form. Like all of his mature symphonies, it comprises four movements, only the second of which, the slow movement, is in a contrasting key. It also supplies superb examples of the ways in which binary form, borrowed from dance music, could be manipulated to create various Classical formal conventions. In order to facilitate understanding, we shall proceed in our discussion from the simple to the complex, beginning with the third movement.

It is in Haydn's third movements that the origins of binary form in dance are most obvious. Labeled **Menuetto** (= minuet), they comprise, in fact, two stylized dances in a characteristic triple meter. The term *Trio* for the second of these dances survives from an earlier Baroque practice in which this dance was performed by a trio of instruments. Although the practice was no longer observed by Haydn's time, he and his contemporaries tended to treat winds as solo instruments for the second dance, as one sees here. In performance the trio is followed by a return to the minuet, traditionally played today without repetitions. The resultant overall structure is thus *ABA'*.

The binary form, as Haydn employs it in this movement, comprises a clear order of events. In the first repeated section (often called the first strain), a musical statement is made. The second section (or strain) consists of a departure from this opening statement—a departure that often comprises both key and musical material—and a subsequent complete return to the opening statement. The series of events we have just outlined is usually referred to as "rounded binary form."

These stylized dances, which in Haydn's hands become longer and far more complex than functional dances, provide an ideal introduction to his inventiveness and wit in enlivening simple forms through manipulation. It goes without saying that any such manipulation carries the risk of obscuring a convention if introduced too early in a piece. Thus it is that Haydn wisely saves this kind of wit for later in the form. In the minuet it consists of tacking on a sizable section following the end of the return (mm. 24–38)—a section that all but doubles the length of the second strain, in fact. Haydn takes a different tack in the trio where he defers, at almost interminable length, the expected return in the second strain. The proportions of the form are such that a return could easily—and comfortably—have been introduced at measure 55. Instead it appears some fifteen

measures later, only after each wind player has had his solo, and following an emphatic fermata, or hold, on the dominant.

Also noteworthy in this movement is the fact that the first strain of the minuet comprises a single phrase, while the first strain of the trio, more conventional in nature, comprises two balanced phrases in an easily perceived antecedent-consequent relationship—even though the two melodic phrases differ by only a single note. Typically the melodies in Haydn's trios seem intended to evoke country peasant dances.

In the second movement we see another way in which binary form could generate larger forms. Haydn employs an old French folksong, "La gentille et jeune Lisette," as the theme for a set of four variations—a gesture that was sure to endear him to his Parisian audiences. The theme, as well as each variation, is in binary form, as was customary in Classical style. In variation technique, something must change and something else must remain the same. A history of the technique would thus trace which musical elements—melody, harmony, rhythm, etc.—belong in each category. In the Classical era the constant is the overall harmonic structure of the theme, which means the key as well. The original melody may or may not be present in successive variations. In this case it is all but omnipresent, being embellished by changes of color (m. 23), the addition of passing tones (m. 96), or the addition of a countermelody (m. 73). Local harmonic changes may occur if the composer includes, as Haydn does here, a variation in the minor mode (m. 45). In parts of only one variation, however (mm. 27 and 41), does Haydn momentarily depart from the stated theme.

The process of closure in a theme and variations is of particular interest. The question is: If one employs a series of identical structures—binary forms, that is—how does one signal the listener that the end has arrived? Haydn's solution, employed by his contemporaries as well, is to break the structure in the last variation. Here the second strain is not repeated, and the lock-step structure is broken at measure 114 by cadential action and a concentration on the opening of the theme.

In Haydn's first movement we see how the binary form, through great expansion, becomes an elaborate convention that was to be employed within the symphony, in chamber works for all sorts of combinations, and as independent pieces such as opera and concert overtures. Called variously *sonata form*, *sonata-allegro form*, or *first movement form*, its derivation from binary form is clear if one notes all of Haydn's indicated repetitions. The expanded first strain is now called the *exposition*; the two parts of the second strain are now called the *development* and the *recapitulation*, respectively. The *exposition* is clearly divided into two key areas and normally comprises, in the following order: a statement of a theme, a bridge passage to the second key area, a statement of what is usually a new theme in the second key, and a closing section made up of cadential action to signal the end of the exposition. The *development section* ranges widely through different keys, avoiding the tonic, and uses as material elements of the thematic material introduced in the exposition and, perhaps, some new thematic material. The *recapitulation* repeats the material from the exposition, usually in the same order, except that the second key area has been transposed to the tonic, thereby righting the tonal imbalance established in the exposition. Occasionally, as here, there may be a slow introduction that often resembles the opening of a French overture (see Vol. I, no. 64) through its use of dotted rhythms. There may also be, though there is not here, a coda that follows the recapitulation.

Haydn carefully differentiates his thematic statements from connective tissue such as bridge passages and closing sections. The former usually consist of several short, balanced phrases as in the first theme here, which comprises three phrases (mm. 12–23). Bridge passages, by contrast, consist of more continuous action, are usually *forte,* and involve one or two motives (mm. 42–61). In this bridge passage Haydn employs scale passages first heard in the slow introduction (m. 4). Development sections tend toward more continuous action as Haydn works over various thematic elements.

Often, as here, Haydn will employ the same theme for both key areas in the exposition, thereby creating a monothematic sonata form. The two forms of the theme will usually be subtly distinguished by a change of color. In this instance the theme in the second key area is entrusted to the oboe, both in the exposition (mm. 78–96) and in the recapitulation (mm. 238–256).

This movement abounds in examples of Haydn's wit. One notes first the unexpected *forte* passage in the dominant minor where the second theme should occur in the exposition (mm. 62–70). The outburst is righted by a return to bridge material (mm. 70–77) that prepares for a statement of the "real" second theme. This same *forte* passage, now in the major, serves to open the development section (mm. 114–133). Then there is the false return, in the wrong key, beginning at measure 134 in the development. And finally, the assiduous preparation for the recapitulation (mm. 191–211), which unfortunately prepares the wrong key. With no warning the listener is literally dumped back into the tonic. One will also note that Haydn employs material from the closing section of the exposition (mm. 105–107) for one section in the development (mm. 180–190).

The fourth movement employs a special kind of rondo that Haydn appears to have developed. A rondo comprises an alternation between a main theme, called the *rondo theme,* and two or more contrasting sections: *ABACA, ABACADA,* etc. The rondo theme always appears in the tonic, contrasting sections being in other keys. Haydn's version of rondo form, usually called *sonata-rondo,* combines elements of both sonata and rondo form, having two themes and a development section arranged in the following order:

Theme	A B A		C	A B A
Key	I V I		other keys	I I I

Two other characteristics of the sonata-rondo are (1) the use of a binary form for the rondo theme, and (2) the stressing of at least one of the returns to the rondo theme, in this case the return following the development (C).

This particular example is noteworthy in several respects. First, the second theme (m. 38) is clearly derived from the first, or rondo theme, so that this example approaches a monothematic rondo. Second, the development section (m. 86) grows seamlessly out of the first return of the rondo theme since its opening measures function at the same time as the expected return at the end of a rounded binary form. Third, a superb example of Haydn's rhythmic wit is encountered in the preparation for the return following the development (mm. 146–163). The passage has been written in such a way that downbeats can be heard to lie either in the lower strings or in the first violin part. The listener can easily perceive them either way.

Finally, two notes concerning the performance of this symphony. H. C. Robbins Landon, the great Haydn scholar, reports that an eighteenth-century mechanical clock survives with the trio from the minuet as its tune. (Mechanical clocks were the rage in the latter half of the eighteenth century, many composers writing pieces for them.) Such an instrument is, in a real sense, the phonograph record of the time, since it can indicate how musical notation was then interpreted. This particular clock shows that the apparent grace notes in measures 41, 45, and elsewhere were performed as appoggiaturas, on the beat, and were long—that is, they had the value of an eighth note in this context. Second, the orchestra for the Concert de la loge Olympique at the time Haydn's symphonies were performed had some forty violins and ten double basses, far more than Haydn ever had at his disposal at Esterháza, and almost as many as are found today in major symphony orchestras.

Source: Used by permission of Belwin Mills Music Publishing Corporation from Kalmus Miniature Orchestra Scores No. 109.

Recordings: Numerous available.

Symphony no. 85   Haydn

II

III

Menuetto. Allegretto

IV

══91══

PIANO CONCERTO

Wolfgang Amadeus Mozart (1756–1791)
Concerto in B-flat major, K. 595, movement 1

As a pianist, much of whose income always derived from his own public performances, Mozart was understandably preoccupied with the piano concerto throughout his short lifetime. Among his earliest compositions are arrangements as concertos of seven piano sonatas by other composers, prepared for use on his concert tours. The first keyboard concerto that is entirely his was written in 1773. Most of the later ones were composed for concerts of his own music that, in the fashion of the time, he offered for his own benefit to Viennese audiences. But anonymous concert audiences in any age can be fickle. By the time Mozart composed the present concerto, which dates from the last months of his life, he could no longer attract a paying audience for his music alone. Consequently this one was included in a concert sponsored by a Viennese clarinettist named Bähr. Mozart also wrote concertos for flute, oboe, clarinet, bassoon, and horn.

Those analyzing Mozart's concertos have proposed a variety of ways in which they could be grouped. Among the categories proposed have been the locale of composition and hence chronology (e.g., the Salzburg group versus the Viennese group) or the assumed place of performance (e.g., the intimacy of the salon versus the impersonality of the concert hall). The present work, more intimate than earlier concertos intended for the Viennese concert hall, was performed in the chambers of the then caterer to the Hapsburg court, Jahn, on Himmelpfortgasse (Gate of Heaven Street).

The Mozart concerto represents a new synthesis of a number of different elements. First, there were the formal attributes inherited from the Baroque concerto (see vol. 1, no. 82). Second, there was the Classical style cultivated in the sonata and symphony, which, when applied to the concerto, had an effect on both its thematic and tonal plans. Recently, some have argued that another ingredient in the mix is the opera aria as written in the mid-eighteenth century.

From the Baroque concerto came the overall plan of the work: three movements whose tempos alternated in the order fast-slow-fast. Also from the Baroque concerto came the pattern of alternation between a ritornello performed by the orchestra (*tutti*) and sections performed by the solo or

soloists. The pattern is most obvious in the outer movements of the work. Though there is general agreement about this basic plan of alternation, considerable disagreement exists as to just how many statements of the ritornello occur, and hence how many alternations there are. Most would see four statements of the ritornello in the first movement of the concerto included here, as follows:

1–73	Ritornello
74–167	Solo
168–183	Ritornello
184–234	Solo
235–249	Ritornello
250–344	Solo
345–362	Ritornello

It must be remembered that analyses are normally made after the fact by someone other than the creator, and are an attempt to understand what the composer had in mind—a difficult undertaking at best since composers have traditionally been reticent about their own works, Mozart being no exception. With such an interpretation of this work, however, a rapprochement with the elements of sonata form can be seen. The first ritornello can be considered as an exposition since it contains two theme groups, a transition between them, and a closing section. The one thing it lacks is the dynamic contrast in keys characteristic of the exposition. The first solo section and second ritornello together constitute a repetition of the exposition, again with two theme groups, a transition, and a closing section. This time, however, there is a movement to the dominant, and the closing section is assigned to the orchestra alone. The second solo section, being modulatory, therefore functions as a development. The recapitulation, now entirely in the tonic, comprises the last two ritornellos—the second of which again serves as the closing section—and the included solo section, as follows:

1–73	Exposition	[Ritornello]
74–183	Second Exposition	[Solo/Ritornello]
184–234	Development	[Solo]
235–362	Recapitulation	[Ritornello/Solo/Ritornello]

The first two sections in this analysis are usually referred to as the ***double exposition***, and most reasonably derive from an identical thematic and key plan used in the aria in early operas by Mozart and his contemporaries. Here the second exposition is signaled by the entry of the voice, the solo instrument in this instance. One other element of the aria was regularly employed in the concerto: the **cadenza** (= cadence). This is an elaboration of the final important cadence in the recapitulation and normally consisted of an improvised passage performed by the soloist. Since keyboard improvisation was a dying art in Mozart's time, he felt it necessary to supply written-out cadenzas for a number of his concertos—doubtless primarily for those that were to be performed by other pianists. A cadenza in his hand survives for this work.

The roles of soloist and orchestra in the concerto have varied in different historical periods. In the Classical concerto as written by Mozart and Beethoven, there was a participation of equals. Each leads at times, and at others serves as accompaniment. In the nineteenth-century concerto the tendency is for the orchestra to serve in a subsidiary role only, as accompaniment. This shift in roles can be easily heard if one compares the *Music Minus One* recordings (the orchestra part alone) for a Mozart concerto and for one by Chopin.

It is left to the reader to analyze the double exposition and recapitulation. We note only that this concerto is typical of Mozart in introducing a new second theme for the solo instrument in the second exposition, and that both second themes recur in the recapitulation. We also note that in the opening tutti (mm. 13–15), and elsewhere in the movement, Mozart quotes himself, introducing an idea from the last movement of his Symphony No. 41 (*Jupiter*).

The development section, as so often is the case in Mozart's work, is short. It comprises only fifty of the 362 measures in the movement; but in this short period of time Mozart achieves an intensity and variety of thematic treatments that is remarkable and worthy of close examination. The second exposition, as expected, has closed on the dominant. Typically the following development section first moves away from the dominant—sometimes gently, sometimes abruptly. In this work the sudden shift to B minor (m. 184) from a starting point of B-flat major is startling. The piano plays the opening theme (see mm. 2–5) unchanged in the new key. The wind response from measures 5 through 6—perhaps better termed "a call" since it sounds like a fanfare fragment—is now expanded in the strings (mm. 187–189). The dialogue continues, shifting first to C major and then suddenly to E-flat major (m. 195). The passage from here to the end of the development contains almost continuous contrapuntal writing, and is one of dozens of passages in Mozart's work that mark him as a contrapuntalist on a par with his Baroque predecessors. The opening theme is first heard in imitation in the winds (mm. 196–210) and is followed by an embellished

version in the piano (first heard in measure 74), now in E-flat minor. The piano continues with a long, florid extension made of pianistic figures (arpeggios and scale passages) that sound against fragments of the opening theme in the orchestra. Beginning in measure 218 the two violin parts engage for five measures in a variant of this theme in strict canon. The canon is heard again, now in oboe and bassoon, in measures 228 through 235. The introduction of triplets in the piano (m. 229) intensifies rhythmic activity in preparation for the recapitulation (m. 235). It is by means of such devices that the satisfaction of "return" is sensed by listeners who may know nothing about the workings of music.

In one of the letters to Mozart from his father, Leopold, the father refers to *il filo* ("the thread") in describing the sharing of melodic materials to create an overall sense of continuity. Part of the fascination in listening to any Mozart concerto is to note how smoothly and logically thematic materials move among the various members of the orchestra and are exchanged with the soloist. The opening measures of this development section are illustrative of this sharing of materials, as indeed are many other passages in the movement.

Another letter, this one from Mozart to his father and dating from 1782, indicates Mozart's awareness of the different levels of sophistication among his listeners and the necessity of appealing to all levels. Referring specifically to three recently composed piano concertos, he says: "There are passages here and there from which the connoisseurs alone can derive satisfaction; but these passages are written in such a way that the less learned cannot fail to be pleased, though without knowing why." His success in reaching listeners at any level is still evident today.

The *K* in our title, followed by a number, refers this time (see no. 86) to Ludwig Ritter von Köchel (1800–1877), the Viennese botanist and mineralogist who first cataloged Mozart's works. Köchel listed these works in what he believed to be their chronological order of composition. Professional scholars since have revised Köchel's numberings, but retain the *K* in honor of the magnitude of his achievement at the time, given his lack of expertise and the sparseness of information available to him.

It should be noted that in many recordings the passage from measures 351-357 is inserted following measure 46.

Source: Used by permission of Prentice-Hall, Inc. from William J. Starr and George F. Devine, *Music Scores Omnibus*, 1964, pp. 239–250.

Recordings: Numerous available.

Concerto in B-flat major Mozart

══92══

SYMPHONY

Ludwig van Beethoven (1770–1827)
Symphony no. 3 in E-flat major, op. 55 (Eroica),
movements 1 and 4

The circumstances surrounding the composition of Beethoven's Third Symphony are not altogether clear. What is clear is that when he finished the work in 1803 Beethoven originally intended to label it *Grand Symphony entitled Bonaparte,* probably to honor the person he saw as asserting the rights of mankind against the autocratic political order then prevailing throughout most of Europe. At some point following Napoleon's self-coronation as Emperor in 1804, but before the work was published in 1806, Beethoven decided to retitle it *Heroic Symphony: composed to celebrate the memory of a great man,* suggesting that he had had a change of heart. Other evidence suggests, however, that both before and after the composition and publication of this work, Beethoven's attitude toward Napoleon was decidedly ambivalent, vacillating between admiration and aversion. Whatever his reasons for the original title and for its subsequent change, the heroic character of the work is undeniable.

Many scholars see the *Eroica* as a fusion of two traditions: the sonata principle as brought to perfection by Beethoven's Viennese predecessors, Haydn and Mozart; and postrevolutionary French music by such composers as Méhul and Gossec, which is characterized by high moral purpose and a grand manner. Far surpassing in scale any previous symphony by Beethoven or anyone else, the *Eroica* is longer, louder, and more dissonant. The initial reaction among Beethoven's contemporaries, as reported by his student Czerny, was that the work was "too long, elaborate, incomprehensible, and much too noisy." More recent judgments are that, in spite of its length, the symphony is extremely tightly organized.

The first movement furnishes characteristic examples of the ways in which Beethoven manipulated the formal conventions of his adopted Viennese heritage. It employs the conventions of sonata form, but two sections in particular have been greatly expanded: the development section (mm. 152–397) and the coda (mm. 557–691). The former is the most dramatic part of the convention, with its conflict of themes and keys. The latter, now far more than merely a final confirmation of the tonic, consists of a wide-ranging terminal development that again explores foreign keys before closing the movement.

Beethoven opens with two tutti chords whose several functions suggest how tightly the movement has been constructed. First, they establish both the tonic and the heroic character of the work. If one were to begin instead at measure 3 with the quiet statement of the principal theme by the cellos, omitting these opening chords, no inkling of heroic character would be projected at the outset. These two chords also close the movement. In line with Beethoven's skillful use of rhythmic procedures, these chords have yet another function: to establish a larger metric unit—two measures long, or effectively 6/4—that persists throughout the movement. Almost immediately one hears a syncopation against this larger metric unit, in the violins in measure 10—an even-numbered measure.

For his principal theme Beethoven has chosen a melody that differs markedly from the typical Haydn or Mozart symphonic theme. In place of their balanced pairs of antecedent-consequent phrases, Beethoven employs an idea that is germinal in nature and can readily be developed. Being based on the triad it can also, at an appropriate high point (mm. 655–658), be assigned to the trumpet of his time, a valveless instrument that was incapable of playing anything but the notes of the harmonic series—that is, "bugle calls." Already on the repetition of the theme (m. 15) Beethoven begins to to develop it, concentrating initially on the third measure of the theme. In the course of this second repetition a new syncopated figure, marked by sforzandos, is introduced (mm. 25–35). This figure will assume thematic stature since it reappears in the development at the approach to the climax of the movement (mm. 250–271). Yet another idea, little more than a repeated three-note motive, is introduced as Beethoven modulates to the dominant of the dominant (mm. 45–55) in preparation for the second key area. This idea also plays an important role in the approach to the climax in the development (mm. 220–267). What is fascinating about this latter passage is the gradual transformation in the character of the idea. Initially relaxed and genial—as it was when first presented in the exposition—it becomes increasingly forceful and menacing as Beethoven

increases the interval size between the notes and raises the dynamic level. The transformation of Dr. Jekyll into Mr. Hyde inevitably comes to mind.

One more important idea that can be associated with the first theme area, strongly rhythmic in character, appears in measure 65. This, too, will play a central role later in the movement (mm. 186–220). Looking back over the territory traversed thus far, we see that one of the ways Beethoven ensures long-range drive and cohesion is by means of a rhythmic progression in successive themes. Beginning with half and quarter notes in the principal theme (m. 3), he introduces eighth notes in his third idea (m. 45), and sixteenth notes in the last (m. 65), creating what could be called a rhythmic crescendo.

The second theme area, beginning at measure 83, represents a momentary lowering of intensity; but in time this section leads by steps to another powerful climax that signals the end of the exposition (m. 144).

At the climax of the development (m. 284), and at the farthest remove tonally from his starting key, Beethoven introduces a new theme. Close examination of its bass line reveals, however, that this has been derived from the principal theme by filling in the gaps with stepwise motion. Later, at mm. 326–337, this bass line assumes momentary prominence.

Several other instances of Beethoven's long-range planning in this movement should be discussed briefly. First, there is a diminished-seventh chord at measure 7 that leads quickly back to the tonic. In the recapitulation, however, this same chord (m. 402) leads in an entirely different direction, to F major.

Another passage demonstrating long-range planning is first encountered in the exposition (mm. 57–83). The four-measure opening phrase (mm. 57–60) is followed by another that is clearly a varied repetition of the first. According to the premise of balance that lies behind such repetitions in Classical style, this second phrase should cadence in measure 65. Instead it leads at that very spot to a diminished-seventh chord, and the introduction of a new idea. One must wait yet another eighteen measures for the period to close. The forward drive that results from this imbalance is almost unbelievable. The passage returns in the recapitulation, now in the tonic (mm. 460–486). It begins yet a third time, just when all indications are that the movement is finally reaching a close (mm. 673–680). The strong suspicion raised by this third appearance is that the movement may open out yet one more time. Instead, the second phrase leads now to a dominant seventh chord (m. 681), a final hint of the syncopated passsage first heard at measure 25, and to the closing two chords.

In a similar spot in the closing section of the exposition (mm.

123–131), where the probability is all but 100 percent that the closing cadence is forthcoming, Beethoven introduces, through syncopation, a rhythmic ambiguity that heightens tension to an incredible degree. Syncopation ultimately depends for its effect on an underlying beat. Perhaps you have witnessed a jazz pianist playing without a drummer. If he were to stop tapping his foot, the syncopations on the keyboard would become chaotic and meaningless. If, as in the passage at hand from Beethoven, all parts have the exact same syncopation that systematically omits the first beat of the measure, and if the process is carried on for a sufficiently long time, the listener tends to latch on to whatever remains as somewhere containing a downbeat. No sooner has the listener settled into this certainty than Beethoven introduces a different kind of syncopation (mm. 128-131) that reestablishes the ambiguity and gives the impression of going on for just one chord too many. Even with the clear return of triple meter, Beethoven defers the expected cadence yet another twelve measures, by means of harmonic digressions..

Two final comments on the first movement: The forceful way Beethoven leads into the coda leaves no doubt that the movement, which could well end at this point, is about to open out again. Crude in the extreme—consisting of three sideslipping root-position triads, on E-flat, D-flat, and C—the process is not recommended as a model in voice leading for beginning theory students.

And mention should be made of the famous premature entry of the horn just before the recapitulation begins (m. 394). Thought initially to be an error in counting rests on the part of the horn player, and later to be an error on Beethoven's part, the passage was often "corrected" during the nineteenth century. One possible rationale would argue that heroes are men of action, not given to contemplation or marking time. The transition to the recapitulation had now gone on long enough (twenty-seven measures). The time for action had come.

A final note on Beethoven's attitude toward the limitations posed by his materials. We have already mentioned that the natural trumpet of his day could only play "bugle calls," and that he calls for this instrument at the peroration in the coda of the first movement (mm. 655–658). This is the fourth and final statement of the principal theme, laid out now in four-measure phrases that alternate between tonic and dominant harmonies. Clearly the trumpet can only play the phrase in the tonic, not the ensuing phrase in the dominant. Even so, Beethoven uses it. It is instructive to compare the trumpet part in the score with any modern recording of the work. Invariably conductors "help Beethoven out," adding trumpets—now equipped with valves, of course—to the second phrase in the dominant. Try to imagine what this second phrase would sound like if played as Beethoven wrote it.

Source: Beethoven, *Sämtliche Werke* (Leipzig: Breitkopf & Härtel, 1864-1890). Bd. 1, No. 3.

Recordings: Numerous available.

Symphony no. 3   **Beethoven**

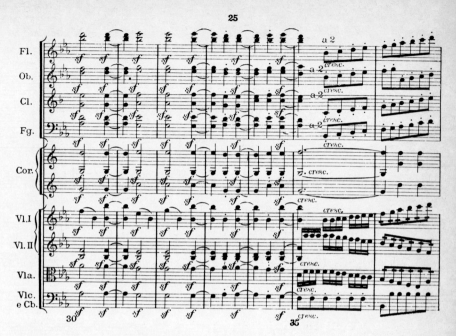

SERIOUS OPERA

Christoph Willibald Gluck (1714–1787)
Orfeo ed Euridice, Act II, scene 1

Time and again over the centuries, opera has been viewed by some as a reprobate that sorely needed to mend its ways. (One can identify serious attempts at opera reform in the seventeenth, eighteenth, and nineteenth centuries.) The reasons for this recurring judgment are not hard to identify. Opera has meant different things to different people throughout its history. Some have looked for and treasured the power that music has to enhance dramatic action. Others, delighting in the sounds of the human voice, have reveled in singing by the latest opera stars, caring little about dramatic plot or its development. Still others have enjoyed the spectacle that was an integral part of many operas staged from the seventeenth through the nineteenth centuries: the burning of Rome, a shipwreck, an erupting volcano. Clearly, whatever approach a composer and librettist took, they could never hope to satisfy all three audiences at the same time. Reformers, including Gluck, have consistently tried to restore the preeminence of dramatic values.

Gluck was a German who had already established himself as a successful composer of both Italian opera seria and French opéra comique by the time he began his fruitful collaboration with the librettist Raniero de Calzabigi in the creation of what are known as his "reform" operas. To this day it is impossible to determine exactly what each man contributed by way of ideas; but there is no doubt that Calzabigi played a major part in the effort. In the famous preface to *Alceste*, the second of the three reform operas produced by the pair, Gluck wrote (or was it Calzabigi's ideas over Gluck's signature?):

> . . . I resolved to divest it [the music] entirely of all those abuses, introduced into it either by the mistaken vanity of singers or by the too great complaisance of composers, which have so long disfigured Italian opera and made of the most splendid and most beautiful of spectacles the most ridiculous and wearisome. I have striven to restrict music to its true office of serving poetry by means of expression and by following the situations in the story, without interrupting the action or stifling it with a useless superfluity of ornaments. . . .

(The preface, which appears in Eric Blom's translation in O. Strunk's *Source Readings in Music History,* continues with a description of other reforms.) It is clear from our quotation that what Gluck was reforming was Italian opera, and specifically opera seria. Gluck's reforms were not created in a vacuum. One sees the effect of his trip to England, where he admired the operas of Handel and was influenced by the great actor David Garrick. Nor were Gluck's reforms without precedent. Some maintain, in fact, that his contribution was primarily to crystallize existing tendencies, taking practices from his immediate predecessors and integrating them into a new whole. Part of his reform consisted of introducing into Italian opera two elements that had always played a central role in French opera: ballet and the chorus. Unlike French opera, however, his use of both was always justified by dramatic action.

The story of Orpheus and Euridice, from Greek mythology, has attracted numerous composers over the centuries, both for opera and for other musical works. (An earlier operatic setting of this myth, by Monteverdi, has been illustrated in vol. I, no. 58). One suspects that its continuing appeal (outside of the love story presented) lies in its exemplification of the incredible power of music. It is simply through his singing and his playing of the lyre that Orpheus is to be able to gain entry to the underworld and to retrieve his wife Euridice.

The first of Gluck's reform operas, *Orfeo,* was written for Vienna and first staged in 1762. It is remarkable for the expressive and noble effect Gluck was able to achieve with the simplest of means. Calzabigi limited the main protagonists to three, eliminating the numerous and often irrelevant subplots involving secondary pairs of lovers that had clogged the action in opera seria. The action moves along with a minimum of text. Individual characters are static—they have a timeless quality, as befits mythological figures—and do not develop as they will in the operas of Verdi and other later composers.

In the Gluck/Calzabigi version of the myth, the action opens with Orpheus and his friends mourning at the grave of Euridice. Orpheus resolves to descend to the underworld to rescue her. Cupid appears and tells him that Zeus will permit him to enter the realm of the dead, and, if he can placate the Furies, Euridice will be returned to him. One other condition is imposed: He must not look back at Euridice as he leads her forth, nor inform her of this restriction.

Our excerpt opens with Orpheus's attempt to gain entry to the underworld (the same scene presented in vol. I, no. 58), and takes place in a cavern near the river Styx. As the curtain rises we see the Furies and Shades, whose dance is at the same time majestic and frightening. At measure 21 an orchestral harp, simulating Orpheus's lyre, signals his entry. Much of the threatening tone in the ensuing chorus by the Furies arises from the fact that they are singing in unison; only gradually, as Orpheus succeeds in placating them, does four-part writing begin to dominate. The opening queries of the Furies are interrupted by another short dance (mm. 34–49), following which they resume their questioning, heightening the tension by now issuing dire threats as well. In measure 64, as the Furies refer to the howling of Cerberus, the three-headed dog that is prepared to devour unauthorized intruders into the underworld, we are given unmistakable proof of its presence by the orchestra. At measure 89 the harp returns and we hear Orpheus's justly famous pleas to the Furies and their cries of "No." Only near the close of the section (mm. 132–133) is there a momentary hint of vocal display (which does not appear in Gluck's original version of the opera). The threatening tone of the Furies gives way to attempts to dissuade Orpheus by depicting the horrors of the underworld; but his pleas become more impassioned as he describes his own hell of despair (mm. 171–192). Note that his agitation engenders a vocal line that is both more complex rhythmically and more disjunct. After one further exchange the Furies relent and depart as Orpheus ventures forth into the underworld.

Seldom in opera has such a moving effect been accomplished with such economy of means. Although this scene (276 measures long) is laid out as a succession of dances, choruses, and solos, continuity is assured early in the scene by linking several successive sections by means of half cadences (mm. 33, 49), which are often accompanied by the performance instruction *attacca.* Gluck uses several simple musical devices to depict the action in the scene. He symbolizes the antagonism between Orpheus and the Furies at the outset by assigning to each a different key, meter, and orchestration. For Orpheus these are E-flat major, duple meter, and an orchestra behind the scenes that consists of harp and strings; for the Furies, C minor, triple meter, and the pit orchestra comprising oboe, bassoon, strings, and occasional trombones and cornetto. As the antagonists reach agreement—that is, as Orpheus's magic begin to work—both parties settle on F minor for the rest of the scene (m. 160ff.). At the same time, however, Gluck assures that the Furies remain in character throughout by assigning to them a rhythmic pattern that recurs over fifty times:

The climax of the scene is both simple and powerful: The granting of entry by the Furies is accompanied by a passage wherein the opening of the gates they speak of is suggested by the contrary motion of the outer voices in measures 239 to 254, a passage that is immediately repeated with the outer voices exchanged (mm. 255–264). The stage directions here make clear the effect Gluck and Calzabigi had in mind:

> The furies and monsters begin to withdraw and, as they disappear through stage exits, they repeat the last stanza of the chorus, which continues as they depart and finally finishes in confused murmuring.

Gluck's reforms of opera seria did not include eliminating the castrato. In fact, the role of Orpheus was written for one of the most famous castrati of his day, Gaetano Guadagni. Twelve years later, in 1774, Gluck prepared a different version of this opera for Parisian performance—a version that therefore sought to accommodate French tastes in opera. Among the changes made were the addition of a number of arias and ensembles, a sizable expansion in the role of the dance, and the substitution of the tenor voice for the male contralto. Some argue that in the process he transformed the character of the opera. In place of the castrato voice, which by its nature has an unworldly quality and is thus considered suitable for mythological figures that are larger than life, Gluck substituted the tenor, which inevitably suggests to these observers that Orpheus is now a human hero. Such an argument runs into difficulty when one considers the other members of the cast. For example, is Euridice to be denied the aura of a mythological being simply because she sings in a "natural" voice? Must she, too, be "altered" to attain this status?

Setting aside the above argument, there is no question but that this opera poses problems for the present-day producer and conductor. Most modern productions and recordings employ the Viennese version, though often with a few additions from the French version. This is done because of the greater dramatic integrity most find in the Viennese version, and in spite of the fact that it calls for the castrato voice. Since castrati are now in short supply, and many modern audiences are troubled by seeing a woman portraying a man onstage, the compromise that is increasingly accepted involves using a countertenor for the role of Orpheus.

We reproduce here a score of the version Gluck prepared for Paris. In this particular scene there are few changes from the Viennese version, though the reader is invited to compare several of the recordings listed below to determine what these differences are. The reader should be warned, however, that regardless of the version being employed, all recordings are in Italian.

Source: Copyright © 1959 by G. Schirmer, Inc. All Rights Reserved. Reprinted by permission.

Recordings: Erato 750423 (Paris version, though sung by a contralto); Angel DSBX 3922 (Viennese version); DGG 139268/9 (Viennese version, though sung by a tenor); Vanguard BGS 70686/7 (Viennese version, though with several additions of vocal display from the Paris version).

Orfeo and Euridice   **Gluck**

Act Two

A frightening, rocky landscape near the gates of the Underworld, veiled in a dark mist occasionally pierced by flames. The dance of the Furies and Monsters is interrupted by sounds of the lyre of the approaching ORPHEUS. When he comes into view they all join in the ensuing chorus.

Une contrée épouvantable, hérisée de rochers, au delà du Styx; au loin s'élève une fumée épaisse, sombre, les flammes y jaillissent de temps en temps. Les spectres et les esprits commencent une danse qu'Orphée interrompt par l'harmonie de sa lyre; à la vue d'Orphée toute la troupe entonne le premier chœur qui suit.

SCENE I

Orpheus. Furies and monsters of the underworld.

No. 18 Dance of the Furies

No. 19 Harp Solo Chorus

No. 20 Dance of the Furies

No. 21 Chorus

(The Furies dance around Orpheus to frighten him.)
(Pendant le chœur les esprits dansent autour d'Orphée pour l'effrayer.)

No. 23 Chorus

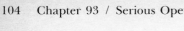

(The chorus answers Orpheus in a somewhat milder manner, showing signs of compassion)
(Le chœur apaisé répond à Orphée avec un peu plus de pitié dans l'expression.)

No. 24 Aria

No. 25 Chorus
(In a milder manner)   *(Encore plus apaisé.)*

94

OPERA BUFFA

Wolfgang Amadeus Mozart (1756–1791)
The Marriage of Figaro, K. 492, Opening scene

Widely acknowledged as the greatest opera composer Western civilization has known, Mozart already had considerable experience composing opera when he joined with the librettist Lorenzo Da Ponte in Vienna to write an opera based on Beaumarchais's play *Le mariage de Figaro.* Their choice was obviously dictated by the controverisal nature of the play. Originally written in 1778, it was kept off the boards in France by Louis XVI until 1784 as politically subversive, since it depicted a philandering aristocrat who was outwitted by his servants. (The role of the play in stimulating thought that was to lead to the French Revolution in 1789 has been noted by many writers.) News of the play traveled fast throughout Europe: Early in 1785, Joseph II, the Austrian emperor, was forced at the last minute to impose a similar ban on its production, in a German translation, in Vienna. Mozart and Da Ponte surely sensed that forbidden fruit is always the most enticing; an opera based on this play, if it could be gotten past the censors, would be bound to have an immediate and widespread appeal and thus be assured of commercial success. Da Ponte claims in his memoirs that he was able to persuade the emperor to relax his ban for an operatic version of the play by assuring him that the more objectionable parts of the play had been removed. (One of the lines in Beaumarchais's earlier play, *The Barber of Seville,* is germane: "What is not allowed to be said these days is sung.") At any rate the opera received its Viennese premiere on 1 May 1786 and was an immediate success. (The emperor's restriction on encores in opera appeared within days of the first performance, and seems to have been directed specifically at the number of these that took place in early performances of *Figaro.*)

Mozart chose to use the conventions of opera buffa (see vol. I, no. 63), but with some significant alterations. Though the language is Italian, and recitative—both *secco* and *accompagnato*—is also present, as is aria style, the original two-act format has been expanded to four acts because of the length of the work. Even so, Mozart hints at the two-act format by employing the characteristic ensemble finale only at the ends of acts two and four. Mozart's increasing use of ensembles elsewhere in the acts—as in the opening scene presented here—points to a lessening in importance of the traditional aria, whose dramatic purpose was to allow characters to react to a situation. Though ensembles are in aria style and have closed forms, they differ from the aria in that action is taking place through dialogue, as we shall see presently. Successive closed forms are numbered (hence the term *number opera*), and recitative is the main vehicle for carrying the action forward through dialogue. As for the plot, it is highly complicated and contains its share of devices from opera buffa, such as costume exchanges and mistaken identities. And like the earlier opera buffa, *Figaro* also owes much to the stock figures from the *commedia dell'arte*: for example, the benighted old doctor and the wily servant.

Opera is intended to be seen as well as to be heard. In making analyses of any opera, we are of necessity ignoring one critically important dimension with immediate appeal, the visual element. Though the matter of the interrelationship between the visual and aural aspects of opera has as yet received little attention, it seems clear that the visual element plays an important part in determining our sense of pacing—of how fast things happen or should happen. In its absence things seem to happen more slowly. (Stravinsky commented on this problem in connection with the recording of *The Rake's Progress,* his last opera.) This, then, is another instance of quoting out of context (see vol. I, no. 1). Still, it is possible to make observations about the relationship between text and music.

The primary role of music in opera has been to reinforce the dramatic situation outlined in the text. The composer has many musical means at his disposal. He might, for example, associate certain types of thematic material with a particular character. Through changes in this material the composer can thus effect "character development." As for the text, in opera arias, as in song, it is often repeated, either for emphasis or to accommodate a satisfying musical form. In opera such repetitions are also necessary to ensure that the listener clearly understands the text. The challenge to the composer is thus to create a work that balances the differing and often contradictory demands of music and drama to create a convincing dramatic whole. Some of the ways in which Mozart accomplishes this aim are revealed by a close examination of the opening scene in *Figaro.*

The curtain rises on a mundane domestic scene. While Susanna sits before the mirror admiring a new hat, Figaro paces the floor measuring the room. (The discrepancy between the Italian original of his "measurements" and various singing translations in English supplies an amusing and instructive example of the problems that arise in performing opera in translation.) The orchestral introduction not only sets the scene and settles the audience, but also serves to introduce the main musical themes of the first ensemble. Figaro is represented by a rather plodding two-note figure with a downward leap that fits the numbers he calls out. Susanna is represented by a contrasting conjunct and suave melodic line that ends in a coquettish arpeggiated figure. We note that Figaro's theme moves from tonic to dominant, and that Susanna's leads back to the tonic.

At first glance there is nothing unusual about these themes. But consider the dramatic situation at the outset. All we learn from the first ensemble is that the two are about to be married. Only in the subsequent recitative do we discover why Figaro measures the room. In other words, the action begins *in medias res,* in the middle of things. The manner in which Mozart suggests this state of affairs is indicative of his keen sensitivity to dramatic values, manifest in all of his mature operas. Each downward leap in Figaro's vocal line starts from a pitch one step higher than before, and therefore traces an upward scale. A lesser composer would probably have begun this line with G (that is, the tonic) rather than A as the upper pitch (m. 20). Mozart implies that the G had appeared before the curtain rose, and that the action is already under way.

We also learn from this opening ensemble that Susanna will be the stronger—and more perceptive—of the two. As the action proceeds Figaro turns from his measuring to join Susanna in admiring her hat—in the process abandoning his stodgy melody as he assumes hers. The number ends with the two of them singing in parallel thirds—a symbol of musical, and hence dramatic unity, for some time. Susanna's melody has triumphed, so to speak.

In the recitative that follows we learn why Figaro has been measuring the room and we begin to sense Susanna's unease about the situation. In the second duet of the opening scene we discover what troubles her as she enlightens Figaro, who in this instance alone appears to be somewhat obtuse. Neither character in this duet has a distinctly different melodic idea. Change in attitude is thus made evident through change of key. As Susanna begins to reveal her suspicions the key shifts from the opening B-flat major to G minor. (Since Mozart reserves this key for his more somber moments, he may well be facetious in this instance.) Susanna's reference to the bell (m. 60), mentioned earlier by Figaro and accompanied there by soft winds, is now accompanied by loud horns. The effect is startling and never fails to elicit a laugh from an audience, even one unaware

that in Mozart's time a cuckold was always depicted with horns. Mozart's audience would have caught his pun—a pretty bad one at that. (The horn crops up time and again throughout the opera with this same symbolic meaning.) We know that Susanna's suspicions have registered with Figaro when his tone changes and he cautions her not to push the theme further. (The slang equivalent of "pian, pian" is "slow down, take it easy.") The tone has changed from the first duet: Even though the two characters share similar thematic material, the suave parallel thirds of the first duet have been replaced here by the choppy rhythms of Figaro's "i dubbi, sospetti" (the doubts, suspicions) in measures 105 to 108 and contrasting rhythms in the two voices in measures 116 to 120 to and 134 to 140).

It has been suggested that Mozart was audacious not only in beginning *Figaro* with servants on stage, but also in having these same two characters sing two successive numbers. It is clear that in so doing he had in mind the dramatic necessities of the plot and was willing to risk offending both critics and the sensibilities of his singers.

In the recitative that follows Susanna informs Figaro that the Count has retracted his abolition of the feudal aristocratic right of defloration, known as the *droit de seigneur,* and plans to exercise it on their wedding night. She tells him to think about *that,* to use his brains; she kisses him, and leaves.

Our discussion has dealt with the relationship between music and text and dramatic situation. Because this is the normal focus for the analysis of music when used in opera, we tend to forget that vocal forms can be as complex and subtle as those employed in instrumental music—and subject to a variety of interpretations. In fact, a composer may find that binary form or rondo fits his dramatic purposes exactly. For example, Figaro's, which follows directly on the excerpt given here, bears a resemblance to the minuet and trio.

Source: Vocal Score by Erwin Stein © 1947 by Boosey & Co., Ltd. Reprinted by permission of Boosey and Hawkes, Inc. English translation by Edward Dent used by permission of Oxford University Press.

Recordings: Numerous available.

Marriage of Figaro   Mozart

A half-furnished room, a large arm-chair in centre. Figaro is measuring the floor; Susanna before a mirror is trying on a hat.

Nº 1 Duet

35
sort of hat for me. Do look here, my dar - ling
fat - to in ver per me. Guar-da un po', mio ca - ro
Figaro
Two foot,
Cin - que,
Fi - ga - ro, Do look here, my dar - ling Fi - ga - ro, do look
Fi - ga - ro, guar-da un po', mio ca - ro Fi - ga - ro, guar-da un
40
Three foot, four foot,
die - ci, ven - ti,
here, do look here, Don't you think my hat is love - ly?
po', guar-da un po', guar-da a-des-so il mio cap - pel - lo,
five foot, That makes
tren - ta, tren - ta
don't you think my hat is love-ly? Do look here, my dar-ling
guar-da a-des-so il mio cap - pel - lo, guar-da un po', mio ca - ro
45
six foot, just six foot three.
se - i, qua-ran - ta tre.
Fi - ga-ro, don't you think my hat is love - ly? don't you think my hat is
Fi - ga-ro, guar-da a-des - so il mio cap - pel - lo, il mio cap - pel - lo, il mio cap -
cresc.
lovely?
-pel-lo.
50
Figaro
Yes, I'm sure it... suits you nice - ly, Just the hat I.... like to...
Sì, mio co - re, or è.... più bel - lo, Sem - bra fat-to in ver per
f p mf p
55
Susanna
Do look here, do look
Guar-da un po', guar-da un
see, just the hat I like to see, Yes, it suits you,
te, sem - bra fat - to in ver per te, sì, mio co - re,
mfp mfp
60
here, Yes, I think it's most be - com-ing, Yes I
po'! O - ra sì, ch'io son con - ten - ta, o - ra
it suits you nice - ly, Yes I'm
or è più bel - lo, Sì, mio

Recitative

No 2 Duet Susanna and Figaro

═══95═══

ORATORIO

Franz Joseph Haydn (1732–1809)
The Creation: Part 1

During the first of Haydn's visits to London he witnessed and was much impressed by the Handel Commemoration, held in Westminster Abbey in May 1791. He apparently resolved at this time to write an oratorio, a resolve that was carried out after his return to Vienna in 1795, following his second visit to London. He was fortunate to have support from aristocratic patrons as well as collaboration with a competent librettist, Baron van Swieten, as he set out on his task. The first performance, which took place before a large audience of nobility in Vienna in 1798, was to lead to many subsequent performances over the years throughout Europe. The work was published in 1800 in both German and English versions. Though it went out of fashion later in the nineteenth century—except in Vienna, where it has been performed almost every year since its premiere—*The Creation* has regained favor in our century.

The Creation appeals on many levels to a wide audience. For those who fancy arias, Haydn includes more than one would find in his Handelian models. The vivid scenes of nature, charming and naive as they may seem to some, are still attractive to the modern audience. For one knowledgeable in musical matters, there are subtleties of structure and harmony, as well as of musical symbolism, that set this work apart from numerous other oratorios of the Baroque and Classical periods.

Much has been written on the associations of specific keys and their relation to the text and scenes being depicted. The first of the three sections of this work is in C major—a key commonly used in Haydn's time for solemn masses and works of splendor and pomp. Haydn delays in a most masterful fashion a presentation of this key until after the amazingly chromatic meanderings of the "Representation of Chaos" and the opening recitative and chorus in C minor. It finally arrives in a blaze of glory as God says "Let there be light."

For storm scenes Haydn favored the key of D minor, as in no. 4 here. By contrast Haydn and his contemporaries associated D major with brilliance, in part because of the open strings used in that key. The chorus "Now heav'n in fullest glory shone," in the third part of this work, uses this key.

Finally, the progression of keys through the three parts is symbolic of the grand theme of the work—the fall of man (the Adam and Eve story) as given in Genesis and in Milton's *Paradise Lost*. (Indeed, the latter work was the direct inspiration for the librettist.) Though C major, the heavenly key, appears at the beginning, the work ends ("falls") in the key of B-flat.

Some of the most vivid pictorialism is found in the accompanied recitatives. An example is no. 4, where each aspect of the storm (wind, rain, thunder, hail, etc.) is first depicted in the music and then described in the text. Later in the work there are equally vivid pictures of the "tawny lion," the "flexible tiger" and even the sinuous (and chromatic) trace of the worm. Haydn shows great self-assuredness in presenting the musical part of the picture first and the text second. With most composers the text appears first or simultaneously with the music.

Throughout the work there are groupings of recitative, aria, and chorus in various permutations. (Similar groupings, though stressing recitative and aria, are found in contemporary opera.) A brief examination of one of these groupings will indicate some of the techniques used by Haydn. Toward the end of no. 2 the angel Uriel says (in the tenor recitative) "and God divided the light from darkness." Following a cadence in C major, an aria for tenor ensues, followed in turn by a chorus that juxtaposes the "gloomy shades of ancient night" ("hell's serpents") and the "holy beams" of the "newly created world."

The short orchestral introduction to Uriel's aria sets the stage for the scene by presenting the opening material of the following vocal line. These few measures also establish Haydn's means of depicting the opposites—light and darkness—that pervade the scene. Representations of light are diatonic and arpeggiated, those of darkness are chromatic and melodically conjunct. A change in tempo marks the dramatic interlude that describes the sinking of the throngs of hell's spirits (in descending chromatic lines) to "endless night." Intensity increases with the entrance of the chorus in dramatic fugal entries that are melodically disjunct in character, with a separate, intense orchestral part. This is not, however, to be a full-fledged fugue. Haydn's model is Handel, not Bach, and the fugal entries soon give way to homorhythmic serenity on the text "new-created world." To round off the scene (and the musical structure) Haydn reintroduces the dramatic references to hell's spirits in abbreviated form, and the scene closes with a final reference to the "new-created world" and authentic cadences in A major, the key of the scene.

The individual expressive devices, such as contrasting chromatic "darkness" and diatonic "light" were not Haydn's inventions. They had been used for a century in both opera and oratorio. Haydn's genius lay in his ability to keep his materials fresh, expressive, and concise. We should note, especially, the wealth of invention in the orchestral writing. With many second-rate composers, orchestral parts in oratorios were limited to stock figures or to simple doubling of the voices. Here they are both supportive and expressively independent—a hard balance to achieve.

Source: Used by permission of G. Schirmer, Inc. from Haydn: *The Creation*, pp. 1–53.

Recordings: Numerous available.

The Creation

Haydn

№ 1. Representation of Chaos.

Nº 2. "In the beginning."
RECIT.

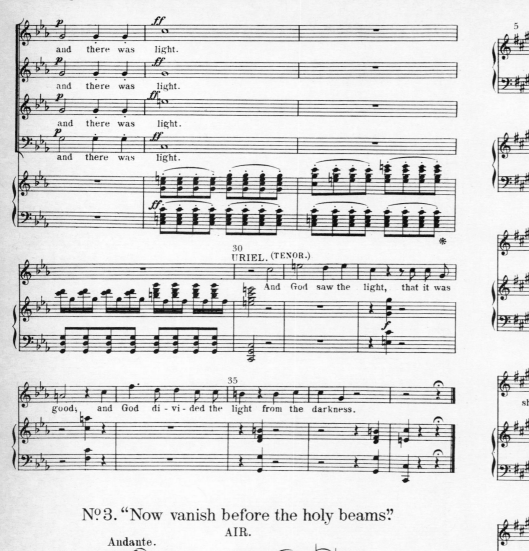

Nº 3. "Now vanish before the holy beams."

AIR.

byss — To end - less night,

To end - less night, To

end - less night.

CHORUS.
TENOR.
Des - pair-ing. curs -

BASS.
Des - pair-ing, curs - - ing rage at-tends their

Des - pair-ing, curs - - ing rage at-tends their
Des - pair-ing, curs - - ing rage, curs - ing rage at-
- ing rage at-tends their ra-pid fall, at-tends their ra-pid fall. des-pair-ing,
ra - pid fall, ra-pid fall. Des-pair-ing, curs -

ra-pid fall, at - tends their ra - pid fall. Des-
tends their ra-pid fall, at-tends their ra-pid fall. Des-
curs-ing rage at-tends their ra - pid fall.
- ing rage at-tends their ra - pid fall.

pair - ing rage, Des-pair-ing, at-tends their ra-pid fall.
pair-ing, curs - ing rage, Des-pair-ing, at-tends their ra-pid fall.
Des-pair-ing, curs - ing rage at-tends their ra-pid fall.
Des-pair-ing, curs - ing rage at-tends their ra - pid fall.

122

Nº 4. "And God made the firmament."
RECIT.

RAPHAEL. And God made the fir-ma-ment, and di-vi-ded the

wa-ters which were un-der the fir-ma - ment from the wa-ters which

5
were a-bove the fir-ma-ment: And it was so.

Allegro assai.

10
Now furious storms tem-pes-tuous rage,

15

Like chaff, by the winds im-pell'd are the clouds,

20
By sud-den fire the sky is in-

flam'd.

25
And aw-ful thun-ders are roll - ing on

high.

Now from the floods in steam as - cend   Re -vi -ving

show-ers of rain,

The drea -ry, waste-ful   hail,

The light and flaky snow.

═══96═══

MASS SECTION

Wolfgang Amadeus Mozart (1756-1791)
Mass in C Minor, K. 417: Kyrie

Austrian mass settings in the late eighteenth century were commonly written in what was known as the *stilus mixtus,* or mixed style. The term indicated that they comprised a mixture of choruses in the Baroque contrapuntal tradition and sections for solo voices that were often in a markedly operatic style. The orchestra often played a prominent role, and trombones were used to double voice parts in the choruses.

The present work, one of seventeen mass settings by Mozart, lies squarely within this tradition. It also betrays his contact with the music of J. S. Bach, a contact brought about in 1782 by Baron van Swieten, a Viennese nobleman and amateur musician who moved in musical c ircles. (It was van Swieten who, several years later, was to prepare the libretto for Haydn's *Creation*; see no. 95.)

The grandest of Mozart's mass settings, this mass was composed as the result of a vow he had made, mentioned in a letter of 4 January 1783, to write a mass in thanksgiving for his marriage to Constanze Weber, which had taken place in Vienna in August 1782. Though partially finished by January 1783, it remained incomplete, and consists of a Kyrie, Gloria, and only part of the Credo. (Mozart was to reuse the music, unchanged, in 1785, for his oratorio *Davidde penitente*.) The Kyrie and Gloria were performed in Salzburg in October 1783, during the first visit of the new couple to Mozart's family and home town. It is possible that Constanze was the soprano soloist.

The Kyrie presented here displays the wide disparity of styles possible in *stilus mixtus*. The overall form, reflecting the textual form, is three-part: an opening and closing choral section, in an austere Baroque style, with the text *Kyrie eleison*; a middle section for soprano solo, with occasional support by the choir, in a decorated *galant* style, with the text *Christe eleison*. The outer sections bear a certain resemblance to the exposition and recapitulation in sonata form. In the first section the tonal movement is from tonic to dominant, the shift of key being accompanied by the abandonment of contrapuntal writing with a *forte* dynamic. The final section repeats these events, though the tonic persists throughout.

The Baroque qualities of the outer sections are manifold: (1) the use of a double fugue (mm. 13-16), (2) the retention of the basso continuo, (3) the importance of sequence both within each subject and as a means of extension (mm. 21-24), (4) the regularity of rhythmic pulse, and (5) a linear type of orchestration, like that of J. S. Bach, in which the choral lines are each reinforced by instruments from different families. Also to be noted is Mozart's use of trombones, especially the rare soprano form. His only use of these instruments is in sacred music or in operatic scenes concerned in some way with the supernatural. In so doing he follows a tradition in the symbolic use of the instrument that dates from the sixteenth century.

By contrast the Christe is completely lacking in conrapuntal writing, has a variable and generally slower harmonic rhythm, and uses instruments for the sake of their color (mm. 51-69). The virtuoso character of the solo vocal line is apparent both in the richness of figuration (mm. 65-68) and in the size of leaps expected from the singers (mm. 52-53).

Source: Used by permission of European American Music Distributors Corporation, sole United States agent for Ernst Eulenberg, Ltd.

Recordings: Deutsche Grammophon DGG 2532 028; Epic SC 6009; Turnabout TV 34174; Philips, 6747 374-6747 389.

Translation: Lord, have mercy. Christ, have mercy. Lord, have mercy.

Mass in C Minor   Mozart

97 and 98

PIANO PIECES

Frederic Chopin (1810–1849)
Mazurka, op. 17, no. 4; Prelude, op. 28, no. 8

The nineteenth century saw, as never before, the coming to the fore of the specialist composer—one who wrote for one kind of medium, or who stressed a single genre to the exclusion of all others. In contrast to the Viennese giants—Haydn, Mozart, Beethoven, and Schubert—all of whom were universalists in that they wrote everything from short piano pieces to symphonies, masses, and operas, we now encounter composers such as Berlioz, who concentrated on music involving orchestra; Wagner, who focused on music for the stage; and Chopin.

As a composer and performer, Chopin's singleminded attention to the piano resulted in a repertory for the instrument that is probably more widely played today than that of any other composer. Every one of his compositions uses the piano, usually as a solo instrument. He wrote neither choral music nor operas, and his orchestral writing (in the two piano concertos, for example) is undistinguished. Chopin's works for the piano range from short, intimate salon pieces to powerful, elaborate, and lengthy ballades and concerti. The two works presented here, a mazurka and a prelude, illustrate the basic characteristics of his style.

Since Paris was the place to make one's name as a virtuoso pianist in the early nineteenth century, Chopin moved there in 1831, joining the company of other famous virtuosi of the day such as Friedrich Kalkbrenner, Sigismund Thalberg, Franz Liszt, and Ferdinand Hiller. These composers composed vast quantities of showy pieces, many of them fantasies on the latest opera, that were intended to dazzle bourgeois audiences. Chopin—and Liszt in many of his later piano compositions—took a different tack. For both, virtuosity was increasingly placed at the service of musical values. And though Chopin was recognized as one of the great piano virtuosos of his time, he gave relatively few recitals during his lifetime, being content to be known primarily as a composer.

Though Chopin spent most of his life in Paris, he always retained an interest in the music of his beloved Poland. This interest was not on the same scale as Bartók's for Hungary—Chopin never collected folksongs in country villages—but it was unquestionably sincere. Chopin made effective use of the rhythms and melodies of Polish national dances, particularly the mazurka and polonaise.

The mazurka is a dance in triple meter, improvisatory in character, and is remarkable for its range of moods. Often sung as well as danced, many mazurkas employed modal harmonies. First mentioned in the sixteenth century, the mazurka had gained popularity throughout the rest of Europe by the early nineteenth century. The fifty-odd mazurkas that Chopin wrote for piano display a wide range of expression and technical difficulty.

The Mazurka in A minor, op. 17, no. 4 is an example of one facet of Chopin's style in its intimate, almost dreamlike quality. As in most of Chopin's music, its structure is very simple, and comprises a statement, departure, and return, or *ABA* form. Within the sections one also encounters straightforward forms. The opening section (to m. 60) may be viewed as an opening introduction followed by a rounded binary form whose first strain (mm. 5–20) is repeated and varied, and whose second strain (mm. 37–60) is stated once only. The *B* section (mm. 61–92) is clearly set off by changes of key (to the parallel major) and material. This secton has many attributes of the trio found in the classic minuet-trio combination—new key, material, and character—though it is not in binary form. The fifths in the bass bring to mind the drone of the *duda*, a bagpipe used in folk music.

Much of the dreamlike quality of this piece comes from its opening and closing measures, which are extraordinary in several ways. There is no clear sense of tonic; and with notes that are all of the same rhythmic value the sense of accent, and hence meter, is not forcefully projected. Without seeing the score, it is doubtful the listener would suspect that the piece begins on the second beat. (How does one hear an initial rest?) But since humans abhor uncertainty—also known as suspense or ambiguity—the listener would doubtless latch onto the second beats as downbeats since they are the most dissonant chords present. In so doing he would of necessity sense the beginning of the main body of the piece, in measure 5, as an upbeat—which it is not, since one of the common rhythms for the mazurka begins on the downbeat with just such a rhythmic figure.

Chopin was meticulous in his use of expression marks, pedaling, and phrasing, and was critical of performers who failed to observe them. (However, his own performances in Paris salons were often improvisatory in nature; it is reported that he never played the same piece twice the same way.) Note his careful use of slurs and ties throughout the piece, but especially at the demarcations of sections (mm. 44–45, 60–61, 92–93).

It is assumed that Chopin wrote his Twenty-Four Preludes in homage to J. S. Bach since he greatly admired Bach's music, which was then becoming widely known. Like his mazurkas, Chopin's preludes exhibit a wide range of styles, moods, and technical difficulties. The prelude presented here has many of the characteristics of a Chopin *etude* (study or exercise): a piece that explores a single technical problem, involving in this case the projection of a melody that lies in an inner voice and is played only by the thumb. A complex rhythmic relationship between the hands is maintained throughout the piece. (Such continuous action is characteristic of Bach's music, and is found in many of Chopin's piano works. It stands in marked contrast to the style of Classical composers.) The intensity and drive in this piece also stand in marked contrast to the simplicity of the mazurka we have just examined.

In spite of these differences, both pieces have certain stylistic features in common. Much of Chopin's music consists of a harmonic and/or rhythmic pattern that is established and maintained in the left hand, over which the right hand plays a single-line melody. Chopin's knowledge of the harmonic overtones produced by the piano—whether gained pragmatically or through scientific studies—is evident in the way in which the harmonics of the bass patterns serve to reinforce the notes of the melody, and thereby contribute to the lyrical feeling that is so characteristic of much of his writing.

While Chopin's music is often difficult, it is always well written for the instrument; the pianist would say, "It lies well under the hand." And though he was scrupulous in his use of notation—it is often described as very "finished"—a proper performance of his music presents a great challenge to the pianist, who must strike a balance between interpretations that would be either overly sentimental or too straightforward and lifeless. But this problem is not unique to Chopin's music.

Finally, we must mention that Chopin is a central figure in the cultivation of chromaticism in the nineteenth century, a position he shares with Liszt and Wagner. His music is rich in nonharmonic tones, appoggiaturas, and cambiatas. Frequently seventh chords are not resolved according to the "rules" of common practice. Note in the prelude the free treatment of dissonance between the ornate embellishments in the right hand and the accompaniment in the left. Similarly, the seventh chords in the left hand in the *A* section of the mazurka often resolve in an unexpected fashion. In their chromatic movement they often anticipate the sliding chords used later by Debussy.

Source: No. 97: *Complete Works*, X, pp. 42–45. No. 98: *Complete Works*, I, pp. 22–25.

Recordings: Numerous available.

Mazurka   Chopin

Op. 17 № 4.

Prelude   **Chopin**

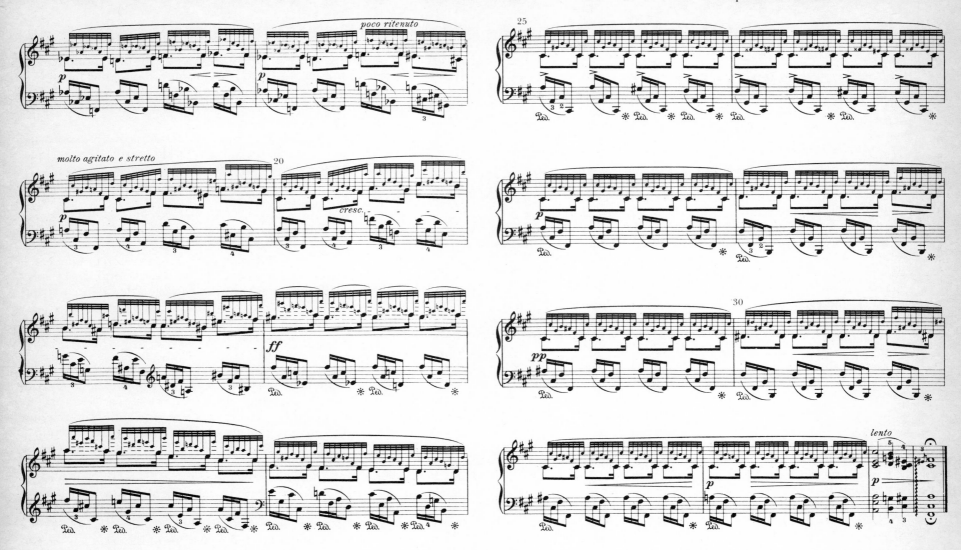

CHARACTER PIECES

Robert Schumann (1810–1856)
Davidsbündlertänze, op. 6, the first three numbers

Though there has always been a connection between literature and music in the West—one thinks of madrigals, motets, operas, and oratorios—the nineteenth century saw the coming to the fore of a new kind of connection that was forged by composers with a strong literary bent: instrumental pieces based on literary themes. Many composers come to mind in this regard: Mendelssohn, Berlioz, Schumann, Liszt, Smetana, Strauss, Tchaikovsky. A number of these composers, and others as well, were also highly articulate with words, producing numerous articles and essays on music and aesthetics, and even the occasional novel. Several earned part of their livelihood (in some cases a sizable portion thereof) as music critics for newspapers and journals—among these were Carl Maria von Weber, Berlioz, Schumann, Hugo Wolf, Smetana, Tchaikovsky.

As a young man Schumann was more widely known as a music critic and essayist on musical matters than as a composer. (He championed the music of Chopin, Berlioz, and Brahms to German audiences.) His continuing concern was what he saw as the mediocrity of music in Germany. One of his vehicles for elevating taste was an imaginary league that he created and called the *Davidsbund* (League of David). Its purpose, straight from the biblical story of David and Goliath, was to fight the Philistines in music. The *Davidsbund* first appeared in an essay Schumann published in 1833. It was also to crop up in two of his early compositions for piano, *Carnaval* and *Davidsbündlertänze* (Dances of the League of David). (Though *Carnaval* bears a higher opus number, and was the second of these two works to be published, it was composed some two years before the *Davidsbündlertänze.*)

Schumann was, to say the least, a complex human being. He invented *personae* to represent two distinct sides of his personality. Eusebius was the contemplative dreamer, Florestan the impetuous stormer of the heavens. Schumann initially intended to write a novel in the style of his favorite Romantic author, Jean Paul, in which these *personae* were to appear as charac-

ters. Though he abandoned the idea, Eusebius and Florestan soon appeared as members of the *Davidsbund* and also thereafter throughout his early critical writings, each in turn giving his view of the composition under review. They also appear in the two early piano compositions mentioned here, each time being associated with a piece in the appropriate mood. In the *Davidsbündlertänze,* composed in 1837, Schumann identifies their presence by an initial at the end of each dance.

Schumann also delighted in aphorisms and old proverbs, sprinkling them liberally throughout the music journal he edited from 1835 to 1844. One such proverb appears at the head of the *Davidsbündlertänze*:

> In each and every time
> joy and sorrow are joined:
> stay faithful to joy
> and sustain sorrow with courage.

Though Schumann's title indicates that this work is a set of dances, it bears no resemblance to the dance suite of the Baroque era. Most dances here are waltzes, though the second one is a *Ländler,* a slow dance in triple meter that was originally a folk dance in Austria and Southern Germany but was to become fashionable at the Hapsburg court in Vienna towards the end of the eighteenth century. Schumann's purpose seems to have been to invoke the spirit of the dance.

The work comprises a set of eighteen dances, the first three of which are presented here. Schumann has ensured a larger unity to the set by both thematic and tonal means. On a thematic level he creates a cyclic form by quoting the third dance in its entirety within the seventeenth. And B minor emerges as the tonic of the cycle, being explicit in the second and fourth dances, and appearing as the first tonal goal of the third dance. Most of the dances have simple, straightforward formal schemes, usually some sort of *ABA* form. Much of the interest in the music derives from the subtle variation of material and from a richness of rhythm that often involves a conflict of accents between the hands (see especially no. 1). In general, Schumann's pianistic style is leaner and less flamboyant than that of his contemporaries—but because of its subtleties, his music is no less easy to play.

Schumann's music has often been characterized as poetic. It also gives the impression of being incredibly rich in meanings, musical and otherwise, many of which one suspects were known to Schumann alone. As a writer it was second nature for him to quote others for the sake of enriching meaning. He applied the same technique to his music, quoting himself and others. Some of these quotations have been identified; for example, the first dance opens with a quote from a mazurka by Clara Wieck, the gifted young composer and pianist who three years later was to become Schumann's wife. The mazurka is the fifth piece in her *Soirées musicales*, op. 6, which had been published in 1836. The same piece is alluded to at the opening of the third dance, which also contains (mm. 47–49) an allusion to the "Promenade" from Schumann's own *Carnaval*. One suspects that other quotations of this sort lie buried throughout the work.

Our selection is taken from the work as it appeared in the first edition. Schumann revised the work for a second edition published in 1850. Apparently somewhat self-conscious about what must have appeared to him on maturer thought to be youthful indiscretions, he retitled the work *Davidsbündler, Eighteen Character Pieces for Piano* and removed the old German proverb that headed the piece, along with all references to Eusebius and Florestan. He also broadened a number of the dances by introducing repetitions, and changed some expression marks. For example, in the first edition the marking for the third dance is *Etwas hahnbüchen* ("somewhat rudely"); in the second edition this was to become *mit Humor*. As one will discover in listening to different recordings of this work, pianists today perform both versions—and even sometimes another one of their own making that borrows from each.

Source: *Werke*, serie VII, vol. 1, pp. 96–101.

Recordings: Numerous available.

Davidsbündlertänze   **Schumann**

100 and 101

CHARACTER PIECES

Franz Liszt (1811–1886)
Harmonies du Soir from *Etudes d'exécution transcendante* (S. 139)
and *La lugubre gondola* (S. 200/1)

Though Liszt has long been recognized as a central figure in nineteenth-century musical romanticism, it is only in recent years that the true measure of his accomplishments has come to be known. The greatest—and most famous—piano virtuoso of his time, he is still known primarily as a composer of piano works that continue to dazzle audiences by their incredible technical demands. But the scope of Liszt's work was far more universal than this. In addition to his many piano transcriptions of operatic tunes by others, which were among the most fashionable pieces of his time and useful for his many concert tours throughout Europe, he composed at least one piece in every genre known to the nineteenth century, among these opera, oratorio, mass, symphony, and song. An ardent champion of the new in music—and himself a bold experimenter, as we shall see—he ensured the wide dissemination of a number of new and controversial orchestral works by arranging them for piano. (Before the day of the phonograph and the tape recorder, this was the public's primary means of getting to know new orchestral works.) And throughout his long career he was to meet most of the major composers of his time, and to become close friends of a number of them, including Chopin, Berlioz, Wagner. Robert Schumann was to write that "the greatest artistic experience of my life was to hear Liszt." Some fifty years later, Debussy heard him in Rome and sought his advice.

Our selections by Liszt demonstrate two aspects of his wide-ranging styles and interests. The first, *Harmonies du Soir*, shows both the technical demands he made upon pianists and the manner in which color could be exploited on the piano, and comes from a work that went through several revisions before it emerged in the form presented here. In 1826, at the age of fifteen, Liszt completed twelve of a projected forty-eight etudes, or technical studies, in all the major and minor keys, and published them under the title *Etude en douze exercises*. His model was probably the *Well-Tempered Clavier* of J. S. Bach, often called the "forty-eight" and available since the beginning of the century in a number of printed editions. Five years later Liszt was deeply impressed by a performance by the great Italian violin virtuoso Paganini and decided to emulate him by expanding the technical and expressive range of writing for the piano. The result was a reworking of the etudes of 1826, which task was completed by 1837. This second version was published in 1839 under the title *Vingt-quatre grandes études*. (Only twelve of the twenty-four etudes announced in Liszt's title were completed.) After he abandoned his career as a touring virtuoso Liszt undertook yet another revision of these works that consisted, in the main, of removing some of the greatest technical difficulties and adding descriptive titles to most of them. This version was published in 1852 under the title *Etudes d'exécution transcendante* ("Transcendental Etudes"). What has been transcended here is the level of technical proficiency previously expected of pianists.

Harmonies du Soir (Evening Harmonies) is the eleventh piece in the set. Although it poses a number of problems for the pianist, the chief one concerns the use of the pedals. There were typically two on the grand piano of Liszt's time: One, called the loud pedal, lifted all dampers at the same time, thereby allowing the strings to continue to sound after the finger was removed from the key; the other, called the soft pedal today and indicated by the term *una corda* ("one string"), shifted the hammers to one side so that they struck only one of the two or three strings supplied for each pitch; in so doing both dynamics and tone quality were altered. Since Liszt's piece depends on color for much of its effect, he has indicated pedaling with great care. The feeling of evening calm projected in the first part of the piece requires careful control of pedaling to achieve the right amount—but not too much!—of blurring of the harmonies. Liszt's widely spaced chords pose another problem for the pianist. Not everyone has Liszt's hands, which, easily spanning the interval of a tenth, allowed him to play parallel tenths without difficulty. The more powerful sections of the piece (for example, the passage marked *trionfale* that begins at measure 80) require another kind of control, namely the ability to project power without pounding. In this regard, Liszt was noted for the clarity and control of his playing, even in those passages that many regard today as bombastic.

This piece is also noteworthy for the ways in which chords have been used, and is illustrative of one of the major developments in nineteenth-century music that first became evident in the works of Schubert. As the century progressed composers increasingly used harmonies for the sake of their value in creating color rather than, as in the classical period, to create a sense of tonic. Chromatic harmonies were the primary agent in this process. But such a use necessarily involves a trade-off: The more one uses harmonies for the sake of their color, the more one runs the risk of weakening their power to create a tonal center. Thus one should expect that in many nineteenth-century pieces tonality will assume a secondary role in creating a sense of musical structure. In his piece Liszt employs not only chromaticism but also, particularly at the climax, the parallel, or "gliding," chords that were to be so common in Debussy's music.

During the last fifteen years of his life Liszt spent his time, on a fairly regular basis, in one of three cities: Weimar, Budapest, and Rome. He had already in 1865 given in to a recurrent urge for spiritual security by entering holy orders, thus renouncing the extroverted and colorful life that had earlier made him the equivalent of television personalities today. Liszt's compositions during these final years, especially those for piano, stand in marked contrast to his earlier works, both in their technical demands and in their forward-looking harmonies. In December 1882, while visiting his daughter, Cosima, and her husband, Richard Wagner, in Venice, Liszt composed the second piece we present here, *La lugubre gondola*. As is typical of many of his works, it exists in several versions, one of them being for violin, violoncello, and piano. We present the first version, which is for piano solo. Liszt's inspiration was the Venetian funeral gondola, which was to be used for Wagner early in the following year. There is no attempt at display here. In its place we find an austerity of mood and degree of dissonance that are remarkable for the time the piece was written. (One might suspect that it had been written by Bartók, who was thoroughly acquainted with Liszt's work.) Much of its mood can be attributed to Liszt's use of augmented triads, which are by their nature ambiguous as to tonal function. The opening accompanimental figure in the left hand outlines an augmented triad, a harmony Liszt was to use increasingly in his later works and which stays with us throughout much of the piece. The somber opening melody in the right hand is quite independent of this accompaniment, so that striking dissonances occur on the downbeats of measures 8, 12, and 16, for example. Beginning at measure 39 the opening section is repeated, but now a step lower rather than in the tonic/dominant relationship that was favored in earlier music. A contrasting third section follows (m. 77 to the end) that also contains an augmented fifth in the left hand. As in the first two sections, the relationship between melody and accompaniment continues to be highly dissonant. The resultant form is *AAB*.

In its austerity and absence of technical demands this piece is far removed from "Harmonies du soir." While our first piece points to Debussy, the second points to Bartók and beyond.

The letter *S* followed by a number in the title refers to Humphrey Searle, who has catalogued the works of Liszt.

Source: No. 100: *Werke*, Series II, vol. 2, pp. 82–89. No. 101: *Werke*, Series II, vol. 9, pp. 174–177. Used by permission of Gregg Press International.

Recordings: No. 100: Numerous available. No. 101: Philips 6514 121, *The Final Years: Late Piano Compositions*, Artist Direct *Liszt 1–30, Piano Works*.

Harmonies du Soir   Liszt

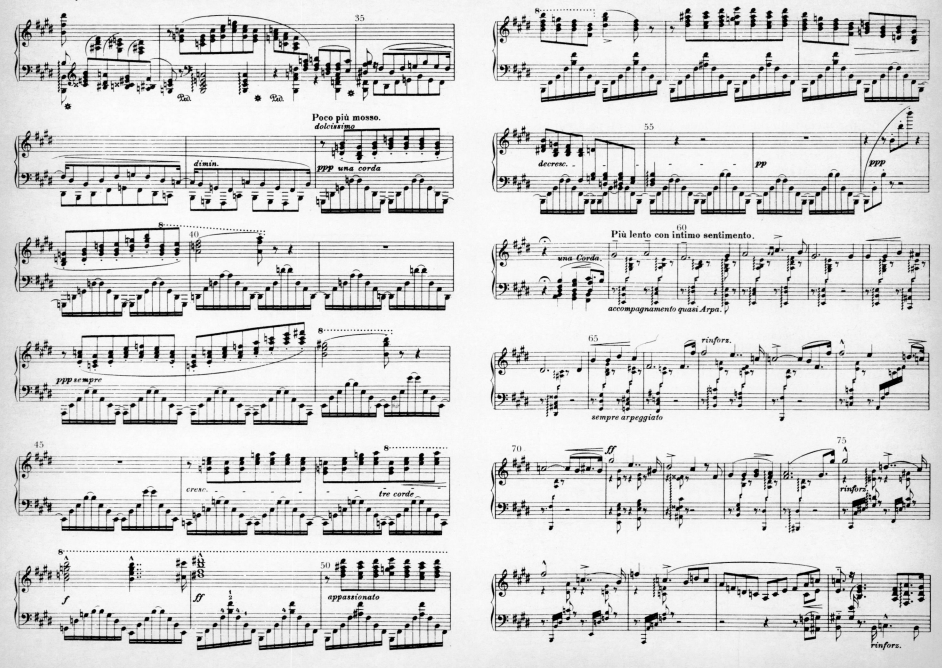

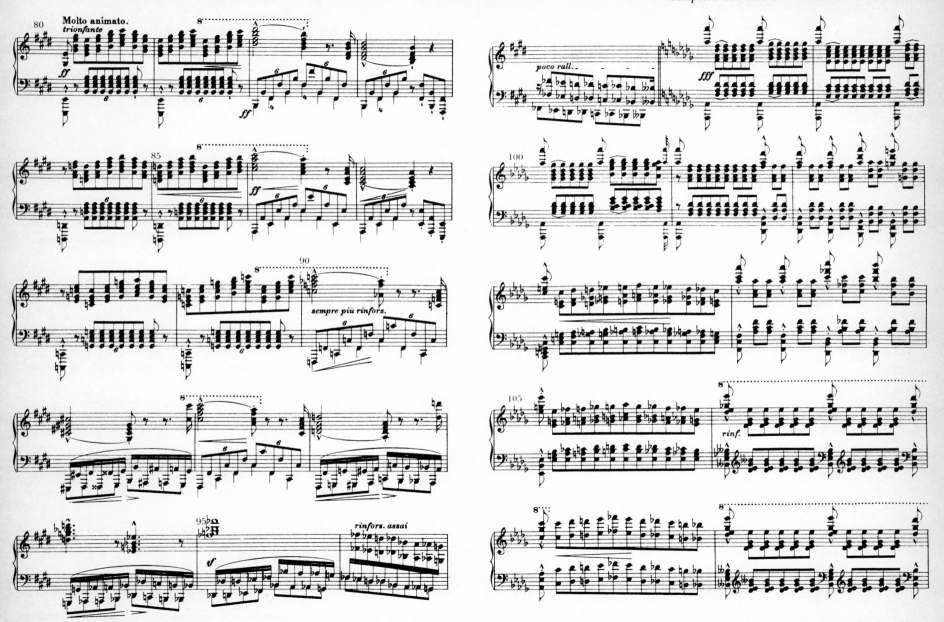

La Lugubre Gondola

Liszt

=102=

CHAMBER MUSIC

Johannes Brahms (1833–1897)
Quintet in B minor for clarinet and strings,
op. 115: movement 2

Nineteenth-century Europe was peopled with an incredible mix of strong musical personalities. At one extreme were such composers as Berlioz and Wagner, the avant-garde of their day who, striving for intensely personal languages, appeared to be pushing music to its limits in every conceivable direction: length, loudness, technical demands, and emotionality. At the other extreme were those like Schumann and Brahms who, keenly aware of their Classical heritage, sought to build on it. Both of the latter therefore continued to cultivate one kind of Classical music that increasingly lost favor during the nineteenth century: chamber music. It is generally acknowledged that Brahms was the more successful of the two in comprehending the nature of the process that made for a sense of organic growth and cohesion in Beethoven's large-scale instrumental works, and hence was the more successful as a composer of instrumental forms, whether for orchestra or for chamber ensembles. For him the key lay in imposing tight constraints on a musical personality capable of writing lengthy works filled with a succession of glorious Romantic themes, such as his Piano Quartet in G minor, op. 25, published when he was thirty. The present work, one of his last pieces of chamber music, shows how tight the constraints he imposed could be. It also demonstrates, as Schoenberg was to observe, that Brahms had a progressive side and was not, as some would have it, a posthumous composer, born too late and yearning after a vanished past.

Late in life Brahms became fascinated with the potential of the clarinet as a chamber instrument, primarily, it appears, because of the sensitive playing of Richard Mühlfeld, a clarinettist in Meinigen from whom he learned the capabilities of the instrument. The result of this new love was two clarinet sonatas and the clarinet quintet that is excerpted here.

In the hands of an expert player the clarinet part can be made to stand out from the strings or, alternately, can blend into the string sound in a supporting role when necessary. Brahms used the instrument in both ways.

Given here is the slow second movement of the quintet. Its overall form is simplicity itself: *ABA*. The outer sections, in B major, are serene in character—although perhaps somewhat melancholy because of Brahms's penchant for turning to the subdominant in minor form in his harmonies—and contrast markedly with the intensely dramatic middle section. The powerful sense of cohesion in the movement can be traced to a typical Brahmsian technique that is common in his mature works: the use of a three-note melodic motive, stated at the outset and repeated in various guises throughout the movement. As initially stated in the clarinet, the motive consists of a descending minor third followed by a descending major second. It can also appear, as in the middle section, as a major third followed by a minor second. Characteristically, Brahms will repeat such a motive at the high point of a phrase or whole section, as in the violins in measures 20 and 85. In the latter instance the clarinet has a much more elaborate version spanning over three octaves. The motive can also appear in inversion, as in the violin in measures 126 to 127, and in the cello in measures 55, 61 and elsewhere—and twice with one or two notes displaced by an octave (mm. 22–23 and 70–71). Its connection with later twelve-tone technique becomes even stronger when one begins to encounter retrograde versions of the motive, as in the clarinet in measures 5 and 6 and 42 to 46 (focusing here solely on the sustained pitches) and in the cello in measures 84 to 85. One obvious example of the motive in retrograde inversion appears in the clarinet at the end of measure 71. Other examples of any one of these four forms can be sought by the reader.

One other element in Brahms's style deserves brief comment: his use of rhythm. Brahms's barlines often belie the meter that one hears in his music; for example, the sequence pattern beginning at measure 27 is clearly in duple meter. And one could make the case that he indulges on occasion in polymeter—that is, more than one meter at a time, a practice that is usually identified with twentieth-century composers. The patterns in the music in measures 17 through 20 suggest that the meter of the violins is 3/4, that of the viola 9/8, and that of the cello 2/4. (Could the clarinet be projecting 6/8? And what is the harmonic rhythm here?)

Source: *Sämtliche Werke,* vol. 7, pp. 163–171.

Recordings: Numerous available.

Quintet in B minor   **Brahms**

═══103═══

OVERTURE

Felix Mendelssohn (1809–1847)
Overture to *A Midsummer Night's Dream*, op. 21

For the early German romantics, Shakespeare was a kindred spirit, a true Romantic. Enthusiasm for his works ran so high that by 1801 sixteen of his plays had been translated into German by August Wilhelm von Schlegel and Ludwig Tieck, including what Tieck called Shakespeare's "Romantic Masterpiece," *A Midsummer Night's Dream.* In 1826, as a boy of seventeen, Mendelssohn fell under its spell, being drawn, as were others of his day, to the play's elements of fancy, its elfin world. (He was to return to the play in 1842 to write incidental music for a planned production at the royal palace in Potsdam.)

As a *wunderkind* and member of a wealthy and cultured Berlin family deeply concerned with nurturing his musical gift, Mendelssohn had been composing since the age of eleven. By 1826, when the present work was composed, he had mastered the art of writing triple fugues and had produced numerous works that included several concertos, a number of string symphonies, sonatas, piano quartets, and his first great work, the Octet for strings. That Mendelssohn had been carefully trained in the Classical style is evident from the form of this overture, which is almost a textbook example of sonata form. Yet the work is thoroughly infused with a Romantic spirit. A number of years later Mendelssohn said of the work:

'[The overture] follows the play closely . . . so that it may perhaps be very proper to indicate the outstanding situations of the drama in order that the audience may have Shakespeare in mind or form an idea of the piece. I think it should be enough to point out that the fairy rulers, Oberon and Titania, appear throughout the play with all their people. . . . At the end, after everything has been satisfactorily settled and the principal players have joyfully left the stage, the elves follow them, bless the house, and disappear with the dawn. So the play ends, and my overture too.'

Though Mendelssohn does not specify in what ways an overture that employs the conventions of sonata form "follows the play closely," his intent in composing the work seems clear: He is using a literary work as a point of departure for a purely instrumental piece. He is thus among the earliest of many nineteenth-century composers with a strong literary bent—among them Berlioz, Schumann, Liszt, and Strauss—and the overture is a direct ancestor of the later program symphony and symphonic poem. (A strong literary bent of another sort is manifest in such composers as Schumann and Berlioz, both of whom also led active lives as music critics.)

The point of contact between play and overture appears to lie in the three different types of characters: the fairies, led by their king and queen, Oberon and Titania; the three pairs of lovers, Theseus and Hippolyta, Demetrius and Helena, and Lysander and Hermia; and the rustic craftsmen involved in the play-within-the-play, Quince, Snug, Bottom, Flute, Snout, and Starveling. Mendelssohn has three distinctively different thematic groups in the exposition, each of which can be related to one of the sets of characters. Following a brief introduction in the winds, the fairies are introduced by the strings (m.8). Their music can best be described as gossamer in character and employs a style which resembles a *perpetuum mobile* and which Mendelssohn was to use time and again, especially in his scherzos. Following a bridge passage that prepares the dominant key area, a warm, rich melody representing the several sets of lovers is stated by the violins (m. 138). A loud orchestral tutti, heavy-footed and obviously oafish in character, which opens with dronelike reiterations of the interval of the fifth (an interval characteristic of such folk instruments as the bagpipe and hurdy-gurdy) heralds the arrival of the rustic craftsmen (m. 194). Their presence is confirmed by the graphic braying of an ass, clearly an allusion to Bottom's predicament. All of this takes place within the exposition of a sonata form, which now has a customary closing section on the dominant.

Earlier we said that this is almost a textbook example of sonata form. It is left to the reader to determine where the other divisions of the form lie. The structure of the first theme is, however, not typically Classical since it comprises a closed binary form, complete with all repetitions. A comparison of the end of the development section here with that in the first movement of Beethoven's *Eroica* (no. 92) will show two very different treatments of this part of the convention. It will also show the level of Mendelssohn's musical sophistication at this young age, since the opening chord of the introducton, reintroduced at this point, has been reharmonized in a most ingenious fashion. The obvious good humor of the work leads to a manipulation of the convention quite remarkable for a seventeen-year-old. The end of the recapitulation could hardly be more emphatic. Mendelssohn

uses every possible sign to indicate that the piece is now over. But does the piece end?

Mendelssohn employs the Classical orchestra with winds in pairs and natural horns and natural trumpets. The one unusual instrument, used for comic effect in the recapitulation, is the *ophicleide*, a brass instrument that is a descendant of the serpent and the precursor of the tuba.

Source: Kalmus/Belwin Mills Edition.
Recordings: Numerous available.

Overture to A Midsummer Night's Dream   **Mendelssohn**

15
20
25
30
Flauto I.
Flauto II.
Oboe I.
Oboe II.
Clarinetto I in A.
Clarinetto II in A.
Fagotto I.
Fagotto II.
Corni in E.
Trombe in E.
Ophicleïde.
Timpani in E.H.
Violino I.
Violino II.
Viola.
Violoncello.
Basso.
pizz.
p
pp
stacc.
pizz.
arco

35
40
45
50
Flauto I.
Flauto II.
Oboe I.
Oboe II.
Clarinetto I in A.
Clarinetto II in A.
Fagotto I.
Fagotto II.
Corni in E.
Trombe in E.
Ophicleïde.
Timpani in E.H.
Violino I.
Violino II.
Viola.
Violoncello.
Basso.
pp
pizz.
arco

55
60
65
70
Flauto I.
Flauto II.
Oboe I.
Oboe II.
Clarinetto I in A.
Clarinetto II in A.
Fagotto I.
Fagotto II.
Corni in E.
Trombe in E.
Ophicleïde.
Timpani in E.H.
Violino I.
Violino II.
Viola.
Violoncello.
Basso.
pp
ff
arco
tr

75
80
85
90
Flauto I.
Flauto II.
Oboe I.
Oboe II.
Clarinetto I in A.
Clarinetto II in A.
Fagotto I.
Fagotto II.
Corni in E.
a 2.
Trombe in E.
Ophicleïde.
Timpani in E.H.
Viol.I.
Violino I.
Viol.II.
Violino II.
Viola.
Violoncello.
Basso.

95
100
105
110
Flauto I.
Flauto II.
Oboe I.
Oboe II.
Clarinetto I in A.
Clarinetto II in A.
Fagotto I.
Fagotto II.
Corni in E.
Trombe in E.
Ophicleïde.
Timpani in E.H.
Violino I.
Violino II.
Viola.
Violoncello.
Basso.
cresc.

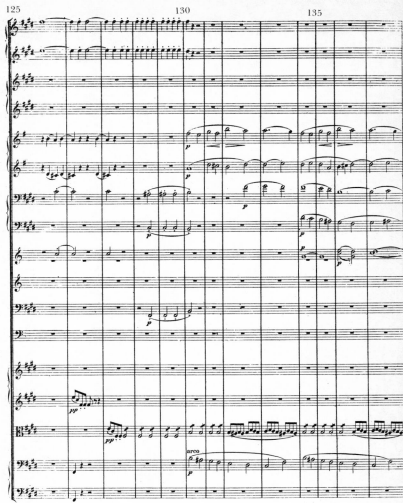

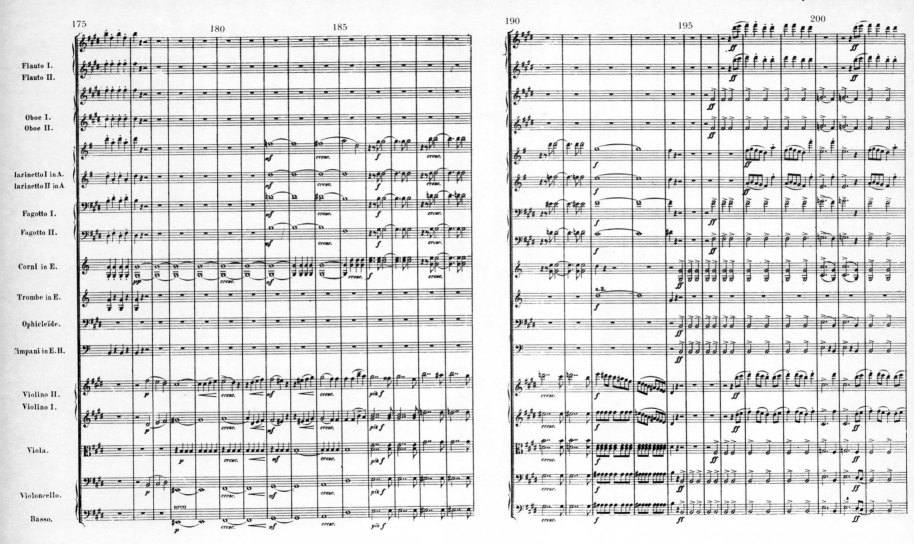

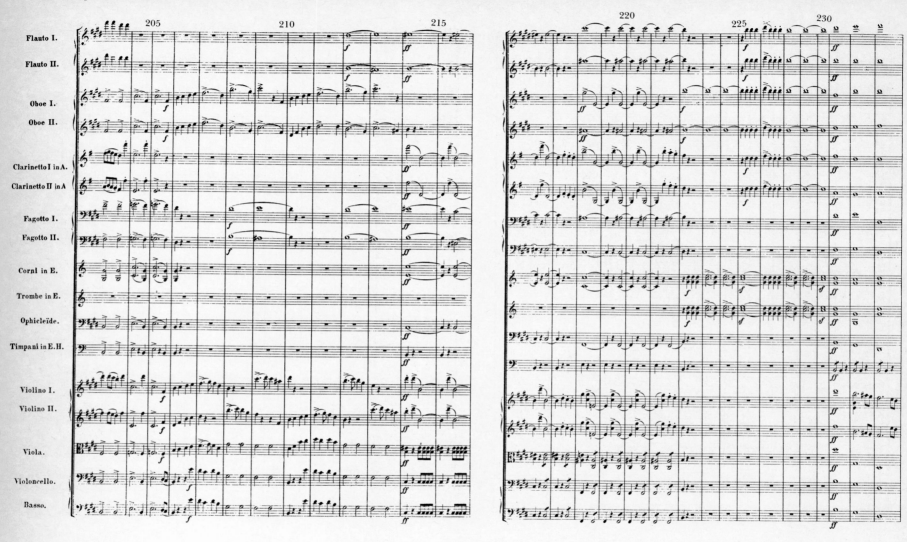

235
240
245
250
255
Flauto I.
Flauto II.
Oboe I.
Oboe II.
Clarinetto I in A.
Clarinetto II in A.
Fagotto I.
Fagotto II.
Corni in E.
Trombe in E.
Ophicleïde.
Timpani in E.H.
Violino I.
Violino II.
Viola.
Violoncello.
Basso.
a 2.
divisi
pp stacc.

260
265
270
Flauto I.
Flauto II.
Oboe I.
Oboe II.
Clarinetto I in A.
Clarinetto II in A.
Fagotto I.
Fagotto II.
Corni in E.
Trombe in E.
Ophicleïde.
Timpani in E.H.
Violino I.
Violino II.
Viola.
Violoncello.
Basso.
pp

295
300
305
310
315
Flauto I.
Flauto II.
Oboe I.
Oboe II.
Clarinetto I in A.
Clarinetto II in A.
Fagotto I.
Fagotto II.
Corni in E.
Trombe in E.
Ophicleïde.
Timpani in E.H.
Violino I.
Violino II.
Viola.
Violoncello.
Basso.
con tutta la forza
a 2.
ff
dim.
poco a poco
pp
divisi
sempre pp
tr

340
345
350
355
360
365
370
Flauto I.
Flauto II.
Oboe I.
Oboe II.
Clarinetto I in A.
Clarinetto II in A.
Fagotto I.
Fagotto II.
Corni in E.
Trombe in E.
Ophicleïde.
Timpani in E.H.
Violino I.
Violino II.
Viola.
Violoncello.
Basso.
pp
arco
pizz.

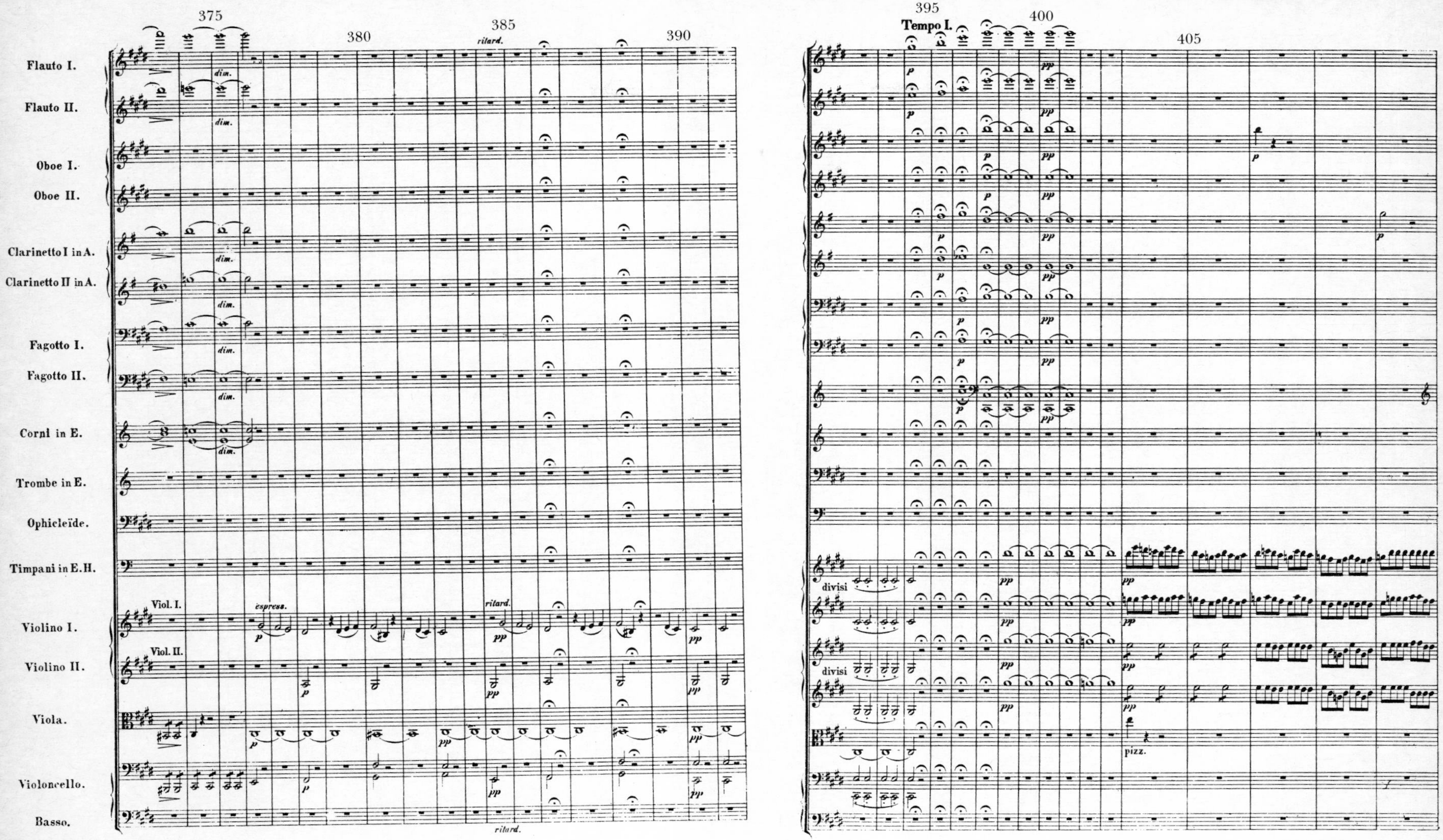

410
415
420
425
Flauto I.
Flauto II.
Oboe I.
Oboe II.
Clarinetto I in A.
Clarinetto II in A.
Fagotto I.
Fagotto II.
Corni in E.
Trombe in E.
Ophicleïde.
Timpani in E.H.
Violino I.
Violino II.
Viola.
Violoncello.
Basso.
pizz.

430
435
440
445
Flauto I.
Flauto II.
Oboe I.
Oboe II.
Clarinetto I in A.
Clarinetto II in A.
Fagotto I.
Fagotto II.
Corni in E.
Trombe in E.
Ophicleïde.
Timpani in E.H.
Violino I.
Violino II.
Viola.
Violoncello.
Basso.
pp
p
arco
pizz.

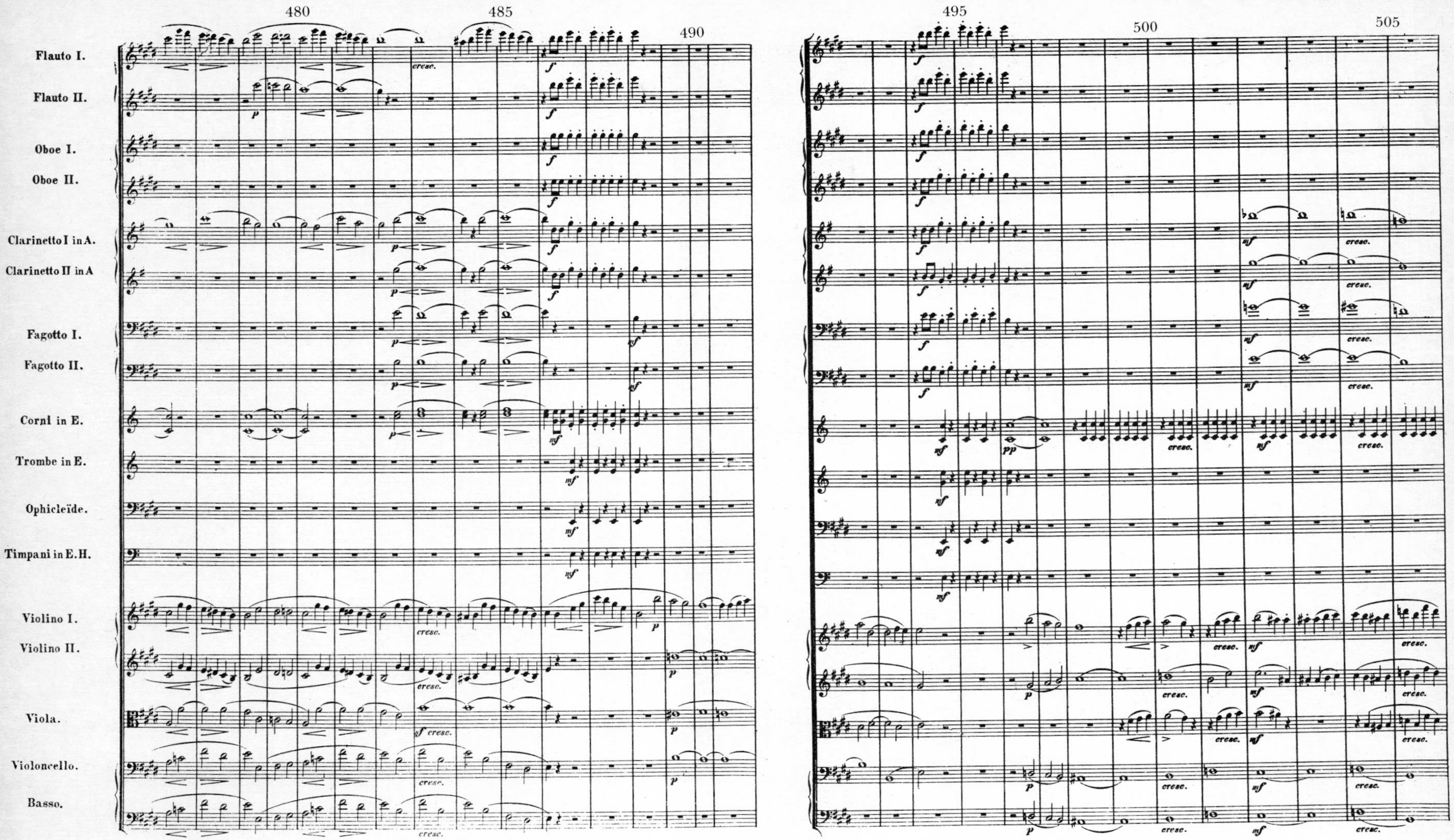
480
485
490
495
500
505
Flauto I.
Flauto II.
Oboe I.
Oboe II.
Clarinetto I in A.
Clarinetto II in A
Fagotto I.
Fagotto II.
Corni in E.
Trombe in E.
Ophicleïde.
Timpani in E.H.
Violino I.
Violino II.
Viola.
Violoncello.
Basso.

510
515
520
525
530
Flauto I.
Flauto II.
Oboe I.
Oboe II.
Clarinetto I in A.
Clarinetto II in A.
Fagotto I.
Fagotto II.
Corni in E.
Trombe in E.
Ophicleïde.
Timpani in E.H.
Violino I.
Violino II.
Viola.
Violoncello.
Basso.
cresc.
più f

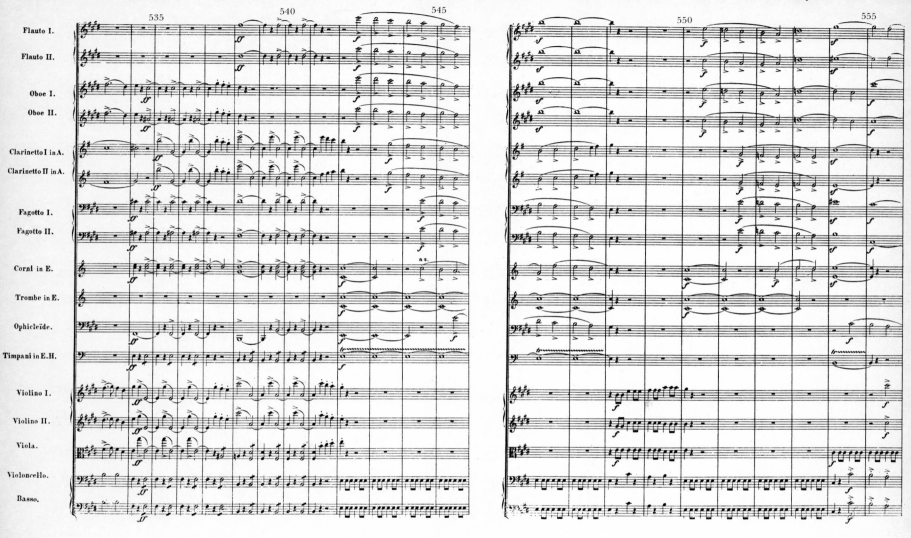

560
565
570
575
580
Flauto I.
Flauto II.
Oboe I.
Oboe II.
Clarinetto I in A.
Clarinetto II in A.
Fagotto I.
Fagotto II.
Corni in E.
Trombe in E.
Ophicleïde.
Timpani in E.H.
Violino I.
Violino II.
Viola.
Violoncello.
Basso.

615
620
625
630
Flauto I.
Flauto II.
Oboe I.
Oboe II.
Clarinetto I in A.
Clarinetto II in A.
Fagotto I.
Fagotto II.
Corni in E.
Trombe in E.
Ophicleïde.
Timpani in E.H.
con tutta la forza
Violino I.
divisi
Violino II.
Viola.
Violoncello.
Basso.
divisi

=104=

SYMPHONY

Hector Berlioz (1803–1869)
Symphonie fantastique, op.14: movement 3

Berlioz is recognized today as the leading French musician of his time. This has not always been so. In fact, during his lifetime he failed to gain recognition as a composer in France, in part because of the startling originality of his compositions, but also because of the somewhat acerbic tongue he often used in pursuit of his ideals, and which he occasionally directed at those who were in a position to help his career. As a consequence, his major source of income throughout his life was music criticism. But from 1835 on he was to augment these earnings as an orchestral conductor, appearing in Germany, Austria, Russia, and England. Along with Carl Maria von Weber, Felix Mendelssohn, and Richard Wagner, Berlioz was thus one of the first of the new breed of specialist conductors that continue to dominate musical life even today.

Like Mendelssohn (no. 103), Berlioz was an ardent admirer of Shakespeare's plays, and turned to them for such works as the *King Lear Overture,* the dramatic symphony *Romeo and Juliet,* and the opera *Beatrice and Benedict,* which was based on *Much Ado about Nothing.* What Berlioz admired in Shakespeare was his freedom from formal constraints, a trait that was to become central to his own music. Berlioz also knew and admired Beethoven's symphonies. In fact, it has been argued that the *Symphonie fantastique,* the work under consideration here, represented a deliberate attempt on his part to employ the framework of a Beethoven symphony for the expression of dramatic and poetic ideas.

The origins of the *Symphonie fantastique* show Berlioz as a prototypical Romantic figure, one who could easily become infatuated with a woman at first sight, romanticize her in his thinking, and then suffer hopeless longing for her as unattainable. Such a state of affairs proved a stimulant to his compositional powers. The immediate impetus for the work arose from a performance of *Hamlet* by a traveling English company, witnessed by Berlioz in Paris in the fall of 1827. On the spot he fell head-over-heels in love with the Anglo-Irish actress who played Ophelia, Harriet Smithson, though he was not to meet her for another five years. The circumstances leading to their first meeting are the stuff of which romance is made. Miss Smithson, again performing in Paris in December 1832, was coaxed into attending the second performance of the *Symphonie fantastique,* which took place at that time. In the course of the performance it began to dawn on her that she was the object of Berlioz's love—she was the one to whom he referred in his symphony. (Though Berlioz was ultimately to wed Miss Smithson, the marriage fell apart several years later.)

Thus the *Symphonie fantastique* has strong autobiographical overtones. (Berlioz's original title for the work was *Episode in the Life of an Artist, Fantastic Symphony in five parts*; in a later edition he reversed the order of the two parts of the title.) It is also one of the earliest examples of program music— that is, music that is intended to depict nonmusical events. To assist the audience in its listening by filling in what he believed would not be clear from the music, Berlioz had leaflets that gave the program distributed to audiences. The fact that he altered the program several times reflects not only Berlioz's changing views on his as-yet-unattained love—at one point he chose to believe some gossip concerning a liaison between Miss Smithson and her manager—but also revisions he made in the score. We give here the version of the program he made for an edition of the score that was printed sometime after 1858; included, however, are only the portions that lay out the overall program and the section that pertains to the movement presented here.

A young musician of morbidly sensitive temperament and fiery imagination poisons himself with opium in a fit of lovesick despair. The dose of the narcotic, too weak to kill him, plunges him into a deep slumber accompanied by the strangest visions, during which his sensations, his emotions, his memories are transformed in his sick mind into musical thoughts and images. The loved one herself has become a melody to him, an *idée fixe* as it were, that he encounters and hears everywhere.

Part III

SCENE IN THE COUNTRY

One summer evening in the country, he hears two shepherds piping a *ranz des vaches* in dialogue; this pastoral duet, the scenery, the quiet rustling of the trees gently brushed by the wind, the hopes he has recently found some reason to entertain—all concur in affording his heart an unaccustomed calm, and in giving a more cheerful color to his ideas. But she appears again, he feels a tightening in his heart, painful presentiments disturb him—what if she were deceiving him?—One of the shepherds takes up his simple tune again, the other no longer answers. The sun sets—distant sound of thunder—loneliness—silence.

That Berlioz's views concerning the necessity of supplying an audience with a program were to change is evident from notes in two different versions of the program. In the leaflet distributed at the first performance he wrote:

The distribution of this program to the audience, at concerts where this symphony is to be performed, is indispensable for complete understanding of the dramatic outline of the work.

Some twenty-eight years later, a similar note in a later edition of the score was to read:

if necessary, one can even dispense with distributing the program, keeping only the titles of the five movements. The symphony by itself (the author hopes) can afford musical interest independent of any dramatic purpose.

What is significant in each of these notes is Berlioz's use of the word "dramatic," for even though the *Symphonie fantastique* is intended as a concert work, he introduces for dramatic effect several devices that are more readily associated with opera. One such is the offstage oboe heard at the outset; another extremely evocative example is that of the timpani chords near the end, which suggest distant thunder.

These timpani chords are but one example of the new kinds of sonority that Berlioz, as a master orchestrator, sought. To cite a few others, there is the sound of the muted violas, divided and playing tremolo at measure 11; his tendency to play off one family of instruments against another, as in measures 133 through 139; and his use of extremely high sonorities, as in measures 106 through 110. Berlioz delighted in the sound produced by large performing ensembles; he had hoped for an orchestra of 230 players for the first performance of this work, but had to settle for 130—a number that is still markedly larger than the typical symphony orchestra today.

The form of this movement is quite straightforward and can, in large measure, be predicted from the program description Berlioz supplies. Both theme and tonality play a part in creating a structure that bears little resemblance to any of the Classical formal conventions. A short introduction and coda frame the main body of the movement, which contains four parts: an opening section (m. 20) with a broad melody of the sort that confounded many of Berlioz's critics since it lacked the antecedent-consequent structure common to Classical melodies; a contrasting section (m. 87) in which the *idée fixe,* the binding thematic element in all five movements, reappears, but in an incomplete form; a return of the broad opening melody (m. 117), initially presented here in an embellished form; and a fourth section (m. 150) in which Berlioz uses one of his favorite devices, the contrapuntal combination of two melodies. (Another example of this melodic combination is encountered in measures 133 through 138.)

In spite of its many forward-looking aspects, this movement is highly traditional in its employment of the stylistic elements of the pastoral convention, which can be traced to the late seventeenth century and had been used by such earlier composers as Corelli, Handel, and Bach, particularly in works intended for Christmas. (See the pastoral symphonies in Handel's *Messiah* and Bach's *Christmas Oratorio*.) The elements of the convention comprise a prominent role for the oboe, long associated with shepherds, to which Berlioz now adds the English horn; the use of compound meter, either 6/8 or 12/8; the prominent use of parallel thirds (see mm. 33, 49, 113, 146, etc.); and bird calls. To this tradition Berlioz adds a new element, the *ranz des vaches,* which is a kind of melody played on the alphorn by herdsmen to call their cattle. (Brahms also used one of these melodies, now scored for horn, in the slow introduction to the last movement of his first symphony.) But it would appear that Berlioz's greatest debt here is to the slow movement of Beethoven's *Pastoral* Symphony. In addition to introducing the calls of the nightingale (mm. 67–69) and quail (mm. 69–77), and hinting at a trilled figure Beethoven had used (mm. 125–127), Berlioz quotes the hemiola rhythm Beethoven employed in approaching two major cadences, even using it for the same purpose (mm. 60–63 and 164–168).

Source: Kalmus/Belwin Mills Edition.

Recordings: Numerous available.

Symphonie Fantastique   **Berlioz**

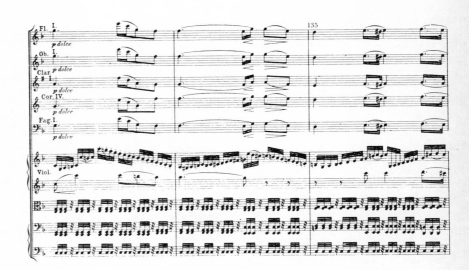

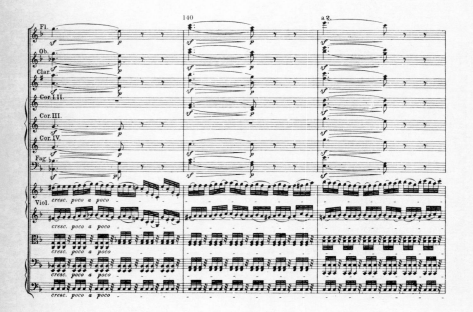

=105=

SYMPHONY

Peter Ilich Tchaikovsky (1840–1893)
Symphony no. 4, op. 36: movement 3

From the eighteenth century, art music in Russia had been dominated by imported musicians and styles, primarily those from Italy. In the first half of the nineteenth century there were efforts on the part of Glinka and the five composers who followed in his footsteps to create a Russian national style based on native literary materials, folk songs, and Slavonic chants. Of the five, all self-taught amateurs and often referred to as "the mighty handful" (see no. 112), the greatest is generally considered to be Mussorgsky.

Tchaikovsky comes from a tradition rather different from that of Glinka and his followers. A member of the first graduating class from the new conservatory in St. Petersburg, and hence trained as a professional, he had received his training from non-Russian musicians. (Upon graduation he was immediately appointed to teach harmony at the conservatory then being founded in Moscow.) Although he knew the five nationalist composers, and made extensive use of Russian folk songs in his music, his conservatory training assured that his orientation would always be to the mainstream of European music, which was one reason for his success outside Russia. (His first piano concerto was premiered in Boston, his violin concerto in Vienna, and among the concert tours he made was one to the United States in 1891, where he conducted orchestras in Baltimore, Philadelphia, and New York, and visited Washington and Niagara Falls.)

Tchaikovsky's output was to include operas, symphonies, symphonic poems, chamber music, and songs. His symphonies, one of which is extracted here, are generally considered to belong to the conservative tradition in nineteenth-century symphonic writing, which means that, like such other composers as Mendelssohn, Schumann, and Brahms, he accepted the conventions of the genre as developed by Classical composers. And like these others he is generally considered to have been more successful with movements other than the first, which, traditionally using the conventions of sonata form, demanded the use of developmental procedures that were not always suited to the sort of lyrical thematic material favored by Romantic composers. Tchaikovsky himself was aware of the problem, saying of his music, "The seams show," and "There is no organic union between separate episodes."

The fourth symphony, finished in 1878, adopts the four-movement pattern of the Classical symphony. Like Tchaikovsky's two other late symphonies, the fifth and six, it has a poetic meaning that can be related to events in his life at the time, but this is only disclosed through reading his letters to friends. Here the first-movement introduction opens with a stern fanfare that Tchaikovsky said symbolized fate. The fanfare recurs several times, at structural points, during the first movement, and also reappears in the fourth movement, lending a kind of thematic unity to the work as a whole. (The same technique, involving all movements, is used in his fifth symphony; see also no. 104.)

The third movement illustrates a number of characteristics of Tchaikovsky's style and is among the best of his symphonic movements. Unlike the first movement in this symphony, it lacks the emotional extremes that trouble many in Tchaikovsky's later works. Here all is light and grace. Tchaikovsky's rich melodic gift is everywhere present, as is his tendency to use bright and sharply differentiated orchestral colors. Often the latter is accomplished by playing off one orchestral family against another. Here each family has its own thematic material, that assigned to the brasses being a sort of augmentation of the opening of the string theme. The tonal plan here is unorthodox by Classical standards, being based on the interval of the major third: F—A—C–sharp/D–flat—F. (A similar key-plan, based on the minor third, is encountered in the first movement: F—A–flat—C–flat—D—F.) Not surprisingly, the return to the tonic is signaled by a return to the opening theme. An extended coda follows (m. 349) wherein snatches of all three themes return. Successive entries in the dialogue among families here are usually a major third apart so that, in a sense, the key-plan of the movement is recapitulated as well.

One final and fascinating feature of this movement should be mentioned. The movement is entitled Scherzo, a word that originally meant "joke." That Tchaikovsky had this meaning in mind is clear from one passage (mm. 17–57) that employs a rhythmic technique that is usually associated with Haydn (see no. 90) or Beethoven or Brahms. The technique involves the consistent displacement of accent, which is felt initially as syncopation. A close look at the passage will show that it consists of a series of afterbeats. If one tries to beat the quarter-note pulse without looking at the music, one will find it all but impossible to maintain the original pattern. Those who try almost invariably end up interpreting these offbeats as beats before the passage has ended. At measure 57, of course, everything comes out right—but with a jolt.

Source: Kalmus/Belwin Mills Edition.

Recordings: Numerous available.

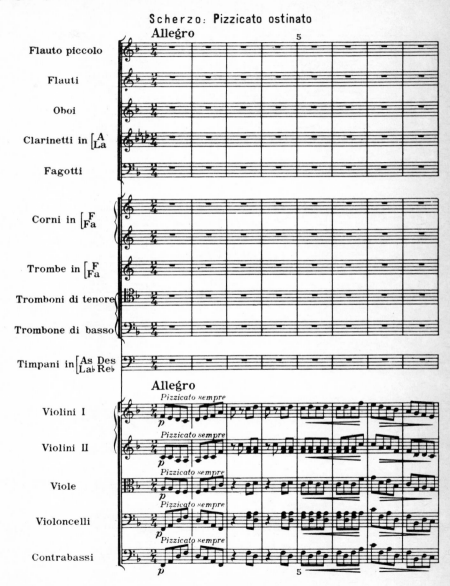

Symphony no. 4   **Tchaikovsky**

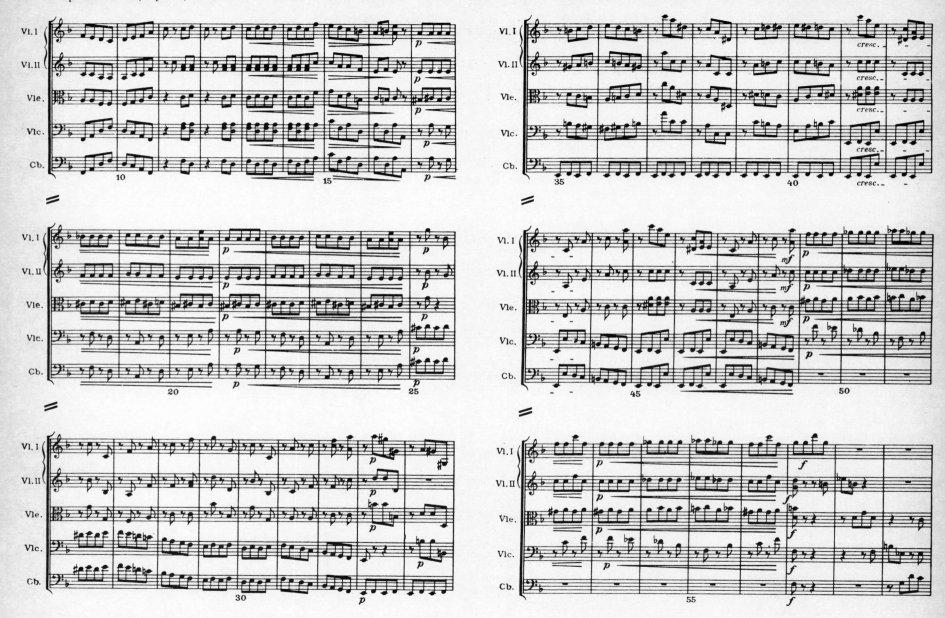

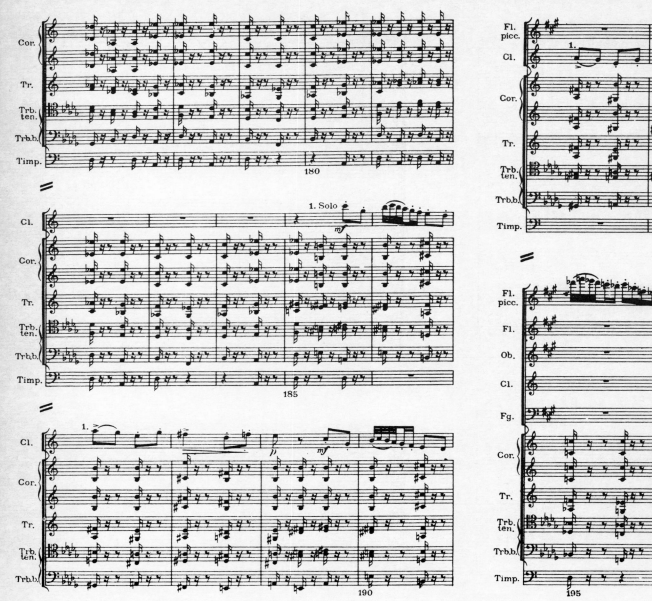

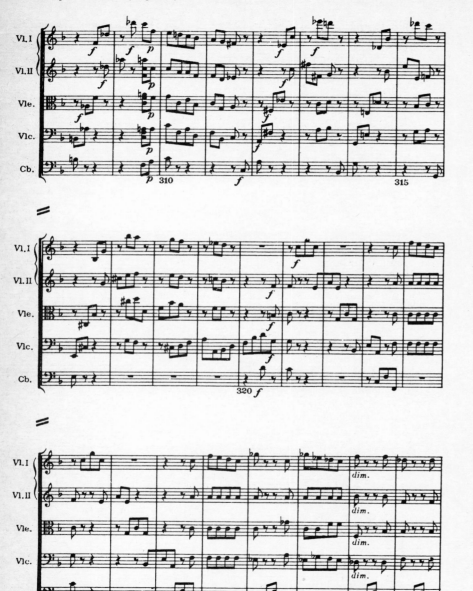

=106=

CONCERTO

Antonin Dvořák (1841–1904)
Cello Concerto in B minor, op. 104: movement 2

Dvořák's Cello Concerto (1895) is the last of his three concertos, and was composed during the final year he spent in New York City as director of the National Conservatory of Music. It is widely acknowledged to be one of his best works, and one of the greatest concertos written for the cello.

The scale of the work is such that it is usually characterized as a symphonic concerto, and is ranked with the four concertos of this sort written by Brahms. Unlike the typical nineteenth-century concerti composed by such virtuoso cellists as Dotzauer, Klengel, and Romberg as vehicles for their own concert tours, in which the orchestra normally supplied the thinnest of accompaniment for virtuosic display, Dvořák's concerto displays a careful balance between solo instrument and orchestra in the handling of themes, and a thematic and tonal structure closely resembling that found in his symphonies.

In a sense the cello was a natural as a solo instrument for the nineteenth-century composer. Along with other instruments in the middle register, such as the English horn and the French horn, it had been assigned an increasing share of the thematic materials in orchestral works, producing in the process an orchestral sound whose center of gravity shifted downward from that associated with Classical style, in which the violin, oboe, and flute had dominated. But it is with good reason that there are far fewer cello concertos than violin or piano concertos. Being a middle-register instrument, the cello's range lies right in the middle of the range of pitches produced by the orchestra, which means that it is easily drowned out, especially by the larger orchestras that were increasingly favored in the late nineteenth century. Dvořák was surely aware of this. Although requested by his friend, cellist Hanus Wihan, to write a concerto for the instrument, he appears to have resolved to try only after having heard the American composer Victor Herbert perform his second cello concerto in Brooklyn in 1894. Dvořák's success in overcoming the difficulties inherent

in the combination is attested to by his close friend Brahms, who said of the concerto: "Had I known that such a cello concerto as that could be written I would have tried to compose one myself." (Brahms had, however, written a double concerto for violin and cello some eight years earlier.)

The main concern in writing such a work, then, is achieving balance between the solo instrument and the orchestra. It will be noted, first of all, that in orchestral tuttis (mm. 39 and 65), which are as loud as any in Dvořák's music, the solo cello is silent. Also, the violins have been assigned a very discreet role, only occasionally playing higher than the cello, as in measures 43 through 48 where they supply a light, arpeggiated accompanying figure, or in measures 57 through 60 where they alternate in dialogue with the solo instrument. Otherwise it is the clarinet—one in A, whose sound is somewhat less bright than the more familiar one in B-flat—or the flute that carries the main burden in projecting an upper voice over the cello. Effective use is also made of three trombones as accompanying instruments in the lower register (mm. 15–21). Dvořák assigns the cello a variety of roles. Although it leads much of the time, it occasionally also provides an elaboration of thematic material being presented by other instruments (mm. 69–75) or a countermelody against this thematic material (mm. 76–82).

Dvořák has written well for the solo instrument, employing a number of techniques that are peculiar to string instruments. In measures 107 through 119, labeled *Quasi cadenza* (see no. 91), in which the solo cello presents an elaborated version of the opening theme, Dvořák calls for the simultaneous use of **arco** (sounds produced by the bow) and ***pizzicato*** (plucked sounds). This is to be done in the context of another string technique called **double stops** in which the performer plays two notes at once, simultaneously bowing and fingering two adjacent strings. Here and there during the passage the performer is also told to pluck one or more of the two remaining strings, not difficult to do here since they are always open strings. The passage in measures 118 and 119 is also characteristic of string writing, and involves rocking the bow rapidly across three strings at once. In measures 162 through 166 Dvořák calls for the use of **harmonics**, indicated by the circles placed next to the note heads. Harmonics have a very pure, ethereal sound and are produced by touching the string lightly with a finger at the appropriate spot, rather than by pressing the string against the fingerboard. It is instructive to compare several recordings of this concerto to hear how different cellists interpret Dvořák's instructions in these two passages. Although Dvořák uses the cello primarily as a melodic instrument, there is another characteristic passage of string writing in measures

69 through 74, in which the solo instrument embellishes the melodic line presented by the winds. If one sees this work performed, one will be struck by the number of times the cellist employs what is called thumb position, in which the thumb of the left hand is placed on the fingerboard, rather than behind the neck (see especially measures 27ff. and measures 54ff.)

The movement has a three-part structure that employs the by-now-familiar pattern of statement-departure-return. We leave it to the reader to discover its outlines, observing only that there is also a coda in which allusions to the middle section appear—though they are now thoroughly transformed in character (see measures 149 through 154, as well as measures 119 through 121).

Recordings: Numerous available.

Cello Concerto in C Minor   Dvořák

II

Adagio ma non troppo (♪ = 108)

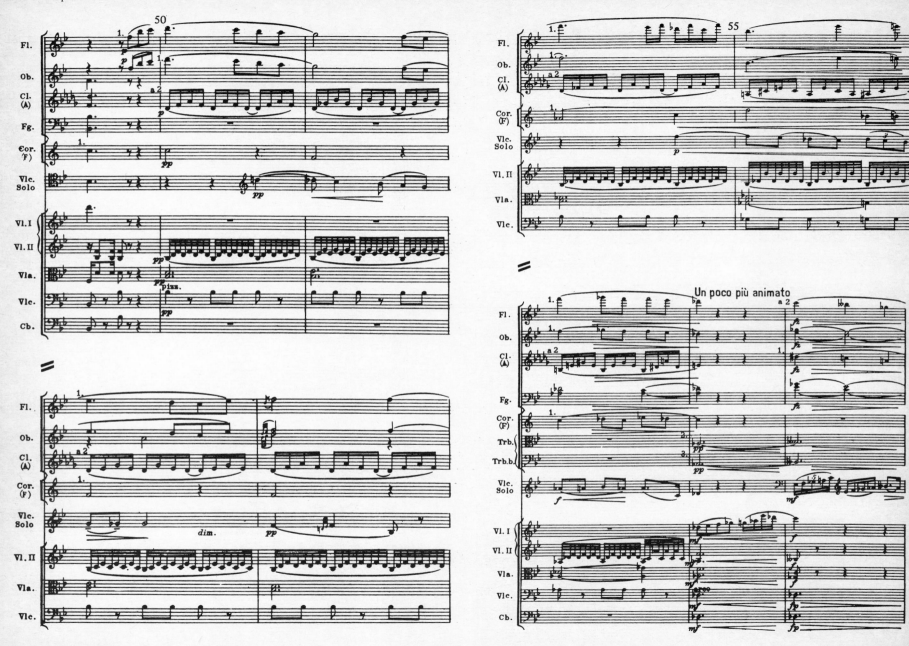

107 and 108

SONG

Franz Schubert (1797–1828)
Gretchen am Spinnenrade (D. 118)
Der Doppelgänger (D.957/13)

The nineteenth century saw extremes in the size of musical compositions. On the one hand were the monumental operas of such composers as Berlioz and Wagner, which called for huge resources and could last upwards of five hours. On the other were the small songs and piano pieces that might last less than one minute. Franz Schubert was a master of these smaller forms, especially of songs, called in German *Lieder*. He wrote over 600 Lieder. Given here are two of Schubert's songs, the first from 1814 near the beginning of his career—and generally considered to be his first masterpiece—the second from the year of his death. Both demonstrate in myriad ways Schubert's gifts as a songwriter.

Gretchen am Spinnenrade takes as its text a song from Part I of Goethe's *Faust*, which had been published in 1808. In the play, Gretchen, the innocent, wooed and won by Faust, sings as she sits at her spinning wheel, bemoaning his absence and recalling in vivid detail their love. Goethe's skillfully wrought poem has a gradual crescendo of sentiment both within each of its three stanzas and throughout the entire poem, with its climax coming at the very end. And each of the three stanzas has been preceded by a refrain, *Mein Ruh ist hin*. Eroticism lies just beneath the surface in the poem, the ending surely referring to "the little death."

Schubert's masterful setting of Goethe's poem captures the growing intensity of the poem by a variety of musical means. The piano part—accompaniment is not an appropriate term since it is in no sense subsidiary to the voice—simulates the movement of Gretchen's spinning wheel while at the same time suggesting the depth of her restlessness. The piano, and thus the wheel, halts momentarily at the end of the second stanza as Gretchen recalls Faust's kiss. Vocal lines rise gradually throughout each stanza, the melodic climax appearing toward the end of each. The most intense climax, repeated for emphasis, appears at the end of the final stanza. The bittersweet nature of the relationship is suggested by

215

Schubert's easy movement from minor to major and back, a stylistic trait found in many of his songs. Also characteristic of his harmonic language (which the reader is invited to examine closely) is the use of Neapolitan key relationships for the sake of intensification (see mm. 26–30).

The form of Schubert's song matches that of Goethe's poem with one change of utmost importance: Schubert adds a fourth, partial statement of the refrain to end the song. Successive stanzas can be characterized as having a progressive form since they grow in length, and each stanza, taking as its point of departure the opening melody and harmony of the refrain, proceeds melodically and tonally in another direction.

Schubert's handling of the refrain demonstrates his keen understanding of the way the sense of expectation works in the listening process in music. As laid out at the beginning, the refrain moves from D minor to C major. In repeating it before the two later stanzas, he confirms its nature. Thus the final, partial statement can only be heard as incomplete, both textually and musically—even though it ends on the original tonic, D minor. The endless character of Gretchen's distress had been vividly projected.

Der Doppelgänger takes as its text a poem by Heinrich Heine, one of the most popular of the German Romantic poets, and is of a type Schubert favored because of the bite in its final stanza. Schubert appears to have set the poem a few months before his death, and included it in a two-volume collection of songs he entitled *Schwanengesang* ("Swan Song") that was published posthumously.

The central role of the piano is equally clear here: By the simplest means—the low and hence dark register, the repetition of a four-chord cell that lacks a third in the first and last chord—it vividly suggests the bleakness of the scene described: the quiet night and the empty streets, as well as the bleakness of the poet's life. The vocal line in the first stanza reinforces this sense of bleakness by its insistence on F-sharp as the beginning and ending note for each phrase. The rising intensity of feeling in the poem is also reflected in the vocal line as it rises to higher pitches in the second stanza.

Schubert has furnished a through-composed setting for the three stanzas of the poem; that is, the music is not repeated in successive stanzas, instead being ever new. He has ensured internal cohesion in the first two stanzas by using a varied repetition of the same material for each pair of two lines in the poem. This pattern of repetitions is abandoned for the third stanza as the piano part traces an upward chromatic progression that matches the impassioned cry of the poet. It is hard to conceive of an apter or more economical musical setting of Heine's poem.

The *D* followed by a number in our titles refers to Otto Erich Deutsch, who catalogued Schubert's works.

Sources: Schubert, *Werke*, XIII, pp. 191–196 (*Gretchen am Spinnenrade*) and XVII pp. 180–181 (*Der Doppelgänger*).

Recordings: No. 107: EMI/Electrola 037–30965, *Willst du dein Herz mir schenken*; EMI/Electrola 063–02598, *Elisabeth Schwarzkopf singt Lieder*; EMI/Electrola 065–99630, *Schubertiade*; EMI/Electrola 067–270067–1, *Lucia Popp Singt Schubert Lieder*. No. 108 DGG 2531 325, *Schwanengesang*; DGG 2720 022, *Lieder*; Angel 36127, *Schwanengesang*.

Translations:

a) *Gretchen am Spinnenrade*
My peace is gone, my heart is heavy; I shall never again find peace.
Any place he is absent is my grave. I have lost all joy in life.
My poor head is confused, my poor wits have been mangled.
My peace is gone . . .
I look only for him from the window, for him only I go from the house.
His upright stance, his noble manner, the smile on his lips, the power in
　　his eyes, and the magic of his words, the touch of his hand, and ah!
　　his kiss.
My peace is gone . . .
My bosom longs after him; ah, might I but clasp and hold him,
and kiss him as I wish, at his kiss I would pass away.
My peace is gone . . .

b) *Der Doppelgänger*
Quiet is the night, the streets are still;
In this house my beloved once lived;
Long ago she left the town,
Yet the house still stands in the same place.

Another man also stands there and stares upward,
And wrings his hands from grief.
It horrifies me when I see his face;
The moon shows me my own features.

You double of mine, pallid companion,
Why do you ape the pain from my love
That tormented me in this place
Many a night in former times?

Gretchen am Spinnenrade   **Schubert**

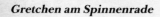

Der Doppelgänger   Schubert

109

SONG CYCLE

Robert Schumann (1810–1856)
Dichterliebe: op. 48, the opening three songs

Of the nearly 260 songs for solo voice that Schumann is known to have composed, some 150 were written in a single year, 1840. It was also in this year that he and Clara Wieck, long in love, were finally able to marry in spite of the continuing disapproval of Clara's father. *Dichterliebe*, a cycle of sixteen songs on poems by Heinrich Heine, was composed in nine days at the end of May of that year, some three months before Schumann's wedding. Schumann selected the poems from Heine's *Buch der Lieder*, which was first published in 1827. He seemingly chose those that bore some relation to his personal situation at the time with the intent of creating a larger work that was to be made up of a number of small works that shared some sort of common poetic theme, which is what a **song cycle** is. The close relationship between art and the life of the composer that is manifest in this cycle is not unique in Schumann's output. In fact, the listener often senses from his music, whether vocal or instrumental, that it contains some poetic meaning known only to the composer.

In *Dichterliebe* we see Schumann at his best: a natural lyricist, most at ease with small forms, whose sophisticated and subtle musical style was almost invariably placed at the service of some extramusical idea. The most obvious difference between his concept of a song and Schubert's (see nos. 108 and 109) lies in the role of the piano. Whereas the piano always plays a supporting role in Schubert's songs, some have argued that Schumann's consist of lyrical piano pieces with a voice part grafted on. Such a judgment receives support from the role of the piano in the first three songs given here, wherein the vocal line is doubled throughout by the piano—though often with different rhythms.

The richness and subtlety of Schumann's language is particularly evident in the first two songs in the cycle. Although the structure here is created by functional harmony, the way in which the tonic is defined differs from eighteenth-century common practice. Here the tonic, F-sharp minor, is never made explicit by the tonic triad but only implied through the harmonic progresson IV-V. (A similar technique is used in Vincent Youmans' "Tea for Two".) This same IV chord then serves as the pivot for a move-

ment to A major as the voice enters. An identical progression of thought in each of Heine's strophes, with the climax at the very end, leads Schumann to supply a strophic musical setting whose melodic high point in the voice also occurs at the end. And as each strophe ends, the opening harmony and key, IV in F-sharp minor, unfolds again. The ending of the song furnishes another example of the subtlety of Schumann's art. It ends on a dominant seventh, and appropriately so given the lack of resolution or fulfillment suggested by the final word, "longing." But the song does not really end here. Schumann counts on the listener's hearing this final chord sounding on in his memory in the silence between the first and second song. The opening of the second song supplies a resolution, but in an unexpected fashion. It opens with a major third in the piano, which because of its context and because it lacks a fifth could be heard as part of either an F-sharp-minor or an A-major triad. Schumann initially seems to confirm the first of these interpretations as the bass line moves downward by step to F-sharp. But the line then continues on so that this interpretation is immediately negated by a IV—I—V—I progression in A major. This is a most effective way to bind together such short pieces into a larger whole. Schumann relies on key relationships for the same purpose later in the cycle, using the descent of the fifth between the second, third, and fourth songs, and again between the fifth and sixth. The reader is invited to examine these later songs closely for further evidence of Schumann's sensitivity to his texts. By way of a guide we note that he appears to show a preference for the antecedent-consequent phrase structure that had been so common in Classical style.

Source: *Werke*, Serie XIII, Vol. 2, pp. 88–95.

Recordings: Numerous available.

Translations:

1. In the beautiful month of May
   as all the buds were bursting,
   In my heart love arose.

   In the beautiful month of May,
   as all the birds were singing,
   I confessed to her my yearning and longing.

2. From my tears sprout
   many flourishing blossoms,
   and my sighs become
   a chorus of nightingales.

And if you love me, dearest,
I send you all the flowers,
and before your window shall sound
the song of the nightingale.

3. The roses, the lily, the dove, the sun
   I once loved them all in the rapture of love.
   I love them no longer,
   I love her alone—sweetheart, beautiful, chaste, the only one;
   she herself, the rapture of love, is rose, and lily, and dove, and sun.

Dichterliebe   Schumann

=110=

SONG

Hugo Wolf (1860–1903)
Der Feuerreiter from *Gedichte von Eduard Mörike*

Although time and again Wolf tried his hand at large-scale works, composing one complete opera and a considerable amount of instrumental music, he was to prove most successful, to his dismay, as a writer of songs, of which he composed some 250. His songs were written in bursts of creative activity—sometimes two or three were composed in one day—during a short and tormented lifetime that included intermittent bouts of depression and ended in insanity. A great admirer of Wagner's music, Wolf successfully adapted for song Wagner's chromatic harmony, his declamatory vocal lines, and elements of his leitmotif technique (see no. 116). In the eyes of many critics his songs are on a par with those of Schubert, Schumann, and other outstanding lieder composers of the nineteenth century.

Wolf attached great importance to his selection of texts. His practice was to publish collections of songs with texts by one poet, honoring the poet by placing his name prominently on the title page. When he served as pianist in the performance of his own songs, he regularly prefaced each song with a reading of the poem, thereby indicating where he thought the emphasis should lie. His musical settings of these poems show a remarkable sensitivity to their mood, manifesting this through both harmony and rhythm, and an equal sensitivity to the proper declamation of the words. It should also be noted that his songs were written for "voice and pianoforte," not for "voice with pianoforte accompaniment." Usually, in fact, the voice and piano go their separate ways. Sometimes, as in *Der Feuerreiter*, the piano part seems like a reduction of an orchestral score. Indeed, Wolf subsequently arranged this song for chorus and orchestra. (He often transcribed the piano parts of his songs for orchestra.)

Der Feuerreiter was composed in 1888, one of Wolf's most prolific years, and was published the following year in a collection of fifty-three songs on poems by Eduard Mörike. The text, like several others in the collection, is taken from one of Mörike's novels, *Maler Nolten*, which he had published in 1832. One character in the novel describes a strange figure,

223

known as "the mad Captain," who is alleged to have lived during the Thirty Years War, and who inhabited an ancient tower next to the local inn. We quote Mörike: "People say that he had been a Captain in one of the imperial regiments but had forfeited his rights as a citizen as the result of some sort of crime. His fate made him a loner who associated with no one. Year after year he never appeared on the streets, except when a fire broke out in the town or neighborhood. He could smell a fire at an instant. When he did, he could be seen at his little window, deadly pale, wearing a red cap and pacing restlessly back and forth. At the first sound of the alarm—indeed, often even before it sounded, and before anyone knew exactly where the fire was—he would take a skinny mare from the stable and ride at full gallop, with an infallible instinct, directly to the scene of the disaster." The actor who tells this tale in the novel then sings, at the request of the assembled company, the ballad of the Fire-Rider, which is the text set by Wolf.

Fascinated by the tale, Wolf did considerable background reading in the fields of folklore and mysticism before composing his setting. Wolf turns the bizzare tale, with its fire, crowds, bells, and wild ride, into a musical work of compelling intensity and excitement. At times his setting may strike one as too grand to be handled by just voice and keyboard. As we shall see, certain musical motives are identified with persons or events in the poem, calling to mind the leitmotif technique we shall encounter in Wagner's music. These associations of music and ideas operate within and among many of Wolf's songs.

The way in which Wolf has set Mörike's poem is both characteristic and worthy of close study. Though the poem has five strophes, Wolf largely ignores this structure in his setting, focusing instead on the ongoing meaning of the poem. But he chose not to ignore Mörike's refrain, *hinterm Berg*, setting this text each time to the same musical idea. In the process he has created a rondolike form. And Wolf matches the subtle changes Mörike makes in the refrain text.

But there is one very effective large-scale musical repetition, evident solely in the piano part, that draws our attention to the connections in meaning between the third and fifth strophes. Here theme, key, and texture serve to establish identity, and to remind us that these are the only two strophes in which references to the supernatural occur.

Wolf's piano part carries the main burden of the drama and is rich in pictorial detail. It opens with a triplet figure that may have been inspired by a similar tale of a wild ride on horseback in Schubert's famous *Der Erlkönig*. The rising line in measures 1 through 16 surely signifies not only the growing excitement of the scene but also the soaring flames. Rhythmic intensity and harsh dissonance are used in measures 15 through 19 to sug-

gest the jostling and confusion of the crowd. (When criticized for his acerbic dissonances, Wolf responded that they could all be explained by accepted "rules of harmony.") The use of repeated quarter notes for the firebell is both simple and effective (mm. 19–21). And the piano supplies a vivid picture of the Fire-Rider springing on his horse and riding forth (mm. 27–34) at the opening of the second strophe.

The change in character in the third strophe elicits a similar change in musical style (m. 47). The tempo now becomes *etwas ruhiger* ("somewhat calmer"), and the dotted rhythms of the wild ride are replaced with even rhythms that project a long-range crescendo to the dramatic climax of the song (m. 61–68). As the Fire-Rider rides into the flames, at the end of this strophe, dotted rhythms reappear in a most assertive fashion.

With the fourth strophe, as the text gradually draws our attention back to the surroundings, Wolf matches textual references with musical references—the crowds (mm. 84–87), the bell (mm. 87–91)—in each case transforming them in character.

A close look at the last thirty measures of the piece will reveal yet other evidence of how masterful Wolf's setting is.

Source: *Werke,* Vol. IV. Translation used by permission of Methune and Co. Ltd., London, from Eric Sams, *The Songs of Hugo Wolf* (1961), p. 83.

Recordings: Numerous available.

Translation:

Do you see? There, at the little window? It's his red cap again! There must be something wierd afoot; he's moving up and down! All at once, everyone's jostling, over the bridge, down to the meadow. Listen! the fire alarm bell is shrilling—behind the hill, behind the hill, the mill's on fire!

Look! There he rides raving sheer through the gate. It's the Fire-rider, on his bony mare. Through the smoke and heat he rides cross-country like the wind. The bell peals on and on—behind the hill, behind the hill, the mill's on fire!

So often he had smelt the red smoke from miles away and ridden out to conjure the flames blasphemously, with a fragment of the One True Cross, but this time—look out! There from the rafters the Devil is grinning at you in the flames of hell. May God have mercy on his soul! Behind the hill, behind the hill; he's running wild in the mill!

Soon the mill burst into ruins. But the rash rider was never again seen from that hour. People and carts come thronging back home away from all that horror. And the little bell rings itself out—behind the hill, behind the hill—fire . . . !

Later on, the miller found by the cellar wall a skeleton, with a cap on, seated bolt upright on the bones of a mare. Fire-rider, how coldly you ride in your grave! Hush! It's all flaking away in ash. Rest in peace, rest in peace, down there in the mill.

Der Feuerreiter

Wolf

===111===

SONG

Modest Mussorgsky (1839–1881)
On the River, from the song cycle *Sunless*

In an earlier commentary (no. 105) we mentioned the efforts in Russia in the first half of the nineteenth century to create a national music that was based on native literary materials, folksongs, and Slavonic chant. These efforts culminated about 1860 in the formation of a loose alliance of five composers, often referred to as "the mighty handful," who shared this common purpose, and who stood apart from contemporaries like Tchaikovsky, whose orientation was mainly toward the mainstream of European music. Balakirev was the spiritual and musical mentor of the group, the other four composers being Borodin, Cui, Mussorgsky, and Rimsky-Korsakov. Largely self-taught amateurs, none of the five had received conservatory training. Such a lack could and did result in a certain crudeness in their compositions such as faulty voice-leading and incorrect harmonic progressions, as many have observed. On the other hand, it had its positive side as well since these men were not predisposed by such training to the accustomed ways of thinking about music or of putting a piece of music together, and were thus able to experiment freely without fear that their efforts would not be "correct." History has judged Mussorgsky to be the most original and most gifted of the five. His influence on later composers has, in fact, been profound.

Mussorgsky is best known today for his opera *Boris Godunov,* which is now recognized as a masterpiece. As such it would be a logical choice for consideration here. But like most of his works it is problematic for a variety of reasons. First, the work underwent a number of revisions as Mussorgsky sought to make it acceptable to the selection committee of the Imperial Theatre, a committee that was accustomed to the Italianate repertory then being performed in the theatre. Second, as a result of his attempts to evolve a musical style that would reflect the realism in art he so treasured—a realism that was also being sought by such contemporary Russian novelists as Dostoyevsky, Gogol, and Turgenev—his music was often seen as crude by his contemporaries, even by his close friends in "the mighty handful." As a result, most of his works were revised after his death by Rimsky-Korsakov, the revision consisting of removing what might be viewed as crudities that could make the work unacceptable to Western audiences. Since it is this revised version of *Boris* that is most often performed and recorded today, we must look elsewhere for indications of Mussorgsky's true intentions. Even though his songs suffered the same fate at the hands of Rimsky-Korsakov and others, his original versions are available and have been recorded. Furthermore, they present in microcosm the principles of realism that he sought in his operas.

The early songs by Mussorgsky are undistinguished, and are in the Romantic tradition then fashionable. But from the mid-1860s Mussorgsky turned increasingly toward depicting realistic pictures of life, often the life of the peasant. For these songs he often wrote his own texts, and employed folk-song-like melodies, frequently borrowing their irregular meters. Some were comic, even satiric; others were extremely poignant in their clear sympathy with the peasant's hard lot. The titles indicate this new interest: "The Street Urchin," "Gathering Mushrooms," "The He-Goat: a little anecdote from high society." His song cycle *Sunless* represents a turn in a different direction. Consisting of a group of six songs on texts by Prince Arsenyi Golenitschev-Kutusov, a young poet with whom Mussorgsky was then sharing living quarters, it is more personal and inward-looking than most of his earlier songs. The alternation between boredom and desperate loneliness in the poems is evident from their titles—"Within four walls," "Thou didst not know me in the crowd," "The idle, noisy day is over," "Boredom," "Elegy," and "On the River"—and appears to reflect the nature of Mussorgsky's life at the time. Because of the loss of the family fortune, brought about by the emancipation of the serfs in 1861, Mussorgsky was forced to support himself by holding tedious government jobs. In the year the cycle was composed, 1874, he was holding a position as assistant head clerk in the Forestry Department of the Ministry of Imperial Domain. His mother, to whom he was devoted, had died in 1865, and his opera, *Boris Godunov,* had twice been rejected by the management of the Imperial Theatre before finally being accepted for performance early in 1874. But even this acceptance proved to be a mixed blessing. Though the work was popular with audiences, press reviews were almost unanimously unfavorable, even the one from the hands of César Cui, whom Mussorgsky thought of as a close friend and supporter.

"On the River" is the final song in the cycle. Its setting of a text that is morbid in the extreme with its hint of imminent suicide, gives a fascinating picture of the range of Mussorgsky's musical language. The serenity of the scene, and the resignation of the speaker, are aptly conveyed in the voice part, which is restricted to a narrow range that only once (m. 28) exceeds an octave as the poem mentions the passions that underlie the calmness. Though the vocal line here is more lyrical than many in Mussorgsky's songs, its shape and rhythm still reflect his concern with realism as it follows the inflections and rhythms of the speaking voice.

The piano part, with its striking harmonies, is equally effective in conveying the mood of the poem. Mussorgsky undergirds the entire song with a pedal on C-sharp, that is expressed in a variety of triplet figures. Above this pedal appear harmonies that are used primarily for their color and may or may not be related according to the rules of functional harmony. For example Mussorgsky juxtaposes harmonies built on D and G-sharp, a tritone removed from each other, in measures 7 and 8. Others stand in the relationship of the third (mm. 10–13). He also uses augmented triads (m. 18) and, in one instance, a harmony that involves all notes of the pentatonic scale (m. 37). Perhaps the most striking effect involves the use of dominant seventh chords without resolution, on scale degrees that are a major third apart (mm. 16, 24, 32, etc.). It is clear from the lines of text with which this progression is associated that Mussorgsky used it to convey the magical attraction the river holds for the speaker. In these effects Mussorgsky, of course, anticipates Debussy, who knew and admired his music. Mussorgsky's manner of building the piece from a succession of small cells comprised of alternating harmonies was also extensively used by Debussy and stands at a far remove from the developmental process then favored by Germanic composers. Sometimes these cells are a measure long (mm. 6–9, 14–15), sometimes two (mm. 10–13, 26–29). Stravinsky also fell under the spell of the songs in this cycle and some fifty years later contemplated orchestrating them, but never carried out the project.

SOURCE: *Modest Mussorgsky: Complete Works,* ed. Paul Lamm (Moscow, 1928; reprint by Edwin F. Kalmus, n.d.), vol. 13, pp. 19–24.

RECORDINGS: EMI SLS 5055, *Russian Songs*; Angel 3575 D/LX, *Mussorgsky Melodies*; EMI 137–173 164–3. *Mussorgsky: Sämtliche Lieder*

TRANSLATION:
The pensive moon,
The distant stars in the blue sky, admire their images in the waters.
I silently stare at the deep waters:
My heart feels their magical secrets.
The gentle waters ripple and become still;
In the moving of the waters lies a powerful enchantment:
I hear thoughts and careless passions.
An unknown voice disturbs my soul;
it frightens me, raises doubts, yet caresses me.
Does it bid me listen, so that I must not move from this place?
Should I flee in confusion?
Does it call me into the depths? I am ready, I will obey!

On the River

Mussorgsky

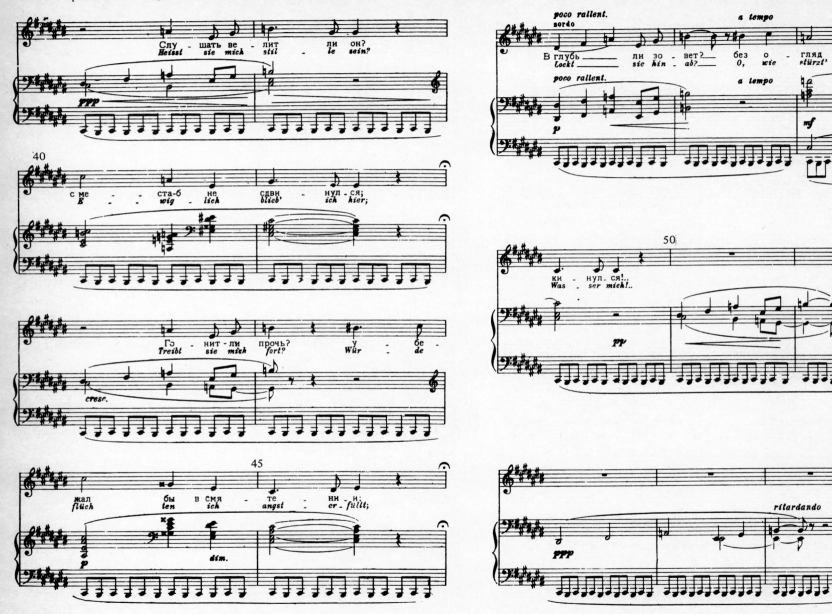

=112=

ORCHESTRAL SONG

Gustav Mahler (1860–1911)
Reveille

Historians of European music often speak of two "Viennese Schools," the first centering on Haydn, Mozart and Beethoven—the Viennese classicists—and the second on Schoenberg and his illustrious pupils, Alban Berg and Anton Webern. Although a century separates these two disparate groups, a case can be made that the music of Gustav Mahler is a connecting link between them. Mahler is sometimes called the last of the German Romantic symphonists. Yet, for all his debt to Beethoven and his admiration of Wagner, there is much in his music that points to the Second Viennese School, the so-called Expressionists. And it is known that as a young man Schoenberg knew Mahler and thought highly of his music.

Like any tag, Expressionism can be a slippery term. Originally applied to a style of painting cultivated primarily in Germany from 1910 through the 1920s, it soon came to be used with music as well, especially for the works of Schoenberg and his two disciples. The definition of the term that best fits the relationship suggested above is a highly intense and personal style in which the distortions of reality replace the ideal norms of beauty sought earlier. (It is no surprise that the musical manifestation of the style should emerge in Vienna, where Freud at the time was investigating the workings of the subconscious.) Many consider musical Expressionism, with its continuing emphasis on the subjective, to be the final phase in the disintegration of Romantic music. Such works as Schoenberg's *Erwartung* and Berg's *Wozzeck* are representative of Expressionism in this sense. Mahler's frequent resort to parody is but one expressionist element in his music.

The Expressionist elements in Mahler's music stem in large measure from his own feeling of alienation. He wrote, "I am thrice homeless, as a native of Bohemia in Austria, as an Austrian among Germans, and as a Jew throughout the world. Everywhere an intruder, never welcomed." The conflicts between pessimism and hope, between torment and exultation, between the simplicity of the country and the sophistication of the city—all are part of his personality and can be found in his music. Some writers speak of him as having neuroses; yet he enjoyed international success as one of the great conductors of his time, especially of opera. He served in a number of the major European opera houses as well as in the Metropolitan Opera in New York for two seasons. (His last post was as conductor of the New York Philharmonic from 1909 to 1911.)

In 1887 Mahler was introduced to a famous collection of folk lyrics, *Des Knaben Wunderhorn* ("The Youth's Magic Horn"), that had been assembled and adapted by Ludwig Achim von Arnim and Clemens Brentano and published in 1805–1808. Like the folk tales collected by the Brothers Grimm, these included some rather bizarre and brutal tales that captured Mahler's fancy: drummer boys sentenced to the gallows, dead soldiers marching homeward, and St. Anthony preaching to the fish. He was to turn to *Des Knaben Wunderhorn* time and again throughout his career, selecting twenty-three of its texts for song settings. His earliest are for voice and piano. Later ones were conceived from the outset for voice and orchestra (though they could be performed with piano) and stand among the earliest and greatest of the new genre of orchestral songs. Several were also to surface as movements in his second, third, and fourth symphonies, which are often referred to as the *Knaben Wunderhorn* symphonies.

In choosing texts from *Des Knaben Wunderhorn* Mahler particularly favored those on military subjects. *Reveille*, one of six of these, was composed in 1899, during Mahler's summer break from his conducting duties, when he usually did his composing. The macabre subject, involving marching dead soldiers, lends itself to the kind of parody at which Mahler excelled. Parody is evident here in the nature of his melodic lines, in his harmonic treatment, and in his choice and use of instruments. Not surprisingly, Mahler's framework for the song is a military march of the sort that John Philip Sousa was composing at the time. It even included the customary trio in a more lyrical vein (mm. 32–72). The song is filled with trumpet fanfares and characteristic march figures (mm. 4–5 and 83–85). And though the harmony is basically diatonic, there are a number of strange passages that make clear that something is awry (mm. 4–6 and 105–107). Since the vocal line is also basically diatonic, the unusual figures that keep cropping up (mm. 21–23 and 87–89) stand out in sharp relief. The effect of some of these can be traced to Mahler's original handling of tonality. Though the strophic structure of the poem is often reflected in the musical setting, Mahler on several occasions modulates towards the end of a strophe rather than in ensuing interludes (mm. 68–72), or even in its middle (mm. 112–120).

Perhaps the most striking feature of the song is Mahler's choice and use of instruments. In addition to the obligatory percussion instruments and the customary pairs of winds, he specifies the contrabassoon. As the lowest wind instrument, its unusual, perhaps even macabre, sound projects easily in the widely spaced open textures that Mahler often employs (mm.

13–15 and 171). Mahler also uses common instruments in uncommon ways. As a sample, we point to the rather crude triple stops called for from violas and cellos in measures 72 through 83; the equally crude bow strokes from all the strings from measure 89 to the end; the instructions to the oboist and clarinettist to upend their instruments, pointing the bells in the air, in measures 90, 96, etc.; the use on the cymbal of a stick with a sponge head in measure 124. But Mahler reserves the most striking effects for the final strophe, when the dead soldiers march by. Here he calls for muted trumpets and horns (mm. 140–162), the shrill sounds of high winds now intensified by the use of the piccolo in an unusual scoring that contains little sound in the middle register (mm. 163–166), and **col legno** ("with the wood") from the violins. In this latter technique, eerie in the extreme, the violins are to bow the string with the wood of the stick rather than with its hairs. (Most violinists do so with great reluctance, fearing that in the process the varnish will be scraped off the stick.) Both Schoenberg and Berg were to continue Mahler's exploration of unusual instrumental sounds in their works.

It is left to the reader to investigate the ways in which Mahler has used thematic materials in the song. We mention only that the impression it gives of being very tightly organized is not without reason. Mahler has created—perhaps unwittingly—a powerful and timeless antiwar statement.

Recordings: CBS 30044, *Mahler's Greatest Hits*; CBS 79355, *Mahler*; Columbia KS 7395, Mahler: *Des Knaben Wunderhorn*; Philips 9500316, *Songs from Des Knaben Wunderhorn*.

Reveille   **Mahler**

1) Piatti attaccati alla Gran Cassa, percossi da una persona

1) sempre *f*

*) Vorschläge so schnell wie möglich
l'appoggiature quanto più possibile presto

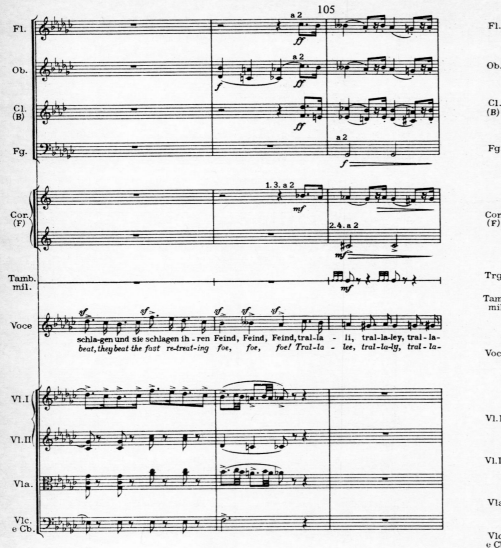

1) Oboen grell schreiend! Schalltrichter heben!
Oboi stridendo nel acuto. L'apertura in aria!

1) Die 2. Spieler setzen ruhig die Dämpfer auf und treten unmerklich ein!
La 2ª metà dei suonatori mettendo la sordina senza dare alcuno accorgimento cominciano a suonare!
2) Becken an der Trommel befestigt
Piatti attaccati alla cassa

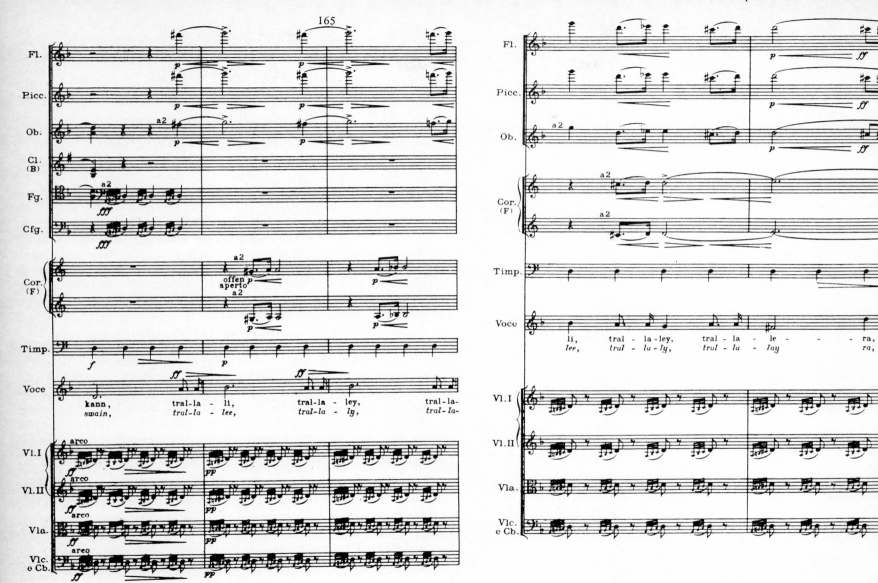

=113=

GERMAN OPERA

Carl Maria von Weber (1786–1826)
Der Freischütz, Act II, scene 2 (*Wolfschlucht* scene)

In the history of opera certain works stand out not only for their intrinsic merit but also for their influence on the music of succeeding generations. One such opera is Weber's *Der Freischütz* ("The Freeshooter"). Right from its first performance in Berlin in 1821, it was hailed in German states as a masterpiece since it appealed in many ways to rising and as-yet-unfulfilled nationalistic sentiments. (Widely performed even today in German opera houses, but seldom in other countries, it is considered by many to be the German national opera.) But *Der Freischütz* also contains a number of stylistic features that were to be widely adopted in nineteenth-century German music, whether it was operatic or not.

Weber made his intentions clear in labeling *Der Freischütz* a Romantic opera. Its subject matter contains many ingredients that were to become the stock-in-trade of later German Romantic composers: nature as an active agent that mirrors the events in man's life, particularly in the struggle between good and evil; and a shift in focus from the heroes of classic mythology to the common people in Germanic folk tales or myths, who moved in a world peopled by demons and apparitions. Weber found the story in 1810, in a newly published collection of tales called *Gespensterbuch*, or "The Ghost Book," assembled by August Apel and F. Laun. This was yet another of those collections of German folk tales and folk songs that were being assembled and published at the time (see no. 112). Not until 1817, however, when he took over his duties as director of German Opera in Dresden, was serious work on the opera to begin. Friedrich Kind, a Dresden poet, was to prepare the libretto.

Briefly stated, the original tale concerns a hunter who sells his soul to Zamiel, The Black Huntsman (i.e., the Devil), in return for seven magic bullets. "Six find their mark, but the seventh belongs to the Evil One." In Kind's version of the tale, set in the seventeenth century shortly after the Thirty Years War, the hunter, Caspar, must either deliver himself to Zamiel after three years, or find someone to take his place. Caspar finds his victim, another hunter named Max, who is in love with Agathe. In accordance with ancient law, she can become Max's bride only if he wins a marksmen's competition. Through Zamiel's intervention, as we learn, Max's aim, normally superb, has been poor in recent hunts. He therefore accepts Caspar's offer of magic bullets and agrees to meet Caspar in the *Wolfschlucht* ("Wolf Glen") at midnight, where the bullets are to be cast. It is this eerie scene that we present here.

As a member of a traveling theater family, and later a conductor of opera, Weber knew well the workings of the theater, and was always intimately involved in all aspects of any production he conducted. In operas like *Der Freischütz* he sought to create a more unified work by several means. First, the orchestra plays a more important role in the drama than that of mere accompaniment to the singer. Here it is used, and very successfully, to create different moods. Second, Weber uses some thematic materials throughout the opera as a means of unifying what is essentially a number opera. Recurring themes, of course, are also a powerful dramatic tool as they serve to remind the listener of some earlier situation in the drama. Wagner, who as a young boy was deeply impressed by Weber's operas, was to use recurring themes extensively in his own operas. Weber also gave an important role to lighting. He speaks of much of the opera taking place in the near dark. (Not until the end of the nineteenth century was the new technology of electric lighting to allow the powerful effects we take for granted in the theater today.)

As the framework for *Der Freischütz* Weber chose the conventions of the German *Singspiel:* balladlike tunes placed within spoken dialogue. But this is hardly a pure type. Several arias are rather Italianate in character, and in the scene under consideration Weber has introduced a technique called melodrama. In this technique, employed earlier by such composers as Jean Jacques Rousseau, the speaking voice either alternates with the orchestra or is heard above it.

We see from an interview with Weber, quoted below, that his intentions were to use music to create strong moods and hence to reinforce the action at any point. To this end, and with great dramatic effect, he focused primarily on tone color and harmony:

> There are in *Der Freischütz* two principal elements that can be recognized at first sight—hunting life and the role of demonic powers as personified by Zamiel. So when composing the opera I had to look for suitable tone colors to characterize these two elements. . . . The tone color of the scoring for forest and hunting life was easy to find: the horns provided it. The difficulty lay only in finding for the horns new melodies that would be both simple and popular. For this purpose I searched among folk melodies, and I have careful study to thank if this part of my task is successful. . . . I had to remind the hearer of the 'dark powers' [Max's words] by means of tone-color and melody as often as possible. . . . I gave a great deal of thought to the question of what

was the right principal coloring for this sinister element. Naturally it had to be a dark, gloomy color—the lowest register of the violins, viola and basses, particularly the lowest register of the clarinet, which seemed especially suitable for depicting the sinister, then the mournful sound of the bassoon, the lowest notes of the horns, the hollow roll of drums or single hollow strokes on them. When you go through the score of the opera, you will find hardly any number in which this somber principal color is not noticeable, you will be able to satisfy yourself that the picture of the sinister element predominates by far and it will be plain to you that *this* gives the opera its principal character.

The orchestral colors described by Weber, especially the use of the horn to evoke the forest, were to become commonplace during the nineteenth century. (Six years after *Der Freischütz*, Franz Schubert was to employ Weber's combination of male chorus and four horns in his *Nightsong in the Forest*.) In Weber's emphasis on horn, clarinet, viola, and cello, we have another instance of the downward shift in the center of gravity of orchestral sound that occurred in the nineteenth century (see no. 106). Weber's skill as an orchestrator was widely admired, a remark by Debussy being typical: "He scrutinizes the soul of each instrument and exposes it with a gentle hand."

Of equal interest to us is Weber's use of harmony. The Wolf Glen scene is saturated with diminished-seventh chords; in fact, the key plan of successive sections in the scene is built on this chord. The chord, of course, was not new, but being ambiguous as to its function, with several possible resolutions and a natural tension-building character, it was to be exploited widely by later nineteenth-century composers.

In spite of Weber's effective use of such orchestral and harmonic devices to depict the wildness of the scene, in at least one respect his music shows a continuing affinity to Classical style. Note how the immediate repetition of individual phrases, so characteristic of classic style, pervades the scene (mm. 13–20, 110–119, 236–239, etc.). To depict the "chaos" inherent in a storm without the music itself becoming chaotic is a difficult assignment. You might compare Haydn's treatment of chaos in the opening of his *Creation* (see no. 95), or the storm scene in Beethoven's Symphony no. 6 (*Pastoral*) to see how other composers solved this problem.

Source: Used by permission of G. Schirmer, Inc.

Recordings: Numerous available.

Der Freischütz   **von Weber**

Flutes & Piccolo, Oboes, Clarinets in A, Bassoons, Horns in D & in C, Trumpets in C, 3 Trombones, Kettledrums & Strings.

A weird, craggy glen, surrounded by high mountains, down the side of one of which falls a cascade. To the left a blasted tree, on the knotty branch of which an owl is sitting. To the right a steep path by which Max comes; below it a great cave. The moon throws a lurid light over all. A few battered pine-trees are scattered here and there. Caspar, in shirt-sleeves, is making a circle of black stones; a skull is in the centre; near by a ladle, a bullet-mould, and an eagle's wing. A thunderstorm is coming on.

Caspar. Dank, Samiel, die Frist ist gewonnen! Kommst du endlich, Kamerad? Ist das auch recht, mich so allein zu lassen? Siehst du nicht, wie mir's sauer wird?

Caspar. Thanks, Zamiel, my respite is won. (to Max) Well, comrade, you've come at last! the toil and trouble you leave to me! (He fans the fire with the eagle's wing, and lifts it up as he speaks towards Max.)

Caspar (wirft ihm die Jagdflasche zu, die Max weglegt). Zuerst trink' einmal! Die Nachtluft ist kühl und feucht. Willst du selbst giessen?

Max. Nein, das ist wider die Abrede.

Caspar. [Nicht? So bleib' ausser dem Kreise, sonst kostet's dein Leben!]

Max. Was hab' ich zu thun, Hexenmeister?]

Caspar. Fasse Muth! Was du auch hören und sehen magst, verhalte dich ruhig. (Mit eigenem heimlichen Grausen.) Käme vielleicht ein Unbekannter, uns zu helfen, was kümmert's dich? Kommt was anders, was thut's? So etwas sieht ein Gescheiter gar nicht!

Max. O, wie wird das enden!

Caspar. Umsonst ist der Tod! Nicht ohne Widerstand schenken verborgene Naturen den Sterblichen ihre Schätze. Nur wenn du mich selbst zittern siehst, dann komme mir zu Hülfe und rufe, was ich rufen werde, sonst sind wir beide verloren.

Max (macht eine Bewegung des Einwurfs).

Caspar. Still! Die Augenblicke sind kostbar! (Der Mond ist bis auf einen schmalen Streif verfinstert. Caspar nimmt die Giesskelle.) Merk' auf, [was ich hinein werfen werde,] damit du die Kunst lernst! (Er nimmt die Ingredienzen aus der Jagdtasche und wirft sie nach und nach hinein.)

Caspar (tosses him the hunting-flask, which Max lays aside). First take a drink! The night air is cool and damp. Will you mould the bullets yourself?
Max. No, our agreement was different.
Caspar. [No? Then stay outside the circle; 'twill cost your life else!
Max. What have I to do, Master Warlock?]
Caspar. Take heart! Whatever you see or hear, keep quiet. (With a secret shudder.) Should a stranger come to help us, what need you care? If anything else comes, what of it? A clever fellow doesn't notice such things!
Max. Oh, how will this end?!
Caspar. Nothing venture, nothing win! Nature does not yield her secret treasures without resistance. Come to my aid only when you see that I myself am trembling, and then call out what I call, otherwise we are both lost!
Max (makes as if he would object).
Caspar. Hush! The moments are precious! (The moon is wholly obscured, save a narrow strip. Caspar takes the ladle.) Now mark what I throw in, that you may learn the art! (Takes the ingredients out of his hunting-pouch, and throws them in one by one.)

Max. Hier bin ich! was hab' ich zu thun?

Max (sharply to Caspar).— Here I am! what must I do?

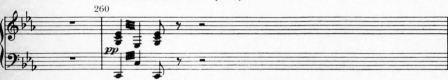

Caspar. Hier, erst das Blei; etwas Glas von zerbrochenen Kirchenfenstern, das findet sich. Etwas Quecksilber. Drei Kugeln, die schon einmal getroffen.
Caspar. First the lead; some broken glass of churchwindows, that can always be got; some quicksilver; three bullets that have hit their mark.

Caspar. Das rechte Auge eines Wiedehopfs; das linke eines Luchses. Probatum est!
Caspar. The right eye of a lapwing, the left of a lynx; a powerful charm.

Caspar. Und nun den Kugelsegen!
Caspar. And now a blessing on the bullets!

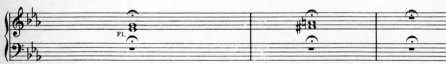

(At the three rests he prostrates himself three times to the earth.)

Caspar. Schütze, der im Dunkeln wacht, Samiel! Samiel! hab' acht! Steh mir bei in dieser
Thou who roam'st at midnight hour, Zamiel, Zamiel, thy pow'r, Spirit dread, be near this

Andante.

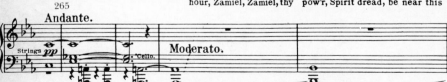

Moderato.

Nacht, Bis der Zauber ist vollnight, And complete the mystic

bracht! Salbe mir so Kraut als rite. By the shade of murderer's

Blei, Segn'es sieben, neun und dead, Do thou bless the charmed

drei, dass die Kugel tüchtig lead. Seven the number we re-

sei! vère:

Samiel! Samiel! herbei!
Zamiel! Zamiel! ap-pear!

(The contents of the ladle ferment and hiss, with a greenish flame. A cloud passes entirely over the moon. The scene is now lighted only by the fire on the hearth, the owl's eyes, and the decayed wood of the oak-tree.)

Allegro moderato.

Horns, Cl., & Strings

'Cello

(Caspar casts the bullet, drops it out of the mould and calls:) Eins! One!
(echo repeats) Eins! One!

(Night-birds come flying out of the forest; they gather round the fire, flapping their wings and hopping about.)

(Caspar casts another bullet and calls:) Zwei! Two! (echo) Zwei! Two!

Poco più mosso.
(A black

Cl. & B. Trombone

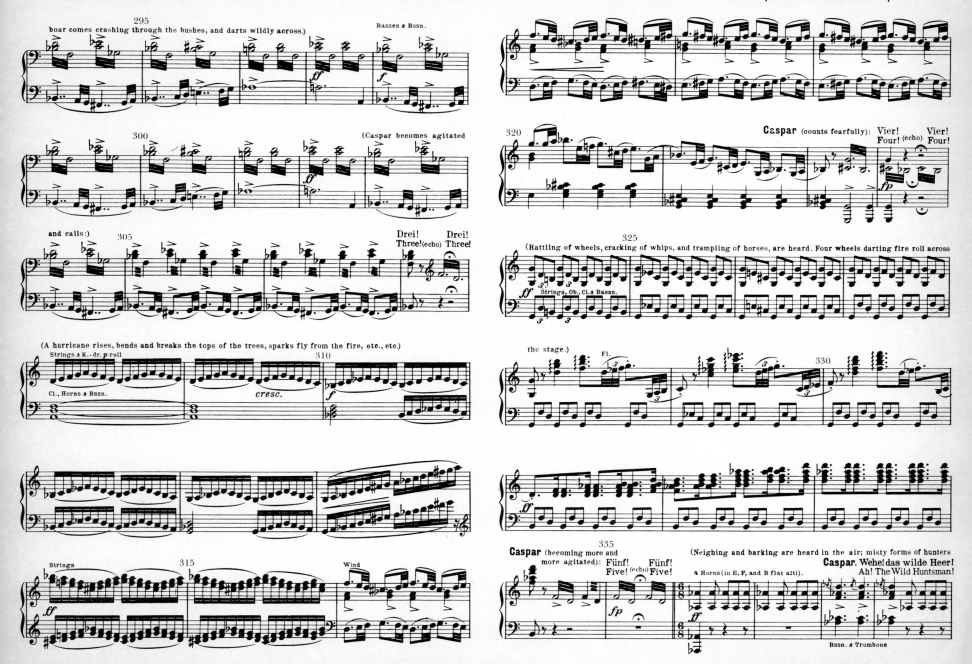

114

ITALIAN OPERA

Gioacchino Rossini (1792–1868)
Il Barbiere di Siviglia, excerpt from Act I

Although Rossini was recognized as the greatest Italian composer of his time, his career must be accounted as extraordinary. Following a period of incredible activity (he wrote over thirty successful operas between 1810 and 1829), he all but ceased composing during his remaining forty-odd years. A number of reasons have been advanced to explain this retirement from the opera scene at the height of his career. The most widely accepted attribute it to Rossini's poor health, which surely was a result of such early hyperactivity, and to his attainment of financial security—not an easy accomplishment for an opera composer of his time who, in the absence of copyright laws, could normally expect income only from the first production of an opera. Though Rossini turned again to composing in the late 1850s, it was not to operas but rather to numerous attractive piano pieces and a fine mass. But his reputation today rests primarily on his operas, the best known being *Il Barbiere di Siviglia* ("The Barber of Seville") and *Guglielmo Tell* ("William Tell"). Many regard the former as the greatest of all comic operas—both Beethoven and Verdi thought highly of it. But recent critics have argued that his serious operas, such as *Tell*, are of equal importance and, in fact, hold a central position in the history of nineteenth-century opera.

The history of opera is filled with accounts of the speed with which composers have written an opera. But few can equal Rossini's achievement in composing and writing out the score of *The Barber* in a mere three weeks. Since the circumstances surrounding the composition of this work reveal much about the conditions under which composers of commercial opera, such as Rossini, had been working since the early eighteenth century, we should examine them briefly.

Rossini was not yet twenty-four, and had already composed fifteen operas over a period of at least seven years by the time he signed a contract on 26 December 1815 to compose the second opera for the forthcoming

Carnival Season at the Teatro Argentina in Rome. The contract states that it was up to the manager of the theater to choose the libretto, "whether old or new," and that Rossini agreed to deliver the score of the opera by the middle of January, "and to adapt it to the voices of the singers, obliging himself, moreover, to make, if necessary, all changes that may be required as much for the good execution of the music as to suit the exigencies of the singers." Rossini further agreed "to direct his opera according to the custom, and to assist personally at all the vocal and orchestral rehearsals as many times as it shall be necessary, either at the theater or elsewhere, at the will of the director; he obliges himself also to assist at the three first performances, to be given consecutively, and to direct the execution at the piano." In this last condition Rossini followed in the footsteps of such earlier opera composers as Mozart, who had presided at the harpsichord in his time. Since the first performance took place on 20 February 1816, the singers had a little over a month to master their parts and the attendant stage business.

As for the libretto, the theater manager, Duke Francesco Sforza-Cesarini, rejected the first one he solicited. He then turned to Cesare Sterbini, who had already supplied a libretto for one of Rossini's operas. Given the shortness of time, Sterbini suggested reworking *Il Barbiere di Siviglia,* a libretto that the composer Paisiello had used for a highly successful opera in 1782, and which had been based on Beaumarchais's popular play, *Le Barbier de Seville* (see no. 94 above for an opera based on Beaumarchais's sequel to this play). To lessen the chances of antagonizing an audience that might still remember Paisiello's opera, Sterbini chose the title *Almaviva, ossia L'inutile precauzione* ("Almaviva, or the useless precaution"), though Rossini's work soon came to be known by its present name. He also attached a long preface to the libretto in the hope of disarming critics.

One of the secrets behind Rossini's speedy completion of the *The Barber* lies in his practice of borrowing numbers from his earlier operas, (usually but not always those that had failed), perhaps reworking them slightly, and changing their text. There are at least nine instances of such borrowings in *The Barber,* including the number given here. The opening of *La calunnia,* for example, was taken from a duet for Arsace and Zenobia in *Aureliano in Palmira,* which Rossini had composed in 1813; the ensuing crescendo passage comes from a duet for Ladislau and Aldimira in Act I of his *Sigismondo,* which had been composed in 1814 and was a failure.

Under the circumstances it is not surprising that Rossini was upset at a projected complete edition of his works, failures and all, in the 1850's. He wrote of the project:

'I remain furious . . . about the publication, which will bring all my operas together before the eyes of the public. The same pieces will be found several times, for I thought I had the right to remove from my fiascos those pieces which seemed best, to rescue them from shipwreck by placing them in new works. A fiasco seemed to be good and dead, and now look they've resuscitated them all!'

Rossini was to be an unwitting victim of the rapid change in attitude toward music that took place during his lifetime, and which was to transform views of a composer's purpose. When he had composed his operas, his expectation was that they, like all earlier operas, would enjoy a short life—but preferably one that was healthy. By the 1850s, however, there had been a marked reorientation towards, and growing interest in, music from the past, which found expression in publications of the complete works of Bach, Beethoven, and Mozart. Thus, what might have been written in haste as a one-time piece by any earlier composer was now deemed worthy of preservation for all time. The end product of this reorientation was, of course, the establishment of what is known as the *standard repertoire,* a body of pieces that is played over and over again to the exclusion of other pieces. To a large extent the standard repertoire still exists in piano music, music for orchestra, and opera.

The circumstances surrounding the premiere in Rome, though peripheral to our concerns here, read like comic opera. We merely mention that we know from Rossini's own account that the first performance was a fiasco, but the second, which he did not attend (feigning illness) was a triumph. Seeing a crowd that carried torches approaching his dwelling following the second performance, and thinking that they had come to set it afire, he sought refuge in a nearby stable. Nothing would persuade him of the crowd's friendly intentions.

Our excerpt is taken from Act I. Basilio is music master to the young and beautiful Rosina, who is the ward of Dr. Bartolo. Bartolo, a character-type straight out of the Italian *commedia dell'arte* (see vol. I, no. 63), plans to marry Rosina, but she prefers her secret suitor, Count Almaviva, whom she knows only as Lindoro. Basilio suggests that Bartolo can eliminate his competition by devising some unseemly gossip about the Count that will embarrass him and perhaps drive him out of town. In the recitative just before the famous aria, "la calunnia" (slander), we hear this exchange:

Bartolo: . . . but slander. . . .
Basilio: What of it? Slander, what is it, don't you know?
Bartolo: No, not really.
Basilio: No? Be quiet and listen to me.

Basilio then launches into his cynical and amusing description of the subtleties of slanderous gossip and their effect on the intended victim. Sterbini has supplied him with a typical opera buffa aria text that contains five stanzas of varying lengths, each of which comprises a complete thought and ends with the rhyme *-ar*. Rossini's setting of this text can only be described as brilliant, even though he uses the simplest vocabulary of diatonic harmonies. The orchestra carries the burden of providing musical cohesion by means of thematic materials, thus allowing the voice great freedom in the way it presents the text. The aria opens with three repetitions of an innocuous four-measure idea that sets the stage for the rising whirlwind to come. In measure 20 begins an example of the Rossini crescendo, one of the best known features of his style. As usual it consists of a repeating four-measure phrase that alternates tonic and dominant harmonies. In this instance several statements move to other keys before returning to the tonic for the final build to the climax. Rossini has skillfully suggested the insidiousness of slander by calling for the violins to play staccato **al ponticello** ("at the bridge") right through to the end of the crescendo in measure 54. (When string instruments are bowed close to the bridge a very eerie sound results that is rich in upper partials but has a relatively weak fundamental pitch.) As the passage proceeds the orchestral texture thickens as other instruments are added, two by two, the horns and trumpets being among the last to enter. Against this background the voice delivers the second and third stanzas of the text, beginning softly and rather haltingly, with long rests between successive phrases, but gradually becoming more insistent with a chattering line of repeated notes that moves finally to disjunct motion. Since the high point of Sterbini's text occurs in the fourth stanza, it is not surprising that Rossini brings it in right before the climax of the aria, in measure 54. After so much tonic and dominant harmony in the crescendo, the Neapolitan sixth chord that serves as the climax (m. 59), at the mention of the "explosion of the cannon," comes as a real shock. Here, for the sake of the imminent return, Rossini moves briefly to the dominant. With the fifth stanza Basilio turns to the effect of slander on the stunned victim, and Rossini returns to the tonic with hints of the opening material in the flute. The reference to a public lashing (mm. 77–80) calls forth another crescendo, this one on a much smaller scale. Cadential material (mm. 105ff.) closes the aria with a climactic sweep that affords the singer the opportunity to acknowledge the applause of the audience. In this short aria, neither harmonically or structurally complex, Rossini has brilliantly etched Basilio's cynical remarks.

That Rossini's comic writing remains fresh even today is a tribute to his taste and wit as he moves rapidly through a series of absurd situations, most of them stock scenes from over a century of *opere buffe*. He never dwells too long on a melodic idea, and he constantly varies the orchestral color. (His writing for woodwinds is especially fine.) His works stand in the long tradition of Italian opera, usually called "singer's opera" since one's attention centers on the voice and beautiful singing.

Recordings: Numerous available.

Il Barbiere di Siviglia   Rossini

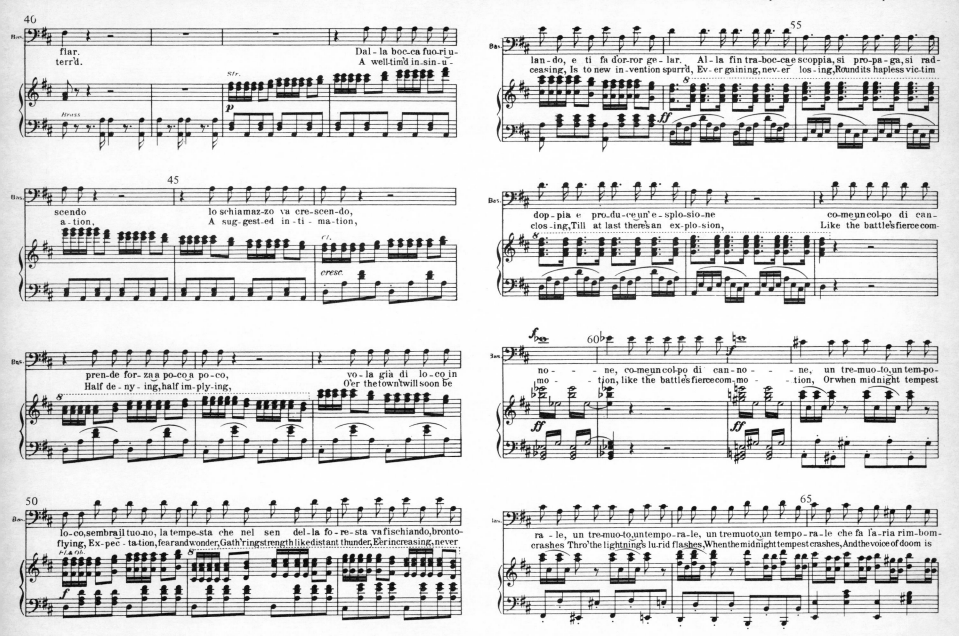

115

ITALIAN OPERA

Giuseppe Verdi (1813–1901)
Il Trovatore, Act IV, scene 1

In an earlier comment (no. 93) we noted that opera has meant different things to different people throughout its history, and as a consequence any composer would be hard pressed to satisfy all of opera's devotees with his works. Of all opera composers, Giuseppe Verdi has had the greatest success in this respect, if one measures success by the fact that four of his operas—*Rigoletto* (1851), *Il Trovatore* (1853), *La Traviata* (1853), and *Aìda* (1871)—have consistently been among the top ten (however this is determined) in at least nineteen major opera houses throughout Europe and

North and South America ever since their premieres. (Other operas among the top ten in these same houses include Rossini's *Barber* [no. 114], Wagner's *Lohengrin,* Bizet's *Carmen,* and one or two operas by Puccini.) Yet, until very recently many critics have given the earlier three of Verdi's operas short shrift because of what were commonly judged to be his ludicrous plots, filled with "blood and thunder," and his hackneyed musical settings that relied heavily on accompanimental figures that seemed best suited to the organ grinder. Such judgments merit momentary consideration.

In the nineteenth century—especially, but hardly exclusively, in Italy—opera was the popular form of entertainment. Even the smallest Italian city could boast an opera house. (Opera was to surrender this leading role only with the emergence in our century of the mass media: film, radio, and television.) In order to be a commercial success, therefore, any opera had to appeal to a broad audience. Only at the risk of losing this audience could a composer depart too far from the conventions of the genre then in use. For Italian opera these conventions included a continuing focus on beautiful singing—resulting in what is known as "singer's opera"—and simple and catchy tunes that would captivate audiences and bring them back for subsequent performances. (Not until the 1880s could one begin to hear recordings in one's home of opera arias by one's favorite singers.) As the most successful Italian composer of commercial opera of his time, Verdi clearly understood and accepted these conventions, initially using Rossini as his model. Though he never abandoned the preeminence of the voice, the increasing financial security he gained from continuing successes allowed him gradually to modify other conventions of Italian opera into a far more personal and subtle art, and to raise standards in general for all Italian opera. It has been argued that much of Verdi's success within Italy might be attributed to his close association with the nationalist movement known as the *Risorgimento,* a "rising up again" that included almost a century of struggle against Italy's domination by foreign powers, and internal strife among regional states, and that was to lead to its unification as a nation in 1870. But such an argument fails to account for the fact that his three operas from the 1850s rapidly made their way outside Italy in spite of the limitations identified by the critics mentioned above, and makes one suspect that these critics may have been applying the wrong standards in forming their judgments. Any judgment of the artistic merits of his operas must begin with a consideration of the role of opera in Italy in Verdi's time and the audiences for which he was writing.

Il Trovatore ("The Troubadour") is the eighteenth of Verdi's twenty-eight operas, and was written on contract for one of the three opera houses then existent in Rome. Verdi took his plot from a play with the same title,

El trovador, by the Spanish playwright Antonio Garcia Guitiérrez (1813–1884), which had first been produced in Madrid in 1836. Focusing on the gloomier side of Romanticism—a side that appealed particularly to Verdi's sensibilities—it was filled with the strong passions of real people that repeatedly stirred his imagination: filial and maternal love, jealousy, and vengeance. (In 1853 he was to write: "I want subjects that are novel, big, beautiful, varied and bold—as bold as can be.") Verdi turned to Salvatore Cammarano, a Neopolitan librettist who had already collaborated with him in three earlier operas, to adapt the play as a libretto. From the sizable body of correspondence between Verdi and Cammarano that survives we gain a fascinating picture of a strong-willed composer who was thoroughly conversant with all matters concerned with the theater, who constantly had in mind dramatic values and matters of pacing, and who was never shy about demanding changes from his librettists in order to realize the dramatic vision he had in mind. (Since Cammarano died before the task was completed, Leone Bardare was entrusted with finishing the adaptation.) The action takes place in northern Spain at the beginning of the fifteenth century during a civil war to determine the next occupant of the throne of Aragon. Since the plot, with its mistaken identities and misunderstandings, is rather complicated, we will give only sufficient details to help in understanding the excerpt at hand. The principal male characters, Manrico and the Count of Luna, are on opposing sides in the civil war. Manrico, a knight, is also the troubadour that gave Verdi his title for the opera. Both Manrico and the Count are in love with Leonora, who loves only Manrico, and who ultimately gives her life in what she believes to be a successful effort to buy his freedom.

Our excerpt—sometimes referred to simply as the Miserere—opens the last act of the opera. Following a common pattern for final acts in many of Verdi's operas, this opening scene included a prayer by the heroine, Leonora. But it includes much more than that. Although this is "number opera" in the tradition of Handel, Mozart, and Rossini, Verdi has drastically altered the conventional makeup of individual numbers for the sake of the overall dramatic effect. The present number is labeled "Scena, Aria, e Miserere," and includes passages of recitativo accompagnato, aria, and chorus. It it clear from Verdi's correspondence with Cammarano that it was the former who suggested the amalgamation into one number of Leonora's aria, the offstage Miserere chorus, and Manrico's ensuing troubadour song from the tower. Other numbers in the opera indicate by their titles a similar amalgamation of disparate elements: Scena, Romanza, e Terzetto; Scena e Duetto; Scena ed Aria.

As for the action here, Manrico has finally been captured by the

Count and is about to be executed. As the curtain rises we see Leonora before the tower in which he has been incarcerated. The sense of impending doom is vividly projected visually through its nocturnal setting, and musically by a short introduction for low clarinets and bassoons. Leonora's cryptic remark as she glances at her ring concerns her plan of action to save Manrico, yet to be revealed. She intends to buy his freedom by agreeing to marry the Count, but then to remain faithful to Manrico by taking the poison she has concealed in her ring. With the tolling of the death bell (m. 62) a male chorus—presumed to be monks, but never identified as such—is heard behind the scenes praying for Manrico's soul. In Leonora's reaction to this doleful combination we see Verdi's consummate gift as a dramatic composer. She sings a short, impassioned aria whose orchestral background of what have been called "volleying chords" effectively projects her sense of dread. This sense of dread is further manifest in her short vocal phrases with their breathless quality and her sighing triplet figures in measures 78 through 80.

The integrity of this particular number is made clear by its key plan. Beginning in F minor, it has a lengthy closing section in F major. It moves internally to A-flat major and A-flat minor before returning to F. Verdi's skillful use of the operatic conventions of his time for the sake of dramatic effect is manifest in several ways. In place of the *recitative secco* that was still employed by Rossini (see no. 114), Verdi now employs unaccompanied recitative (mm. 11–19) for the opening dialogue, perfectly matching the gloomy scene. The more familiar *recitativo accompagnato* follows. Another example of his skill is found at the end of the number. Leonora's exaltation over the gift of her life for Manrico provides a natural and justified opportunity for the vocal display that was so much a part of Italian opera. Her subsequent departure from the stage, accompanied by a full close, allowed for the customary applause by the audience before the following number began, and hence a minimal disturbance in dramatic continuity.

One other aspect of the tradition of Italian opera should be mentioned. In "singer's opera," the performers were accustomed to taking rhythmic liberties with their parts employing a technique that is known as **rubato** (It., "robbed"). These liberties were usually but not always most evident in connection with high notes. If one listens to different recordings of Leonora's aria section in measures 38 through 61, one will note the ways in which rubato is used. One will also see that it takes a skillful conductor to coordinate the orchestral and vocal lines. This is especially true of the passage in measures 50 through 54 where we encounter a common Verdian technique, the joining of the solo voice and an instrument at the interval of a third or sixth.

Source: Used by permission of G. Schirmer, Inc.

Recordings: Numerous available.

Il Trovatore   Verdi

A wing of the Palace of Aliaferia; on one side a tower, with casements secured by iron bars. Dark night.

═══116═══

GERMAN OPERA

Richard Wagner (1813–1883)
Die Walküre, Act III, scene 3, *Wotan's Farewell*

It is probable that more has been written on Richard Wagner than on any other Western composer. Such intense and continuing interest in both his artistic ideas, which he expressed at length in his prose writings and in his music, indicates the forcefulness of his personality and further suggests the pivotal role his music played throughout the latter half of the nineteenth century and well on into the twentieth. Wagner was a controversial figure. Endowed with a sizable ego and a clear sense of his artistic purpose—or perhaps more accurately, his artistic mission—he did more than any other composer of his time to foster a sense of seriousness of purpose in the arts, to the point where some began to view the arts as a surrogate for religion. In the process he was also instrumental in altering the traditional view of the composer's place in society. Earlier the composer had normally been seen as an artisan or craftsman whose main purpose was to supply agreeable entertainment, but many now began to look upon the composer as a spiritual leader. The course of Wagner's career testifies both to this new view of art and to the dramatic change in the social position of the composer that took place during his lifetime. Though in the 1840s Wagner, like Haydn some eighty years earlier, still wore livery as a court servant in his position as conductor of the court opera of the King of Saxony in Dresden, by 1876 he was to see the completion of an opera house in Bayreuth, Germany—paid for with other people's money—intended solely for the performance of his operas, to which came on bended knee the crowned heads of Europe. Such a strong-willed person was bound to arouse strong feelings in others: Some were to become his ardent supporters, others equally vehement detractors. His spell was such, in fact, that it is only in the last forty years that it has been possible to begin to view his works dispassionately.

Wagner's most impressive work is his *Ring of the Nibelungen*. Characteristically bold in concept, in almost every aspect the work reflects the grandiose side of Romanticism. It consists of a cycle of four music dramas (Wagner's term for his later operas) that last in aggregate almost fifteen hours and were intended to be performed on four successive evenings in a special festival. As was his custom, Wagner wrote both text and music, working on the *Ring* off and on over a period of twenty-eight years. (He interrupted work on the cycle to compose two other operas, neither of which is much smaller in concept: *Die Meistersinger* and *Tristan und Isolde*.) Following Berlioz's lead, Wagner called for a sizable orchestra that includes winds in fours, eight horns, six harps, and a variety of new brass instruments that permitted the extension of available sonorities into new registers: bass trumpet, the so-called Wagner tubas that are entrusted to horn players, both tubas and contrabass tubas, and contrabass trombone. Such an assemblage requires especially large voices that can be heard through the massive orchestral sound—though the excellent acoustics of his *Festspielhaus* in Bayreuth, where his operas are still produced each summer, allow singers to be heard clearly even through the loudest tuttis.

The four operas of the *Ring* consist of a trilogy (*Die Walküre, Siegfried,* and *Die Götterdämmerung*) preceded by a prologue, *Das Rheingold*. Wagner drew his plot from Germanic and Nordic myth, believing that myth, because of its universality, would have the greatest meaning and broadest appeal to an audience. His choice of subject doubtless reflects his participation in the abortive revolution that took place in Dresden in 1849. (While most of his revolutionary associates, including the Russian anarchist Bakunin, were captured and imprisoned, Wagner managed to escape to Switzerland, where he remained an exile from German states until 1861.) The plot of the *Ring*, which encompasses several generations of characters, is far too complex to summarize here; but its theme, which is simplicity incarnate, is readily understandable: The corruption that arises from man's greed for money (gold) leads to his greed for power and subsequent renunciation of love, for Wagner mankind's only redeeming force. Though the plot is peopled with gods and goddesses, dwarfs and giants, toads and dragons, and mortals, and contains numerous stunning stage effects, it is widely agreed that Wagner's intent in the *Ring* was to create a monumental allegory that had relevance to the social conditions of his day. One interpretation, by the English playwright George Bernard Shaw, sees Wagner attacking contemporary middle-class values in capitalist societies.

Wagner wrote the text for the *Ring* from 1848 through 1852. The music for *Die Walküre*, the work excerpted here, was composed from 1854 to 1856, and is thus roughly contemporaneous with Verdi's *Il Trovatore* (no. 115). (Even a cursory glance will reveal that the two come from very different worlds.) Since it is in *Die Walküre* that one encounters the most intense interaction between gods and mortals, many find this work to be the ideal *entrée* into the *Ring* cycle. The title of the opera, rendered in English as

"The Valkyries," refers to the eight daughters of Wotan, the king of the gods in Germanic mythology. (The "Ride of the Valkyries," which opens the third act, is probably the most frequently performed orchestral excerpt from Wagner's operas.) It is their task as goddesses to bring fallen heroes from the battlefield to Valhalla, the home of the gods. One of them, Brünnhilde, is Wotan's favorite. In the scene presented here she has just disobeyed his command. As the punishment that Wotan, even though he is a god, must by law impose on her, she is to be changed into a mortal and to be placed, defenseless, in a deep sleep. Whoever wakes her will have her as his wife. Brünnhilde pleads that she be surrounded by fire so that only a hero can claim her. Acceding to her wish, Wotan begins his emotional farewell.

Listening to the excerpt with score in hand, you will observe that:

1. It is the orchestra that supplies continuity here by means of a very rich texture of musical ideas, and the vocal part is merely one of many strands within this texture. (The ending of the scene, 160 measures to the end, called the "Magic Fire Music," is often performed as an orchestral excerpt without Wotan's vocal line. The absence of his line in no way affects the musical continuity.)
2. Certain melodic and/or harmonic ideas, often associated with a specific instrumental color, recur many times in the orchestral part, and occasionally in the vocal line.
3. On occasion the harmony is highly chromatic, to the point where the key areas are constantly shifting.
4. The composer gives explicit stage directions that make extraordinary demands on stage directors, who must find a way to make flames issue from a rock and, directed by Wotan's spear, surround Brünnhilde. Needless to say, these flames had to be harmless to both singers and audiences in buildings where fire was a recurrent and recognized hazard.
5. Although it deals with an unlikely world of gods and mortals, the scene is intensely emotional and evocative. One feels that the composer has somehow projected Wotan's tortured inner state through his music.

Of the above characteristics, the third, Wagner's chromatic harmony, had the greatest impact on music of the late nineteenth and early twentieth century. The disintegration of tonality that led to atonality had its roots in Wagner's extended chromaticism and his deceptive and delayed—endlessly delayed—cadences. In these practices he was an important predecessor of Schoenberg, Berg, and Webern, who are often referred to as the "second Viennese school."

The second characteristic, the use of recurrent melodic, harmonic,

and timbral ideas, has always fascinated Wagner's audiences. Called leading-motives (or, in the German, **Leitmotifs**) by one of Wagner's admirers, these ideas can be shown to be related to certain characters, or to recurring dramatic themes in the libretto, and were extensively used by Wagner to recall past events. Some commentators have compiled elaborate catalogues of the 100-odd leading motives found in the *Ring*, giving each a label, and would have us believe that the listening process consists in the main of identifying them as they go by. Without memorizing them, in their view, one could not hope to understand or enjoy the works. (Debussy, whose views on Wagner were decidedly ambivalent, referred to Wagner's leading-motives as "calling cards.") But it is wise to keep in mind that the verbal tags that have been attached to these motives are not Wagner's. Nor is there a single view as to what each one means. For example, the motive stated in measures 69 through 84 is sometimes referred to as "Wotan's love for the Walsungs," sometimes as "Brünnhilde's justification," or even as "Brünnhilde's submissive resignation." Furthermore, many leading-motives change character, appearing in a number of variants that seem to grow one out of another, and thereby appear to be consciously related to other leading-motives. (See Donington's book, mentioned in the footnote, for a discussion of this phenomenon.) Let us look more closely at their use and the way in which they gain meanings in the scene under discussion.

Wotan's farewell has three large sections, each of which begins with a statement by Wotan and ends with an extensive orchestral passage. Preceding his first statement there is an orchestral passage that includes a lengthy reference to the Ride of the Valkyries in the brasses (mm. 1–7), and closes with a brief reference to a motive that we will soon learn is associated with Brünnhilde's sleep (mm. 8–9). In Wotan's first speech he gives some of the reasons that he will miss Brünnhilde. As he mentions a "bridal fire," the ring of fire that will soon surround her, the strings introduce for the first time, in slightly disguised form, a motive (mm. 48–49) that will assume importance as Wotan's kiss puts Brünnhilde to sleep and changes her from goddess to mortal (mm. 130–137), and that is sometimes labeled "magic sleep." This leads without break into the motive that will be associated with the "magic fire" (mm. 52–55), in which we can all but see the flames licking skyward as Wotan says "a blazing flame shall surround the rock." Later, as Wotan mentions that she can be awakened only by "one freer than I, the god!" the brasses introduce a motive (mm. 61–65) that serves as a prophecy since it is only in the next opera that we will learn that it is associated with the hero Siegfried, Brünnhilde's savior. The fact that the brasses underscore Wotan's vocal line here makes the prophecy even more portentous. In the orchestral passage that closes this first section we hear a motive that had been associated earlier with the enduring love between Wotan and

Brünnhilde. Its appearance here suggests that this love will survive the stern punishment she is about to undergo.

In the second section, usually called the "farewell song" (mm. 94–156), Wotan's remarks become more personal as he prepares to put Brünnhilde to sleep. The "sleep" motive, first heard in measures 8 and 9, now begins to dominate the musical fabric, appearing primarily in the violas and cellos. Wotan's vocal line here is more tuneful and hence more memorable than his lines earlier in the scene, and for good reason. Wagner will refer to two of its segments (mm. 94–98 and 111–114), primarily in the violas and cellos, on two occasions later in the scene (mm. 141–151 and 221–229), to remind us of Wotan's sorrow as he administers the necessary punishment to Brünnhilde. As he takes her head in both hands to kiss her, a motive earlier associated with the "renunciation of love" returns in the English horn (mm. 122–126). In addition to reminding the audience that Wotan's act signifies such a renunciation, Wagner may well be suggesting that Wotan is himself aware of it. The orchestral passage that concludes this section opens with the "magic sleep" motive mentioned earlier, and closes with another (mm. 155–157) that has been variously labeled "fate" and the "curse."

The final section of the scene opens with a powerful motive in the low brass (mm. 160–162) that has been variously labeled "law" or "the treaty" and refers to the law that Wotan is bound to obey in dealing with Brünnhilde's disobedience. As he invokes Loge, the god of fire, Loge's motive reappears in the strings (mm. 163–170). It is left to the reader to trace Wagner's use of leading-motives in the remainder of the scene and to determine their dramatic significance.

It should be clear from the above that what makes the scene work dramatically is its music, and that it is the leading-motives that establish the richness of meanings in any instant in the action, in much the same way that themes do in a Beethoven symphony. Since Wagner's later operas, including those in the *Ring*, have been characterized as examples of "symphonic opera," we should consider briefly the ways in which the term "symphonic" may apply here. First of all, Wagner abandoned the conventions of number opera that he was to observe in all his earlier operas up through *Lohengrin*. Now the music is continuous throughout each act, ceasing only as the curtain falls. Furthermore, through the use of leading-motives he found a means to unify not only individual scenes but also entire operas—and even the Ring cycle as a whole—by thematic means, following a practice that was increasingly to be found in contemporary symphonies. As an avowed admirer of Beethoven, Wagner drew from Beethoven's symphonies what he saw as the most dramatic part, the development sections, as his model on how to proceed. Here the periodic phrase structure, still com-

mon in many of Beethoven's exposition of themes, was to give way to a continuous fabric of musical ideas that were continually developed, and in which tonality was constantly changing. In large measure such a description fits Wagner's basic technique in his later operas.

One final point. Much has been made of Wagner's extensive use of chromaticism, to the point where his continuing and skillful use of tonality has received little attention. Since this scene brings to a close an opera that has lasted an entire evening, it is not surprising to find Wagner increasingly focusing on a single tonic, E, as the scene progresses. Though he often moves to other keys, E major recurs time and again at cadential points (mm. 48, 61, 99, etc.). The orchestral passage at the end of the first section (mm. 69–93) contains a monumental cadential six-four chord in the tonic (mm. 85–88), followed by its expected dominant chord (mm. 89–93) which, however, resolves deceptively. The "magic sleep" motive zeros in on E in its second and third appearances (mm. 130–138 & 199–203). And from measure 203 to the end E major appears as the dominant tonality. The final authentic cadence (mm. 228–229) is followed by an additional sixteen measures that confirm this as tonic. In a sense, then, most of this final scene is functioning as a closing section, perhaps even with a coda (mm. 156ff)—if one views it from the standpoint of symphonic form.

Source: Used by permission of G. Schirmer, Inc.

Recordings: Numerous available

*Summaries of the plot, as well as interpretations of its meaning other than Shaw's in *The Perfect Wagnerite*, are to be found in Robert Donington's *Wagner's Ring and its Symbols*, and John Culshaw's *Reflections on Wagner's Ring*.

Die Walküre   **Wagner**

Lichte Brunst umgiebt Wotan mit wildem Flackern. Er weis't mit dem Speere gebie-
Bright shooting flames surround Wotan. With his spear he directs the sea of fire

Spit ——— ze   fürch ——— tet   durch-
sharp ——— ness   fear ——— eth   shall

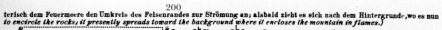

terisch dem Feuermeere den Umkreis des Felsenrandes zur Strömung an; alsbald zieht es sich nach dem Hintergrunde, wo es nun
to encircle the rocks; it presently spreads toward the background where it encloses the mountain in flames.)

fortwährend den Bergsaum umlodert.)

schrei ——— te   das   Feu ——— er nie!
cross ——— not   the   flam ——— ing fire!

205
WOTAN.

Wer   mei — nes Spee ——— res
He   who   my spear ——— point's

(Er streckt den Speer wie zum Banne aus.)
(He stretches out the spear as a spell.)   215

(Er blickt schmerzlich auf Brünnhilde zurück)
(He gazes sorrowfully back on Brünnhilde.)

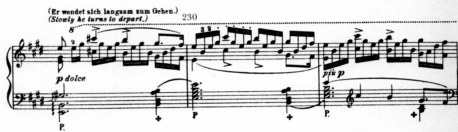

(Er wendet sich langsam zum Gehen.)
(Slowly he turns to depart.)

(Er wendet sich nochmals mit dem Haupt und blickt zurück.)
He turns his head again and looks back.

240
(Er verschwindet durch das Feuer.)
He disappears through the fire.

(Vorhang fällt.)
Curtain falls.   245

=117=

WORK FOR CHORUS AND ORCHESTRA

Johannes Brahms (1833-1897):

Wie lieblich sind deine Wohnungen, from Ein deutsches Requiem, op. 45

Brahms's *Ein deutsches Requiem* (A German Requiem) is one of the great choral masterpieces of the nineteenth century. Completed in 1868, it is the work that established him as one of the leading composers of his day. Its title indicates that it stands apart from the kind of requiem composed by such contemporaries as Berlioz, Verdi, Fauré, and Dvorak, all of whom wrote requiem masses that used the texts of the Roman rite. Brahms, on the other hand, selected his own texts from Luther's translation of the Bible, and had a different focus in mind. The texts of the requiem mass are directed to the departed soul, praying for its eternal rest, but Brahms's are directed to those who survive, offering them comfort in their bereavement. His opening text sets the tone for the entire work: "Blessed are they that mourn, for they shall be comforted." (The English text given below differs in detail from the familiar King James Version since it has been based on Luther's translation.)

The *German Requiem* contains seven movements, three of which include solos for either soprano or baritone in addition to the choir. We give here the fourth movement, for chorus alone. Although one of the shorter movements, it shares with the other six a symphonic character. Form is large-scale, and Brahms has treated both chorus and orchestra as equals in the presentation of musical ideas, often trading roles when an idea is repeated.

As can be seen from our translation below, Brahms has based the movement on three verses from a psalm that contrast the serenity and bliss of dwellers in the Lord's house with the longing to attain that bliss. Brahms has chosen the conventions of sonata form as best suited to his text, using the first verse of the psalm for both theme areas in his exposition and recapitulation (as well as the coda), the second for the development section, and the fourth for the highpoint that occurs towards the end of the recapitulation. The manner in which he introduces the final verse is particularly imaginative and displays his keen recognition of how textual syntax can enhance musical form. First introduced while the second theme is being recapitulated by the orchestra (m. 111), it leads easily into the ensuing highpoint, which is built on new material. This highpoint (mm.143-148) merits a somewhat closer look since it displays a common Brahmsian treatment of rhythm at high points. Though up to this point the meter has almost unequivocally been 3/4, Brahms now introduces a combination of 3/4 (in the bass strings), 3/2 (in the sopranos and altos), and 2/4 (in the tenors, basses, and violas). But this metric complexity has not been unprepared. In the measures preceding the climax he has carefully introduced several statements of 3/2 in the bass instruments, in conjunction with contrapuntal activity in the voice parts.

Brahms's interest in early music, especially that from the Baroque era, is well known, and is manifest in his own music. (He is listed as one of the subscribers for the first scholarly edition of the complete works of J.S. Bach, and was co-editor of similar editions of the works of Corelli and Couperin.) In turning to the past to find models for his own compositions Brahms is the first of several composers—among them Schoenberg, Hindemith, and Stravinsky—who were to do the same in the second decade of the twentieth century, and who are usually tagged as Neo-classicists. Among the many instances one could cite of Brahms's adopting Baroque procedures is the opening of the first movement, which has the characteristics of a motto aria (see vol. I, no. 72). Although the initial choral entry is incomplete musically, it is immediately repeated and joined to a continuing passage that forms a complete musical idea. As in a motto aria, the text, cited above, sums up the affection or, to put it another way, sets the tone for the entire work. Examples of this influence in the present movement are manifest in Brahms's adoption of contrapuntal procedures and include the use of the inversion of the first theme as an instrumental introduction (cf. mm. 1-4 and 5-8), even though this occurs within an essentially homorhythmic texture; the use of imitative texture for part of the development section (mm. 48-55)—including a suggestion of stretto (cf. the early soprano entry in measure 53); and the use of invertible counterpoint in the voice parts in the approach to the climax (mm. 124-140).

One of the marvels of Brahms's style is his ability still to make functional harmony work for structural purposes, even though he employs the enriched harmonic vocabulary of the nineteenth century. For example, the sonata convention in the present movement behaves in an expected fashion, moving from tonic to dominant within the exposition. Outer movements of the work are also clearly anchored in the same key, F major. Inner movements proceed by what appears to be a carefully calculated plan of rise and fall in harmonic tension, depending on the nature of the text and its place within the overall plan. As for examples of how Brahms used an enriched harmonic vocabulary, we cite only three: (1) his rather unusual use of a plagal cadence to close an internal phrase (mm. 12-13); (2) his use of an augmented sixth chord that functions as a passing chord, not a preparation for the dominant (m. 121); and (3) his expansion of the concept of what are variously called applied or secondary dominants by the addition of their preparations (e.g, the progression in mm. 137-139, which could all be easily absorbed within the key of E-flat as V/vi vi ii/vi V/vi V/ii ii ii/ii V/ii.

On hearing the complete *Requiem* one gets the impression of a work that is very tightly unified. Close examination of the music will reveal why this is so. The entire work is based on a three-note intervallic cell first stated by the sopranos of the chorus in its initial entry in the opening movement, and permeating the entire work, usually but not always appearing in conspicuous places (see the discussion of a similar practice in no. 102). Since the three-note cell here is found in any one of four forms, we presume to borrow terminology from a later style that, at least in part, had its roots in what Brahms was doing. The four forms in which this three-note cell is found are known as *prime, inversion, retrograde,* and *retrograde inversion.* The source of our terminology is, of course, twelve-tone technique (see no. 124), which was first extensively used by Schoenberg, who acknowledged his debt to Brahms in other ways. If one takes as the prime form the initial statement of the cell in the first movement (that is, third followed by second, both ascending), it is this form that is presented by the sopranos in mm. 4-5, and followed immediately by the retrograde inversion in measure 6. On the basis of our earlier remarks, it is no surprise that the other two forms of the cell, inversion and retrograde, have just been presented by flute and clarinet in the opening measures. At a similarly prominent spot, the beginning of the second theme (mm. 23-25), the first violin presents the retrograde version. Among numerous later statements of this cell are those by the tenor and bass at the climax of the movement (mm. 143-148), and that by the lower strings (mm. 175-176). A search for further examples of the cell, whether in orchestral or choral parts, will not go unrewarded.

Source: Johannes Brahms, *Sämtliche Werke*, vol. 17, pp. 95-113.

Recordings: numerous available

Translation:

1. How lovely are thy dwelling places, Lord Sabaoth.
2. My soul longs and yearns for the courts of the Lord: my body and soul rejoice in
   the living God.
4. Happy are they who dwell in thy house, who praise thee for ever and ever.
   —Psalm 84

=118=

UNACCOMPANIED CHORAL PIECE

Giuseppe Verdi (1813–1901)

Ave Maria, from *Quattro pezzi sacri*

Though Verdi is known primarily as an opera composer, he also composed some very fine nonoperatic works as well, especially after he completed *Aïda* in 1871. In addition to his monumental *Requiem* (1874) and a very fine string quartet (1873), there are the *Quattro pezzi sacri* ("Four Sacred Pieces") that are among the last pieces he composed. The earliest of these sacred pieces, composed between Verdi's two late operatic masterpieces, *Otello* and *Falstaff,* is an unaccompanied setting of the famous prayer to the Blessed Virgin Mary, Ave Maria. The circumstances surrounding its composition suggest that Verdi was indulging in a highly sophisticated sort of musical play. (But is not all creative activity in the arts really a highly sophisticated form of play?) In a letter in the *Gazzetta musicale di Milano* in August 1888, Adolfo Crescentini, a professor of music in Bologna, presented what he called an "enigmatic scale" that he had constructed, and challenged composers to supply a logical harmonization. (Crescentini was not the only one at the time to be interested in artificial scales; see nos. 119 and 121.) Numerous composers responded with solutions. Apparently both Verdi and his friend Boito, the composer who both coaxed Verdi into writing his final two operas and wrote the librettos for them, had been intrigued by the compositional problems posed by the scale, since in March 1889 Verdi wrote to Boito:

Leaving Milan, I threw into the fire some papers, among them that wretched scale. I still have the first part of the scale, but of the second, done on the spot, I have forgotten the modulations and the arrangements of the parts. . . . If you haven't burned it, send me the A and G chords.

You'll say that its not worth spending time on this trifle, and you're right. But what of it? They say that when you are old you revert to childhood; and such trifles recall the age of eighteen, when my teacher delighted in breaking my brain with such basses. Besides, I think I could write a piece with words on this scale—for example, an *Ave Maria.*

Boito shortly responded:

I was wise to copy out those two pages of the fractured scale, upon which you climbed up and down with such ease. To overcome every difficulty without effort is a grace. There's a sad beauty in these pieces of sung polyphony that bring to mind the evening prayer.

Crescentini's scale has two different forms, one ascending, the other descending, and can only be characterized as challenging in its avoidance of the normal tonal degrees in either direction and in its use of augmented seconds. Verdi lays out the scale in whole notes as a cantus firmus, and repeats it four times, placing it in each of the four voices in turn, and transposing it down a fourth for the last two statements. His solution to the problems it poses are ingenious and rely heavily on suspensions, applied dominants, and augmented-sixth chords. In several cases Verdi also employs what are commonly called "reverse progressions": measures 4 to 5 E minor: V/V—V/II; measures 7 to 8 and 23 to 24 E minor: V—IV. Note also the enharmonic shifts in measures 12 to 13 and 28 to 29. It is left to the reader to untangle the harmonic mysteries of the piece. Needless to say, only singers with ears sharply attuned to the harmonic implications at any point can hope to bring off in performance what can only be called a stunning choral piece.

Source: G. Verdi, *Quattro Pezzi Sacri.* Used by permission of Belwin Mills Publishing Corporation.

Recordings: Numerous available.

Translation:

Hail Mary, full of grace, the Lord is with Thee; blessed art Thou amongst women and blessed is the fruit of Thy womb, Jesus. Holy Mary, Mother of God, pray for us sinners, now and at the hour of our death.

Ave Maria

Verdi

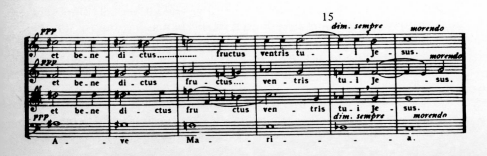

══119 and 120══

CHARACTER PIECES

Claude Debussy (1865–1918)
Voiles and *Des pas sur la neige,*
from *Préludes,* Book I

Throughout the nineteenth century the repertory for the piano showed a continuing expansion of the range of sonorities available on the instrument. Though Chopin was the most important figure in this development, significant contributions were also made by Liszt and Brahms. In the early twentieth century, by far the most notable developments in compositional techniques for the piano are found in the music of Debussy, who is increasingly recognized as one of the most innovative and influential composers of our century. Debussy was already well established as a composer of opera and orchestral works by the time he published any important pieces for piano. His two books of preludes appeared in 1910 and 1913 respectively, and are mature works that contain some of his best known contributions to the medium.

Much of the writing on Debussy's music falls back on such adjectives as "evanescent," "blurred," "coloristic," or "impressionistic." (Debussy was particularly unhappy with the latter term since his taste in art ran to the

Pre-Raphaelites and such Japanese printmakers as Hokusai, not to contemporary French Impressionists.) How he achieved such qualities is our concern here.

Debussy had a masterful understanding of the acoustical properties of the piano, by all indications obtained through pragmatic experimentation—playing and listening—rather than through scientific study. A careful examination of his harmonies reveals how often he uses a bass note or chord whose overtones reinforce the often fragmented melodies—or melodic cells—in the higher registers. Sometimes the performer is instructed to let a chord ring until the sound dies out. (In this regard Debussy was among the first to recognize that silence, properly approached and handled, can be just as powerful a means of sustaining tension as a *fortissimo* passage.) Often his harmonies, used more for their coloristic value than for their ability to establish a tonic, depend for their full effect on the performer's skill in the use of the pedals. As a pianist Debussy was noted for his subtle pedaling, particularly for his use of a technique known as ***partial pedaling***, which forms part of the oral tradition for the performance of his music since it is never indicated in the music. In partial pedaling, the right-hand pedal, commonly known as the "loud pedal," is only partially depressed, so that the dampers are not entirely removed from the strings. In so doing the "decay time" of sounds is affected, more in some registers than in others. (Although partial pedaling is a resource available on all pianos, some touring concert pianists make little use of it because no two pianos are regulated in exactly the same way. It should also be noted that while Debussy played on and wrote for a piano with two pedals, loud and soft, present-day performers of his music sometimes use in addition the third pedal that is common to American concert grands. Known as the "sustaining pedal," it allows the selective lifting of dampers for some notes so that they will ring through while the pianist independently pedals following notes in other voices.)

Each of Debussy's preludes carries a programmatic title—or better, a programmatic postscript, since he places titles at the ends of pieces, seeming thereby to wish to deemphasize their importance in the listening process. (Still, they are there.) Since *Voiles*, the title of our first prelude, can mean either sails or veils, some have argued that Debussy's ambiguity here is deliberate. For one well-known critic, obviously untroubled by any questions concerning the ambiguity of words, the languor and restlessness of the piece evokes a picture of sailboats bobbing at anchor. (One wonders what he would have seen had Debussy entitled the piece "Vapeur.") The ambiguity in Debussy's title is reflected in the music through his use of the whole-tone scale for much of the piece. Since all intervals in this scale are of the same size, the semitones of the diatonic scales being absent, one is de-

prived of the sense of tonal position that these semitones give, and hence of a readily identified tonic. One can demonstrate this easily by playing idly on the piano only the notes of the whole-tone scale, emphasizing no one pitch. The result will be a certain tonal vagueness, which clearly was Debussy's purpose—vagueness being related to ambiguity. (We must call attention, however, to the four chromatic passing tones in measure 31, none of which do much to disturb the pervasive sense of the whole-tone scale.) By using the whole-tone scale for both melodic and harmonic purposes, the amateur improviser can easily reproduce Debussy's sound. But it is another matter to fake his careful and subtle control of materials.

Structural coherence is attained in *Voiles* by a variety of means, all of which will be encountered in later twentieth-century compositions. These include the emphasis on a characteristic interval (here, the major third), a pedal tone, ostinatos, and the return of melodic material. Perhaps the most obvious effect on first hearing is the pedal tone. Beginning in measure 5, Debussy introduces a low B-flat that will be heard throughout most of the piece (see a similar procedure in no. 111 by Mussorgsky, who was highly regarded by Debussy). But note that the final interval one hears, C—E, after the pedal has ceased sounding, has first been heard in measure 5 at the end of the opening section, just as the pedal is introduced, and that the interval of the major third pervades the melodic ideas in the upper voices in measures 1 through 6, 10 through 21, and 25 through 28 before returning in measure 58 to dominate the closing measures. The most obvious return of melodic materials is the recurrence, at the very end, of the descending figure that is heard throughout the opening measures. But careful examination will disclose another, less distinctive melodic idea, first stated in an inner voice in measures 9 through 14, that recurs twice in the course of the piece. Another device Debussy uses to ensure cohesion is the ostinato (see also no. 111), found here in measures 23 through 28 in an inner voice, and in measures 32 through 37 in the top voice.

But Debussy does not use the whole-tone scale throughout. He abandons it momentarily in measures 42 through 47 for the pentatonic scale, at the dynamic high point of the piece, thereby creating an *ABA* form if the piece is viewed solely from the standpoint of the scales he uses. Unlike the whole-tone scale, the pentatonic scale gives a strong sense of tonal position since, like the diatonic scale, it comprises intervals of different sizes, in this case major seconds and minor thirds. A rather strong feeling of E-flat as the tonic emerges toward the end of this middle section. But since Debussy then reintroduces the whole-tone scale, the impression of the entire piece is of an opening uncertainty that gives way momentarily to certainty, but then reverts to uncertainty at the end.

Des pas sur la neige ("Footsteps in the Snow") is a very different piece that shows other sides of Debussy's compositional procedures. Here the dynamic level never rises above *piano*. Even so, the piece has an identifiable climax that is brought about by other than dynamic means. Here we encounter further evidence of Debussy's debt to Russian composers and his avoidance of the developmental process then popular in Germanic music. Debussy's tempo indication and performance instruction at the outset give a clear view of his expressive intent: "Melancholy and Slow; this rhythm should have the sonorous value of a melancholy, ice-bound landscape." The piece is dominated by a monotonous, one-measure cell that employs appoggiaturas and that never departs from its original pitches. In a sense, then, it is functioning rather like an ostinato that is heard at various points in the top, middle, and bottom voice. What is fascinating about the piece is the variety of ways in which this cell has been harmonized, the different guises it assumes. Only once does Debussy seem to repeat an earlier harmonization (see mm. 5–6 and 20–21), but the second statement moves on in a different direction to become the climax of the piece, which is created by increasing the number of voices and by introducing the widest spread between the outer voices. Distinctive melodic material in addition to the ostinato is rather sketchy, though the reader can identify several instances of ideas that recur. But as the piece proceeds, another cell, the descending interval of the third, first stated twice in measures 3 and 4, becomes increasingly insistent (see mm. 21–25 and 28–33).

In retaining a "tune" unchanged, and constantly varying its setting, as Debussy has done with his ostinatolike figure here, he is following in the footsteps of Glinka, the Russian composer who evolved this method for harmonizing Russian folk song, and who was copied by such later Russian composers as Borodin and Tchaikovsky (see the way he deals with the borrowed folk song in the final movement of his Fourth Symphony). Such a way of putting a piece together is, of course, completely contrary to the procedures employed by contemporary German composers, who constantly varied material through its development (see nos. 102 and 116).

As will be evident to the listener, the tonic in this piece is clearly projected.

Source: Claude Debussy, *Préludes*, book I. (*Voiles*, pp. 3-6; *Des pas sur la neige*, pp. 22-23). © 1910 Durand S.A. Used by permission of The Publisher Theodore Presser Company, sole representative U.S. and Canada.

Recordings: Numerous available.

Voiles   **Debussy**

(...Voiles)

Des pas sur la neige   **Debussy**

Comme un tendre et triste regret

30

Plus lent

Très lent

35

morendo

ppp

(... Des pas sur la neige)

≡121≡

CHARACTER PIECE

Alexander Scriabin (1872–1915)
Poème, op. 69, no. 1

In an earlier commentary (no. 116) we spoke of the growing tendency on the part of some in the nineteenth century to view art as a surrogate for religion and the artist as The Messiah. The most extreme manifestation of this trend was embodied at the end of the century in the Russian composer,

Alexander Scriabin. Echoing Wagner, he believed that "the calling of an artist was higher than a king," arguing in 1910:

> Politicians and bureaucrats are *not* to be praised. Writers, composers, authors, and sculptors are the first-ranking men in the universe, first to expound principles and doctrines, and solve world problems. Real progress rests on artists alone. . . . They must not give place to others of lower aims. [Used by permission of Kodanska International, Inc.]

And although he appears to have misunderstood what Wagner was about artistically, Scriabin shared Wagner's view on the purpose of the arts, being quoted as saying in 1904: "Art must combine with philosophy and religion to produce something indivisible. This was the new Evangel to replace the old outworn Gospel." [Bowers, II, 50]

Such views reflected Scriabin's growing preoccupation, from 1902 on, with philosophical and mystical ideas—ideas that were to determine in large measure the kind and character of the large-scale works he subsequently composed. In 1909, echoing the view of a number of contemporary Russian symbolists, he was to say: "I am the creator of a new world. I am God!" [Bowers, II, 193]. But even earlier, in 1906, the extent of his messianic vision is crystal clear from a letter he wrote to his patroness, his only source of financial support at the time, berating her for not having attended a performance of one of his works:

> There will be a time . . . when every person (not just friends) will skip from one pole of the earth to the other just to hear a pause in a composition of mine! [Bowers, II, 48.]

The ultimate manifestation of Scriabin's mature point of view is a projected work that he spoke of, off and on, from 1904, but was never to compose:

> I have an idea to create some kind of a Mysterium. I need to construct a special temple for it. . . . But people aren't ready for it. I must sermonize. I must show them a new path. I have even preached from a boat, like Christ. . . . I have a little group of people here who understand me. They will come with me. [Bowers, II, 50]

The *Mysterium* was to be preceded by what he called the *Prefatory Action*:

> The Prefatory Action would . . . be a stage work of immense proportion and conception. Bells suspended from the clouds in the sky would summon the spectators from all over the world. The performance was to take place in a half-temple [i.e., hemispherical] built in India. A reflecting pool of water would complete the divinity of the half-circle stage [i.e., simulate a sphere]. Spectators would sit in tiers across the water. Those in the balconies would be

the least spiritually advanced. The seating was strictly graded, ranking radially from the center of the stage, where Scriabin would sit at the piano, surrounded by hosts of instruments, singers, dancers. The entire group was to be permeated continually with movement, and costumed speakers reciting the text in processions and parades would form parts of the action. The choreography would include glances, looks, eye motions, touches of the hands, odors of both pleasant perfumes and acrid smokes, frankincense and myrrh. Pillars of incense would form part of the scenery. Lights, fires, and constantly changing lighting effects would pervade the cast and audience, each to number in the thousands. This prefaces the final Mysterium and prepares people for their ultimate dissolution in ecstasy. [Bowers, II, 253]

What Scriabin had in mind is not far removed from the psychedelic experiences sought by some in our day, wherein lights and incense are used to enhance music, creating thereby a total sensory experience. Scriabin attempted to realize this vision in part in his last orchestral work, *Prometheus, Poem of Fire* (1908–1910), in which lights that corresponded in color to the music at any point were to bathe the hall throughout the performance. His orchestral score includes a line that is entitled *Tastièra per luce,* or "light keyboard," which indicates the colors.

Setting aside such grandiose plans, and Scriabin's philosophical arguments on the social role of the arts, we will concentrate here solely on his musical contributions, which are not insignificant. Scriabin was first and foremost a pianist. In addition to teaching piano for several years at the Moscow Conservatory, he undertook numerous concert tours throughout Europe, and made one in 1906 to this country, performing in New York, Cincinnati, Chicago, and Detroit. It is no surprise, therefore, that the majority of his compositions are for piano, and include ten sonatas and a large number of shorter pieces entitled variously prelude, etude, nocturne, poem, etc. Stylistically his point of departure was Chopin, though he rapidly developed a highly personal style of his own. (He also composed a piano concerto, three symphonies, and two symphonic poems. One of the latter, the *Poem of Ecstasy,* received its first performance in New York in 1908.)

In his time Scriabin was recognized as one of Europe's most forward-looking composers. (Stravinsky's *Firebird* [1910] owes much to Scriabin's style at the time.) He is best known today for the so-called "mystic chord" that permeates many of his late works, including the first measure of our example, which comprises a series of augmented, diminished, and perfect fourths, as follows: C—F-sharp—B-flat—E—A—D. In these same works he is also said to have been preoccupied with chords that employed all twelve notes of the chromatic scale, an activity normally associated with contemporaries in the Second Viennese School (see. no. 124). But a recent study by Professor Jay Reise ("Late Skriabin: Some Principles Behind the Style," in

19th Century Music (1983), 220–31) argues that the innovation in Scriabin's late works consists of his introduction of artificial scales while at the same time he retains the dissonance treatment of the past. By artificial scales we mean those other than the diatonic scale, which had served as the foundation of Western music from the early Middle Ages, even though it was to be highly colored by chromaticism in the nineteenth century. (For an earlier instance of a composition based on an artificial scale, see no. 119) The two scales with which Scriabin appears to have been most concerned are the whole-tone scale, of which there exist two forms, a semitone apart, and the octatonic scale, which consists of a regular alternation of whole tones and semitones, and of which there are three forms: C—D—E-flat—F—F-sharp—G-sharp—A—B—C, C—D-flat—E-flat—E—F-sharp—G—A—B-flat—C, and C-sharp—D—E—F—G—A-flat—B-flat—B. The piece we present here employs both whole-tone and octatonic scales.

Reise further argues that Scriabin treats any notes that lie outside these scales as dissonances, so that they almost invariably resolve by half step into one of the scale tones in accordance with the treatment of "nonharmonic" tones in earlier functional harmonic practice. In this matter, therefore, Scriabin appears as a conservative since he observes long-established practice when it comes to the resolution of dissonance.

The piece at hand was composed in 1913, and opens with a whole-tone scale based on C. In measure 10 Scriabin shifts to a whole-tone scale based on C-sharp, and then alternates both forms, measure by measure, through measure 13, ending with the original form. The "nonharmonic" tones in the first two measures are A and D-flat, both of which resolve by half step, either immediately or at some remove. (The A in the left hand in measure 1 resolves at the beginning of measure 2; the A in the right hand in measure 2 resolves at the beginning of measure 3.) The passage in measures 5 through 8 consists of a transposed repetition of the opening measures, the "nonharmonic" tones now being C-sharp and F. Reise argues that the C-sharp and F in measure 9 function as a sort of pivotal area since they anticipate the second form of the whole-tone scale that will be introduced in measure 10. In measure 17 a varied repetition of the first section begins, consisting for the most part of a restatement of the theme a tritone removed, from measure 25 on. The passagework in measure 16, using the whole-tone scale based on C, is answered in measure 32 by the other form of the scale. Once only, in measures 33 and 34, Scriabin uses the octatonic scale here (the second form given above), in a sense presenting a final reinterpretation of the opening measures. In measure 35 Scriabin reverts to the opening whole-tone scale, and hence to the opening sonority, the one foreign tone being G.

Scriabin's use of different scales here brings to mind a rather similar treatment by Debussy some three years earlier in "Voiles" (no. 119), and indicates that experimentation of this sort, whenever an older style shows signs of wearing out, is not restricted to one individual.

Source: Alexander Skriabin, *Ausgewahlte Klavierwerke*, Band III, pp. 88-89. © 1968 by Edition Peters, Leipzig. Reprinted by permission of C.F. Peters Corporation. Quotations from Fabian Bowers, *Scriabin*, used by permission of Kodausa International, Inc.

Recordings: Columbia M 31620, *Horowitz plays Scriabin*; BIS LP 119, *Alexander Scriabin: Piano Works*; Vox SVBX 5474, *Scriabin: Complete Piano Music, Vol. IV*.

Poème   Scriabin

═══122═══

ORCHESTRAL PIECE

Claude Debussy (1862–1918)
Prélude à l'Après-midi d'un faune

Even before Debussy's compositions were widely known, he was recognized as an informed and articulate musician in the most sophisticated intellectual circles in Paris. His close friendship with the symbolist poet Stéphane Mallarmé, whose Tuesday evening gatherings he attended along with such young artists and writers as Paul Gauguin, Claude Monet, James Abbott McNeill Whistler (painter of *Whistler's Mother*), André Gide, and Paul Valéry, led Debussy to compose an orchestral work that was inspired by Mallarmé's most famous poem, *L'Après-midi d'un faune* ("The Afternoon of a Faun"). Debussy's work, which he finished in 1894 at the age of thirty-two, was an instant success and firmly established his reputation as one of France's leading young composers. It has since become the most popular of his orchestral works.

The faun of Mallarmé's poem is a shaggy forest creature from Roman mythology, not unlike the satyr of Greek mythology, with short horns, pointed ears, goats's hooves, and a short tail. By tradition he was a lover of wine and women. In Mallarmé's poem, rich in erotic imagery, the faun dreams of his conquest of two nymphs, one chaste, the other experienced. (He also has a fantasy concerning lesbians.) But the boundaries between dreams and the fantasies of the waking state are never clearly drawn. Such conscious obscurity reflects Mallarmé's belief that the function of poetry was to be evocative:

> It is not *description* which can unveil the efficacy and beauty of monuments, seas, or the human face in all their maturity and native state, but rather evocation, *allusion, suggestion.*

Thus Mallarmé felt that poetry should aspire to the richness of meanings available in music. To this end he often used words for the sake of their sound, and cultivated a language that was clearly intended to establish multiple associations and to suggest a variety of meanings. As a result it is virtually impossible to translate his poem, as any one line will demonstrate. The opening line, for example, seemingly delivered by the faun in a waking state is "Ces nymphes, je les veux perpétuer." In one translation this is rendered as "Those nymphs, I want to make them permanent," in another as "I would eternalize those nymphs." Yet another, equally plausible translation—though more pointed because of its double entendre—might be "I wish to perpetuate those nymphs." But there is no denying the sense of languor that permeates Mallarmé's poem. (The original poem and an English translation are found in William Austin's *Claude Debussy: Prelude to "The Afternoon of a Faun;"* [New York: Norton, 1970]; but see Austin's comments concerning the translation on p. 21.)

Since Mallarmé originally conceived of his poem as a stage work, to be performed by a narrator with actors to mime the parts—he even included stage directions in an earlier version—Debussy originally intended to write incidental music for such a theatrical production, projecting a series of pieces entitled: *Prélude, Interludes, et Paraphrase finale pour L'après-midi d'un faune.* He was to compose only the *Prélude*, however, and supplied the following remarks for one of its early performances:

> The music of this *Prelude* is a very free illustration of the beautiful poem of Mallarmé. By no means does it claim to be a synthesis of the latter. Rather there are the successive scenes through which pass the desires and dreams of the faun in the heat of this afternoon. Then, tired of pursuing the fearful flight of the nymphs and the naiads, he succumbs to intoxicating sleep, in which he can finally realize his dreams of possession in universal Nature.

Though Debussy's intent is clear in this rather bland statement, it was to be more sharply focused in a letter he wrote to a journalist friend at about the same time:

> If the music were to follow [Mallarmé's] poem more closely it would run out of breath, like a dray horse competing for the Grand Prix with a thoroughbred.

We should also note that Mallarmé was apparently pleased with Debussy's interpretation, as he wrote to him following the first performance—characteristically using musical terminology—that

> your illustration of *L'Après-midi d'un faune* set up no dissonance with my text, except to go further, indeed, into the nostalgia and the light, with delicacy, with malaise, in depth.

In recent years Debussy has come to be recognized as one of the pivotal figures in the development of new ways of constructing a piece that do not rely on the developmental processes of nineteenth-century Germanic music. This is our justification for including a late-nineteenth-century piece in a section entitled *Twentieth-Century Music*. Debussy's mature musical style, first fully evident in the *Prélude à l'après-midi d'un faune*, was shaped by a number of earlier events in his life: his thorough training in the Classical tradition in the Paris Conservatoire (1872–1884), much of which he subsequently consciously rejected; his three summers (1880–1882) as household pianist for Nadezhda von Meck, the wealthy Russian who is better known as Tchaikovsky's patroness, and through whom Debussy first learned something of recent musical developments in Russia (see nos. 119 and 120); his two summer trips to Bayreuth (1888–1889) to hear the operas of Wagner, which proved to be both a positive and negative influence on his own music; and his hearing of Javanese music performed by a gamelan, an ensemble consisting primarily of percussion instruments, at the Paris World Exhibition in 1889.

Since Debussy's intent in the *Prélude* was to capture in music the suggestive quality of Mallarmé's poem, it should be no surprise that many find the work elusive; furthermore, it has been argued that any careful analysis of the work is likely to be right—so far as it goes. Our concern here will be to consider a few of the ways in which Debussy attains his goal while at the same time creating a cohesive piece of music.

Right from the outset, through Debussy's juxtaposition of ambiguity and certainty, we are aware of one of the reasons the work has such an evocative air. A solo flute, playing in a low and sensuous register seldom used by earlier composers, presents a slow, languorous line that projects neither tonic nor meter. Tonal ambiguity arises in large measure from Debussy's stressing of C-sharp and G, a tritone apart, as the outer limits of the line. (Both pitches will play important roles throughout the piece.) The lack of a sense of meter can be attributed to the suppleness of his rhythm, which intermixes long notes, sixteenths, and triplets in such a way as to give little sense of an underlying regular pulse. Only in measures 3 and 4 does a momentary sense of tonic and meter gradually emerge as the flute outlines the notes of an E-major triad in regular eighth-note motion. (Hindsight will reveal that the work is anchored in the key of E major.) This opening melody, since it is not a complete 'tune,' contributes to the allusive effect. It will recur nine times throughout the piece, most often, but not always, with the same opening pitch, C-sharp, but each time with different harmonizations and timbres. Here Debussy has borrowed a technique that was widely used by Russian composers such as Mussorgsky and Tchaikovsky, wherein a melody is repeated, not developed, and its setting—both timbral and harmonic—is ever changed.

Other techniques that contribute to the ambiguous or vague air of the work are the occasional unresolved reverse progressions, for instance V-II (mm. 17 and 41–42; the use of deceptive cadences that behave in unusual ways (mm. 61–63 and 84); and use the whole-tone scale either for an entire passage (mm. 31–36) or as the source of the occasional harmony (mm. 56, 64, and 92). And there is the very evocative silence, full of import, in measure 6. But perhaps the most fascinating example of ambiguity is in the form of the piece. Most listeners will sense some sort of return, brought about by both tonal and thematic means (see mm. 79 and 94 for two candidates). But identifying a departure following the opening statement is more difficult. One candidate is measure 31, following an authentic cadence on the dominant, B. Yet the material here is clearly derived from the opening. Perhaps a more likely spot is measure 37, where new material appears in the oboe, part of which will recur in the return (m. 95). But this new material opens much like the beginning flute solo, on C-sharp. (Tracing successive prominent appearances of C-sharp from measure 1 through its final one in measure 109 is a fascinating pursuit. The same is true of the pitch G.) Another candidate is measure 55, again following an authentic cadence. Here is surely something different—even though its key is D-flat or C-sharp. The rather pointillistic melodic technique of earlier measures now gives way to a broad, even Romantic melody, strongly pentatonic at the outset, which is repeated from measure 63—though it now incorporates ideas from earlier in the piece (cf. mm. 67 and 39, 68 and 28). This passage also shows the influence of Russian scoring, particularly that of Tchaikovsky, in that melody is assigned to one family of instruments, accompaniment to another, the roles being reversed in measure 63. From measure 63 on we encounter another new technique, polymeter. Although the winds would appear to be playing triplets, by the grouping of their notes in pairs Debussy has created an effective duple meter, with a beat unit different from that in the main meter. By such a means the accompanying texture here almost surpasses the melody in interest and importance.

We have concentrated thus far on melodic, harmonic, and rhythmic resources. But Debussy's orchestra, and the ways he uses it, are also of utmost importance to the sensuous, elusive quality of the piece. (Debussy was to fuss with orchestration and dynamics right through the première, fine tuning the piece in order to get just the effect he wanted.) The sole percussion instrument used is the tuned antique cymbals that contribute a marvelous effect in the closing measures (mm. 94ff). As for the brasses, Debussy calls only for four horns, and uses them extensively. The sound of three flutes and two harps dominates the opening and closing sections. Except for the middle section with the broad melody, the scoring is almost always subdued, seldom rising above *mezzoforte* in dynamics. Finally, we should note two of the more unusual instrumental effects: the two horns and low violin, from measure 107 on, that almost sound like three horns; the subtle difference between the measures following 11 and those after measure 94, brought about in the latter by doubling the flute and using a fingered tremolo in the strings that alternates two pitches.

Source: Kalmus Music Publishers reprint edition.

Recordings: Numerous available.

Prélude à l'Après-midi d'un faune   **Debussy**

20

=123=

ORCHESTRAL PIECE

Arnold Schoenberg (1874–1951)
Premonitions, from *Five Pieces for Orchestra*, op. 16

Schoenberg's early works, like *Verklärte Nacht* and *Gurrelieder*, were composed in a lush, late Romantic style that displays the strong influence of both Brahms and Wagner. But his increasing use of chromaticism led in 1909 to a stylistic crisis wherein he abandoned any semblance of triadic harmony, and hence of the cadence as a means of creating tonal centers. The new style that evolved has been called, for better or worse, atonality. In later years he was to refer to the central feature of this style as "the emancipation of the dissonance," meaning that dissonance was no longer to be viewed solely in its relationship to triadic harmony. Schoenberg insisted, and rightly so, that this change in his style was evolutionary, not revolutionary—that he was merely carrying to its logical conclusion the implications of Wagner's chromaticism. In so doing he saw himself as fulfilling a historic mission, as can be seen from some remarks he made in 1910.

> I am conscious of having broken through every restriction of a bygone aesthetic; and though the goal toward which I am striving appears to me a certain one, I am, nonetheless, already feeling the resistance I shall have to overcome; I feel now how hotly even the least of temperaments will rise in revolt, and suspect that even those who have so far believed in me will not want to acknowledge the necessary nature of this development. . . . I am being forced in this direction. . . . I am obeying an inner compulsion which is stronger than any upbringing. [Willi Reich, *Schoenberg*, p. 49]

It should come as no surprise that, in following what he saw as a logical next step in the evolution of musical style, he should encounter resistance to the performance of these pieces and, in fact, of others that were to follow. None of them has as yet had a broad appeal for the typical concert-going audience. Yet they are widely recognized today as seminal works in opening up new possibilities in music.

Schoenberg's first ventures in this new style, all composed in 1909, were four works in very different genres: *Three Piano Pieces* (op. 11), a song cycle on poems by Stefan George called *The Book of the Hanging Gardens* (op. 15), the monodrama *Erwartung* (op. 17), and *Five Pieces for Orchestra*. All of them are representative of what is called Expressionism (see no. 112), and have a hypertense quality even for listeners today because of their pervasive dissonance and unusual sonorities. All are also rather short, in part because Schoenberg was clearly feeling his way in a new world of sound, having abandoned a structural principle, tonality, that had earlier been the main means of sustaining large-scale forms. New principles were just then under investigation.

Premonitions is the first of the *Five Pieces for Orchestra*. Like the other four—*Yesteryears, Summer Morning by a Lake (Colors), Peripetia,* and *The Obligatory Recitative*—it was initially untitled. Schoenberg reluctantly added titles at the behest of the publisher, noting that he did not intend to imply that the pieces had "poetic content." We present the piece here in a revised version that he prepared in September 1949. His revision consisted in the main of reducing the number of instruments required in order to facilitate performance by a normal-sized symphony orchestra. In the original version Schoenberg had called for winds in fours (including a contrabass clarinet), six horns, three trumpets, and four trombones. Even with a reduced—though hardly small—orchestra, the piece is filled with brilliant and subtle color effects. The influence of Mahler (see no. 112) is evident in the open-textured, chamber-music-like scoring, wherein the entire orchestra seldom plays at the same time. Also Mahler-like is Schoenberg's use of unusual and somewhat bizarre sonorities—bizarre by earlier nineteenth-century standards, that is: the menacing sound of the muted trombone in a very low register in measures 12 through 14; the rather shrill sound in measures 40 through 42, resulting from a widely spaced scoring that lacks a central core of sound in the middle register; the eerie sound that is produced by flutter tonguing in the bassoons and low brasses in measures 77 to 78, and 127 to 128. One must also note the occasional subtle change in color within a motive, brought about by the gradual addition of other instruments (mm. 1–3, 7–9, and 113–118). The close identification between motive, color, and register should also be noted. For example, some motives are found only in wind instruments in a high register, others primarily in bass string instruments. Other examples will be cited below.

Schoenberg's procedures in this piece represent a middle ground between the sort of thing Brahms was doing (see nos. 102 and 117) and his own fully developed serial technique, which will be examined in no. 134. They indicate a concern with finding ways to give cohesion to a piece of music that no longer relies on functional harmony, and thus on the triad. His early solution was to create an open texture that consisted of a complex of different motives. Much of the motivic material here is derived from one of two three-note cells, each of which consists of a second and a third. The first contains a minor second and a major third, and is heard twice in the cellos at the very outset. Allowing for the principle of ***octave equivalence*** discussed in nos. 102 and 124, this same cell, in inversion, is used as a three-note harmonic unit or chord—D—A—C-sharp—that, beginning in measure 26, sounds throughout the rest of the piece, usually in bassoons and bass clarinet (one wonders when the players are expected to breathe). It also appears in the double basses beginning at measure 64, and in the horns and trombones at the climax in measure 77. The second cell, spanning a tritone, consists of a major second and major third and is first heard in melodic form in the double bass in measure 7. Assuming that this is the prime form, its retrograde form is used as an ostinato that first appears in the cello in measure 34 with different pitches, but then reverts to the original pitches in measure 64. This ostinato is heard almost without interruption throughout the rest of the piece. In measures 79 through 95 it appears in augmentation in the harp and timpani. Again allowing for octave equivalence, the retrograde version also forms the basis of a motive first stated, once only, in the horns in measure 15—F—B—E-flat—that will dominate a later section (mm. 96–103). It should come as no surprise that both the remaining forms of this cell are also present. The inversion is encountered in the trumpets in measure 54 and the horns in measures 60 through 62, the retrograde inversion in measures 120 through 123 in the form D, B-flat, A-flat. It will be noted that the outer pitches of this final statement match those in the original statement of the prime in measure 7.

There are four other distinctive motives that contribute to the larger form of the piece, as we shall see. The first, accompanimental in function, is the harmonic interval of the fifth, whose harmonic role is made apparent by the fact that it is almost invariably presented in two instruments of the same kind, as in the clarinets in measure 1, the horns in measure 36, and in several pairs of instruments in measures 63 through 77. A second motive comprises the four descending notes that trace the successive intervals of the minor second, tritone, and perfect fourth. First heard in the horn and clarinet in measure 5, and transposed to other pitches in measures 21, 40, etc., this motive is presented once in inversion in measure 51. The third motive is a simple pattern of five repeated notes, always played *forte* by muted brasses (mm. 6, 22, and 106). The last one, a more extended eighth-note figure, is first introduced by the cellos in measure 26, and dominates the middle of the piece. Schoenberg treats it like a fugue subject, introducing it in successive voices (m. 38, viola; m. 49, second violin), and even employing several other techniques borrowed from the fugue. There are strettolike passages in measures 57 to 59 and 79 to 90 and, in the latter of these two passages, a statement in augmentation in the trombone, and a further one in double augmentation in the trumpet.

A careful look at pitch relations in the piece will reveal that the term "atonality" is rather inaccurate since the identification of some motives with specific pitches remains relatively stable throughout the piece. We have already mentioned several of these above. In addition, Schoenberg's occasional use of octave writing, especially in the strings, tends to give a temporary emphasis to the pitches involved (mm. 73–77 and 100–103).

Schoenberg's rhythm here is also deserving of close study. Each motive has a distinctive rhythm that is readily recognized. As for meter, though the basic meter is defined at the outset as triple, one scarcely feels it because of the lack of those regularly recurring accents that are such an integral part of most music based on functional harmony. Furthermore, the duple meter introduced in measure 26 in the cellos is deceptive. Because of the ostinato pattern that soon emerges, it quickly turns into a cross-meter that is also triple. But there is no mistaking the momentary quintuple meter created by the repeating motivic patterns in measures 120 through 122.

With such a rich interplay of motives, and an absence of familiar triadic harmonies, one's initial reaction may well be that this piece is all but formless. But maturer consideration will disclose a piece that has a beginning, a middle, and an end, all brought about by motivic play. Ostinatos of various sorts provide much of the cohesion from measure 34 on. And there is a clear sense of return in measures 96 to 112 that results from references to the motives first heard in measures 5 through 16. Futhermore, the motive that appears at the opening of the middle section in measure 25, recurs several times at the very end of the piece (mm. 120–124). The intervening measures (mm. 113–119) gradually build a pair of alternating staccato chords that saturate the texture with all the notes of the semitonal scale.

These are the first pieces in which Schoenberg applied to the orchestra the open-textured writing he considered suited to this new atonal style. But this style had evolved in music for the piano, which involved a single performer. Such a texture was bound to be more troublesome for large ensembles since it relied heavily on a complex motivic fabric rather than on the melody/accompaniment hierarchy that had been the norm in earlier tonal music. Because it was not always self-evident to the orchestral player or conductor which of the many strands might be important in any particular passage, Schoenberg felt it necessary to create a new system of symbols to make his intentions clear, a system that was to be adopted by his student Alban Berg. The symbol ⊢indicates the *Hauptstimme,* or principal voice, at any point in the piece (see the violoncello in measure 1). When this role passes to another instrument, a closing bracket ⌐ (see measure 3) is used. Occasionally Schoenberg indicates the presence of a secondary voice (*Nebenstimme*) by the symbol Ν(mm. 69–77 and 79–98). At such times, all other voices are expected to have a subsidiary role. In the absence of both symbols, as in measures 113 through 128, one must assume that all voices are equally important.

Even though Schoenberg's music has not yet, and may never, prove popular with many concert-goers, there is no denying his central role in the stylistic changes that took place in the first half of the twentieth century.

Recordings: Numerous available.

Premonitions   **Schoenberg**

*) The Low D♮ is obligatory

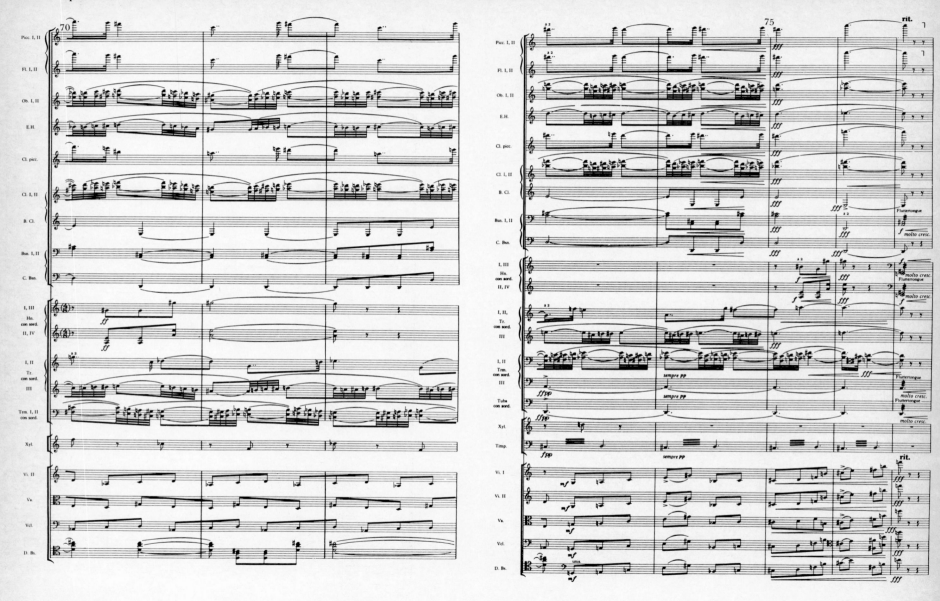

=124=

SYMPHONY

Anton Webern (1883–1945)
Symphonie, op. 21, movement 2

Along with Alban Berg (see no. 128) Webern was a disciple of Schoenberg (see nos. 123 and 134), the three of them constituting the so-called Second Viennese School. All three adopted twelve-tone technique in the 1920's, but with markedly different results. Where Schoenberg and Berg in essence applied the technique to the Germanic musical syntax they had previously employed, in a sense pouring new wine into old bottles, Webern developed a terse, aphoristic style, not unlike Japanese haiku, wherein the implications of twelve-tone technique for the other elements of music appear to have been exhaustively explored. Most of Webern's pieces are very short, some lasting barely a few seconds, so that his complete works fit on four record discs. His two-movement *Symphonie*, completed in 1928 and excerpted here, lasts less than nine minutes. Of the three men, Webern was to have the greatest influence immediately following the Second World War on such young composers as Boulez, Stockhausen, and Babbitt. Even the aging Stravinsky was to fall under Webern's spell in his last works.

Webern's symphony, in sharp contrast to those written in the late nineteenth century, is scored for a chamber orchestra: clarinet, bass clarinet, two horns, harp, and a quartet of strings. Its first movement is in rounded binary form, with repetitions of both strains, and is replete with canons of various sorts. The second movement, presented here, is a theme with seven variations that are performed without break. Both demonstrate his concern with symmetries of various sorts at this point in his career.

The present work is our first example employing twelve-tone technique, also known as twelve-note technique, serial technique, or dodecaphony—but not dodecacophony. (A slightly earlier piece employing twelve-tone technique, by Schoenberg, is discussed in no. 134.) We have already mentioned several earlier works whose features pointed toward a number of elements of this technique (see nos. 102, 117, and 123). We should begin by stating the four postulates that underlie the system as used by most composers, noting first that the arrangement of pitches with which the composer begins is called variously the tone row, the row, or the set. Our source for the postulates is a first-rate study by George Perle (*Serial Composition and Atonality* [Berkeley, 1963], p. 3).

1. The set comprises all twelve notes of the semitonal scale, arranged in a specific linear order.
2. No note appears more than once within the set.
3. The set is statable in any of its linear aspects: prime, inversion, retrograde, and retrograde-inversion.
4. The set, in each of its four transformations (i.e., linear aspects), is statable upon any degree of the semitonal scale.

Most composers have used twelve-tone technique to negate any sense of tonic. This can be achieved if the first two postulates are scrupulously observed, since they guarantee that no one pitch will asume prominence at any point. (In this connection Perle's use of the term "semitonal" rather than "chromatic" should be noted. For more on the implications of this distinction see the end of the discussion in no. 134.) What one soon discovers is that the interval becomes the important concern in establishing relationships in this music. But we must also mention the principle of octave-equivalence, which had long been recognized by tonal composers. (Without such an equivalence a tuba and piccolo could hardly perform in the same piece.) In twelve-tone technique it means that any pitch in the row can be stated in any octave. (The equivalence of pitches, regardless of their octave, can be easily demonstrated by playing successive notes of a familiar tune, say "America," in different octaves. One will discover that the tune is clearly recognizable, though individual notes appear to differ in color or timbre. In other words, there is a close correlation between register and color.) It should also be said that the row serves as the source for all pitch relationships in serial technique, whether melodic or harmonic.

The first step in the analysis of any twelve-tone piece is to identify the row. This we have already done, giving as the top line of the table below the preeminent form that Webern uses in the first movement. Once having identified the row, the most efficient next step is to construct what is called a *matrix*—our table—that shows all possible transpositions of the row in all its possible forms. This comprises a box that contains 144 squares, twelve to a side. The current custom is to lay out all transformations of the original form of the row, or prime (P), from left to right, and those of the inversion (I), from top to bottom, using enharmonic equivalents as needed (e.g.,

F-sharp for G-flat) to facilitate analysis (see no. 134). Once this has been done, all possible transpositions of the row, whether prime or inversion, are determined and the matrix is completed. The numbers along the borders indicate the distance in semitones from the starting pitch of the original form, which is identified as P-O or I-O. (If the initial pitch of P-O is A, as here, then P-1 starts on B-flat, P-2 on B, etc.) We present below such a matrix for the piece at hand. It will be noted that retrograde forms (R and RI) can be obtained simply by reading from right to left or from bottom to top.

Turning now to the structure of the row, and the ways in which Webern has used it in this movement, we note that he has constructed a row whose intervallic structure is symmetrical around a central pivot, the tritone. As a result P-O, for example, is identical to R-6, and I-O is identical to RI-6. This means that there are only twelve forms of the row—and their retrograde forms—that concern us, those numbered between O and 5.

The symmetry we have discovered in the row is manifest in many ways, on many levels, throughout the movement. A close look at the theme, which employs RI-2 and I-2, will show that interval relationships are only one of the musical elements that are symmetrical around the interval of the tritone in measure 6. It is left to the reader to determine which other elements are symmetrical as well, and to determine whether or not these symmetries can be heard. And if one discovers symmetries in both the row and the themes, it is safe to assume that they will be found elsewhere in the movement. For example, Variation 1 is not only palindromic like the theme, but also comprises a double canon by inversion. (A palindrome reads the same forwards and backwards: Dennis and Edna sinned.) Such canons by inversion, or mirror canons, have a vertical symmetry around some central pitch. As for the overall form of the movement, we note that there are seven variations that are framed by a theme and a coda, which means any overall symmetry in the movement should pivot on the fourth variation. Webern himself said as much in a lecture quoted in *The Path to the New Music*, commenting that this variation "is the midpoint of the whole movement, after which everything goes backward." It is left to the reader to determine in what ways this occurs (the particular transposition of the row should not be ignored).

Returning briefly to a consideration of the relationship between different forms of the row, it should further be noted that the last two pitches in P-O are identical to the first two in I-3, which will allow the composer to elide one form of the row with the other. Although this is true of numerous pairs of rows, Webern capitalizes on this particular pair and another, R-1 and RI-4, in moving from Variation 1 to Variation 2, and therefore also from Variation 6 to Variation 7.

One of the dangers of highly organized works such as this one by Webern is that the fascination of tracing row structures and symmetries of various sorts, a purely intellectual exercise, easily draws one's attention away from the fact that this music was written to be heard, and might in addition appeal to the emotions. Analysis can become an end in itself, rather than a useful means to get at why a work affects one as it does. What one hears by way of pitch relations in this piece surely results in large measure from the way Webern has constructed the row. But an analysis of row structure is merely the first step in determining how such a piece "works." And even though Webern may have earned a Ph.D. in musicology, writing his dissertation on the music of the fifteenth-century composer Heinrich Isaac (see vol I, no. 31B), he was a practicing musician, and spent much of his life as a successful conductor of works of all sorts with choruses and orchestras in a number of European cities.

I→	0	9	10	11	7	8	2	1	5	4	3	6	
P→ 0	A	F#	G	Ab	E	F	B	Bb	D	C#	C	Eb	0
3	C	A	Bb	B	G	Ab	D	C#	F	E	Eb	F#	3
2	B	Ab	A	Bb	F#	G	C#	C	E	Eb	D	F	2
1	Bb	G	Ab	A	F	F#	C	B	Eb	D	C#	E	1
5	D	B	C	C#	A	Bb	E	Eb	G	F#	F	Ab	5
4	C#	Bb	B	C	Ab	A	Eb	D	F#	F	E	G	4
10	G	E	F	F#	D	Eb	A	Ab	C	B	Bb	C#	10
11	Ab	F	F#	G	Eb	E	Bb	A	C#	C	B	D	11
7	E	C#	D	Eb	B	C	F#	F	A	Ab	G	Bb	7
8	F	D	Eb	E	C	C#	G	F#	Bb	A	Ab	B	8
9	F#	Eb	E	F	C#	D	Ab	G	B	Bb	A	C	9
6	Eb	C	C#	D	Bb	B	F	E	Ab	G	F#	A	6 ← R
	0	9	10	11	7	8	2	1	5	4	3	6 RI	

Source: Used by permission of European American Music Dist. Corp., Agents for Universal Edition, from A. Webern, *Symphonie*, opus 21, pp. 9-16.

Recordings: Columbia CK4L-232, *The Complete Works of Anton Webern*; Columbia M4 35193, *The Complete Works of Anton Webern*; CBS Masterworks 76911, *Webern: Orchestral Music*; Deutsche Grammophon 2711014, *Schönberg-Berg-Webern*.

Symphonie   **Webern**

10 Min.

1928

═══125═══

SYMPHONIC WORK

Béla Bartók (1881–1945)
Concerto for Orchestra, movement 1

Like J. S. Bach, Bartók is a composer whose reputation following his death is far greater than it ever was during his lifetime. In part this is because, as a Hungarian, he came from a country not known in his time for producing composers of international stature. His artistic development took place during a period of emergent nationalism, a phenomenon that had already resulted in statehood in Russia, Germany, and Italy (see nos. 111, 113, and 115). But until World War I, when Hungary finally gained independence from Hapsburg rule, Hungarian musical life was dominated by Germanic music. As a result Bartók's early works display the successive influences of Liszt, Brahms, and Richard Strauss—even though, as an ardent nationalist, he insisted on speaking Hungarian rather than German in the family and wore native dress when performing in public. (Following the war he was to learn much from Debussy's music.) But of far greater significance to Bartók's artistic development was his discovery in the first decade of our century of the true Hungarian folk song. What had passed for Hungarian folk song earlier had been the music of Hungarian gypsies—what one still hears from fiddlers in Hungarian restaurants, which was often imitated by an earlier Hungarian-born but German-trained musician, Franz (originally Ferenc) Liszt. Though Liszt saw great artistic merit in the music of the Hungarian gypsy, he, like his contemporaries, believed that the folk songs of the Hungarian peasant were merely corrupted versions of gypsy music.

> It seems presumable that the Hungarian peasant, whose inferior musical organization would render him less conscious of the imperfections of his singing, seized upon the melodies which he heard the Bohemians [i.e., gypsies] perform, as a sort of windfall. Leading a primitive life . . . his own voice generally remained sufficiently fresh for the purpose of singing them. . . . Hungarian songs, as they exist rurally . . . are both too poor and too incomplete to produce any new artistic result, and cannot yet even pretend to the honor of being universally appreciated.

With such a patronizing attitude Liszt would surely have dismissed the quarter tones common in Hungarian folk songs as the out-of-tuneness one should expect from untrained musicians. Bartók was far more astute in his perceptions, however, and approached his native folk song with both an open mind and a well-tuned ear. For several years, in collaboration with Zoltán Kodály, he undertook extensive field trips throughout Hungary, to collect folk songs from peasants in the country villages. On his own he also ventured to the Balkans, North Africa, and Turkey. (It must be remembered that the Ottoman Empire, an Arabic culture, had dominated not only north Africa but also the Balkans for a number of centuries, and at one point extended to the very gates of Vienna.) What Bartók found provided him with new models for scales, melodic construction, rhythms, and forms—in short, with a way out of the stylistic crisis that had overtaken Western music through the breakdown of tonality. Outside of the benefit to his own stylistic development, his research in folk song led him to develop a methodology for the classification of melodies that is widely accepted today in the field of ethnomusicology, a discipline that encompasses the study of folk song worldwide.

The *Concerto for Orchestra* was the first work Bartók composed following his emigration to the United States in 1940. (Bartók was among the last of a great wave of European intellectuals to migrate to this country during the 1930s and early 1940s because of political conditions in Europe. Others included the authors Bertold Brecht and Thomas Mann, the physicists Albert Einstein and Enrico Fermi, and the composers Arnold Schoenberg, Paul Hindemith, and Igor Stravinsky.) It was commissioned in the spring of 1943 by Serge Koussevitsky, then conductor of the Boston Symphony Orchestra, on behalf of the Koussevitsky Foundation. At the time Bartók, though well-known throughout Europe as a pianist and composer, was all but unknown in this country; the recitals he had already performed across the country, which always included some of his own compositions, had not been particularly well received. Under the circumstances, it is not surprising that, by all appearances, he chose to fulfill the commission by composing a work that might have a broad appeal to concert-going audiences, American or European. The work, based on elements originally intended for a ballet, has a strong Romantic flavor and was begun on 15 August in Saranac Lake, New York, where Bartók, suffering from leukemia, had gone for the summer. He worked on it, as he said, "practically night and day," so that it was completed by 8 October of that year.

For the first performance Bartók supplied the following description:

> The general mood of the work represents, apart from the jesting second movement, a gradual transition from the sternness of the first movement and

lugubrious death-song of the third, to the life-assertion of the last one.

The title of this symphony-like orchestral work is explained by its tendency to treat the single instruments or instrument groups in a *'concertant'* or soloistic manner. The 'virtuoso' treatment appears, for instance, in the fugato sections of the development of the first movement (brass instruments). . . . As for the structure of the work, the first and fifth movements are written in a more or less regular sonata form. . . .

Bartók's version of sonata form, used in a number of his mature works, is palindromic (see no. 124). The recapitulation (mm. 396ff.) presents the materials of the exposition in reverse order. Bartók's key plan for the main body of the work is characteristic of his mature works, and is a logical outgrowth of his free use of all the notes of the chromatic scale. In place of the polarity of tonic and dominant found in Classical practice he substitutes the interval of the tritone. Thus the exposition, which begins in F, proceeds by step downward (E-flat, C-sharp, C) to B for the second theme. The recapitulation proceeds in a similar fashion (A, G, F-sharp, F) to complete the return. The development also stresses the polarity of the tritone, juxtaposing first D and A-flat, and later E and B-flat. (See a similar juxtaposition in the introduction, mm. 58–75). We should also make note of several of the devices Bartók employs for tonal purposes. In measures 35 through 50 he uses a pedal in timpani and horn, and in the figuration in the lower strings constantly returns to the same bottom pitch, E. A trill that includes tonic and leading tone serves the same purpose in measures 135 through 148, as does the interval of the fifth in measures 149 through 177. Leading tone action is also apparent at the return to the recapitulation (mm. 395–396) where the A-flat in retrospect is heard as a G-sharp leading to A. The final return of the tonic, F, in measure 488 is preceded by a figure in the bass employing a double leading action that circles F from above and below. And there is no mistaking the implied authentic cadence at the very end of the movement.

As for Bartók's musical materials, the interval of the fourth is prominent right from the opening measures. It forms a central part of two of the main themes (mm. 76 and 134), and is used both melodically and harmonically in the great fugato that closes the development (mm. 316–385). (The search for other contrapuntal procedures in this movement will not go unrewarded.) On other occasions (mm. 192–197 and 212–220) Bartók will color a melodic line by setting it in parallel triads. The theme that begins at measure 39 has a characteristic rhythmic structure, opening with short notes on the accent. A very different, but also characteristic, Bartók theme that opens by alternating two adjacent pitches is encountered at measure 154. We should also comment briefly on Bartók's use of different scales. In measures 6 through 21, are two wedges that open out with one form of the whole-tone scale, and close with the other. It will also be noted that the opening of the main theme in measure 76 contains a fragment of the octatonic scale, an artificial scale that alternates whole tones and semitones throughout the octave (see no. 121).

Much has been made of the importance of the golden section (.618) and the related Fibonacci series (0 1 1 2 3 5 8 13 21 34, etc.) as a determiner of formal proportions in some of Bartók's mature works. (One example of the golden section, is a line that is divided into two unequal parts such that the ratio between the shorter and longer part is the same as the ratio of the longer part to the whole. In a Fibonacci series any number is the sum of the two preceding numbers, and the ratio of two successive numbers in the series approaches as a limit the golden section. Both relationships are found in such natural phenomena as the sunflower and pine cone, but were also employed in the design of the Parthenon.) Careful study of this movement of Bartók's *Concerto* will reveal some evidence of their application here, but not in any comprehensive fashion. Using the lengths of time for each section of the movement, supplied in minutes and seconds by Bartók below the score at structural points, a case can be made that the end of the exposition roughly coincides with the golden section of the movement as a whole. In addition, the golden section of this opening part roughly coincides with the end of the introduction and, within this part, the reverse of the golden section (.382) roughly marks the appearance of the second theme in the exposition. But none of these calculations can be considered mathematically precise since each deviates from the golden section up to a limit of 3.4 percent. Readers may wish to search for other signs of Bartók's use of the golden section, or of the Fibonacci series—or they may be content to accept the fact that Bartók—perhaps subconsciously—established these proportions in the process of searching for what he sensed were proper proportions in large-scale works.

Source: © Copyright 1946 by Hawkes & Son (London) Ltd; Renewed 1973. Reprinted by permission of Boosey & Hawkes, Inc.

Recordings: Numerous available.

Concerto for Orchestra   **Bartók**

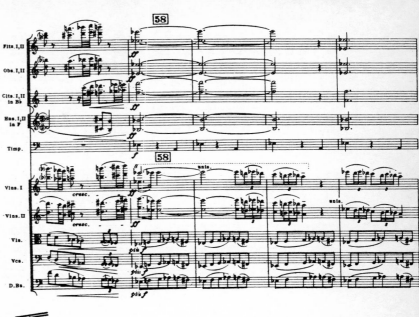

*) always use a soft (cardboard) mute.

SUITE FROM A FILM SCORE

Aaron Copland (b. 1900)
The Gift, from *The Red Pony*

Aaron Copland has composed in a wide range of genres that includes film scores, operas and ballets, and concert works such as symphonies, concertos, and sonatas. After studies as a youth in New York City (he was born in Brooklyn), Copland went to Paris where he was the first of a long series of Americans to study composition with Nadia Boulanger, one of the most influential teachers of our time. Upon his return to this country his career was launched with a performance of his *Symphony for Organ and Orchestra,* which had a widely reviewed premiere in New York in 1925. A composer of great skill and flexibility, Copland writes equally well for the high-school performer and the professional. His most recent works include several excursions into twelve-tone technique. He has also written numerous articles and books, a number of them designed to explain "serious" music, including contemporary music, to the general public.

Many of Copland's works have been written on commission for a particular dance company, a film, or a special occasion. The work we have excerpted here, *The Red Pony,* is one of these. Taken from his fourth film score, it was composed in his late forties, by which time he had evolved a highly personal style and was considered a major figure in American music. The film, made in Hollywood, was based on a story by John Steinbeck. A further commission, from the conductor Efrem Kurtz, resulted in Copland's arranging his score as a concert suite of six movements, which was first performed by the Houston Symphony late in 1948. The titles of the movements are

1. Morning on the Ranch
2. The Gift
3. Dream March and Circus Music
4. Walk to the Bunkhouse
5. Grandfather's Story
6. Happy Ending

Copland's remarks concerning the film and his adaptation of its score as a suite are germane:

> Steinbeck's tale is a series of vignettes concerning a 10-year-old boy called Jody and his life in a California ranch setting. There is a minimum of action of a dramatic or startling kind. The story gets its warmth and sensitive quality from the character studies of the boy Jody, Jody's grandfather, the cowhand Billy Buck, and Jody's parents, the Tiflins. The kinds of emotions that Steinbeck evokes in his story are basically musical ones, since they deal so much with the unexpressed feelings of daily living. It seems to me that Lewis Milestone, in directing the picture, realized that fact and, therefore, left plenty of room for musical treatment—which, in turn, made the writing of the score a grateful task.
>
> In shaping the suite, I recast much of the musical material so that, although all the music may be heard in the film, it has been reorganized as to continuity for concert purposes.

His comments on the movement presented here, *The Gift,* are as follows:

> Jody's father surprises him with the gift of a red pony. Jody shows off his new acquisition to his school chums, who cause quite a commotion about it. "Jody was glad when they had gone."

As Copland's comments indicate, the main focus of both the film and his score is the boy Jody. This work therefore stands in the tradition of those pieces that evoke childhood scenes and yearnings, which include Schumann's *Scenes from Childhood* and Debussy's *Children's Corner.* In each case the music is about children, rather than intended for performance by children.

Writing film scores poses unique problems for the composer. First, he must synchronize his score with the action in the already completed film. More important, since the main focus is the visual image, his music must play a secondary role. But the power of music is such that it can easily become obtrusive, thereby distracting the viewer. Copland's awareness of this latter problem, and his view of what constitutes a good film score are of 'interest:

> The touchstone for judging a Hollywood score: Was the composer moved in the first instance by what he saw happening on the screen? If there is too much sheen, he wasn't; if there are too many different styles used, he wasn't; if the score is over-socko, he wasn't; if the music obtrudes, he wasn't. It is rare to hear a score that strikes one as touching because of the fact that the composer himself was moved by the action of the film. [Aaron Copland, *Copland on Music* (New York: W.W. Norton, 1963), p. 135.]

His particular solution was to adopt a simpler style for his film scores and numerous ballets in the late 1930s.

> I think a more accessible style was brought on by the nature of the things I was asked to do: a ballet score implies that you are looking at something while you are listening to the music, so that you can't give your undivided attention to the music. This suggests a simpler style. The same is true of movie music. [Benjamin Boretz & Edward Cone, *Perspectives on American Composers* (New York: W. W. Norton, 1971), p. 140]

An integral element in this new simpler style was the American folk song, such as those Copland used in the two ballets, *Billy the Kid* and *Rodeo*. In turning to folk song Copland was emulating such other contemporaries as Stravinsky (no. 127) and Bartók (no. 125), in his case consciously trying to create an "American" style. And like the other two, he so absorbed the characteristics of folk melodies that he could write his own, so to speak. Copland said of the present work that

> Although some of the melodies in *The Red Pony* may sound rather folk-like, they are actually mine. There are no quotations of folklore anywhere in the work.

The opening melody in the violins, with its large leaps that rely heavily on the basic interval of the fifth, is typical for Copland at the time, and has been likened to the wide-open spaces encountered in the Far West, with their concomitant sense of loneliness. The analogy may seem farfetched, but it has been widely accepted; similar effects were used by other consciously "American" composers of the time, such as Roy Harris. A series of fourths, another basic interval, has opened the movement in the harp. The only dissonance in this passage is supplied by the vibraphone, which the composer directs to be played with soft hammers. The resultant effect is indicative of Copland's imaginative use of tone color. (It is instructive to compare different recordings of this passage. If played softly, the vibraphone dissonances in measures 3 and 5 sound like unobtrusive harmonics of the chord in the harp and strings. If played with greater intensity, they become obtrusive, giving a harsher quality to the chord.)

Copland's use of scales in this opening passage is indicative of the subtlety of his art. Although he relies mainly on the notes of the pentatonic scale for melodies and harmonies, the scale that lies at the basis of many American folk songs, he fleshes out this scale by filling the gaps so that it eventually becomes diatonic. In measures 7 through 13, for example, he uses a six-note, or hexatonic, scale by adding a new pitch, D; but it is only in measure 26, at the very end of the passage, that he introduces G-sharp, the seventh degree, or leading tone, as a melodic note. (See its earlier appearance, as a dissonance, however, in measure 18. One might wish to examine measures 22 through 38 from this same point of view.)

The form of this movement is straightforward and relates to the events outlined above. The quietness of the opening—reflecting, perhaps, Jody's suppressed excitement—gives way to gradually increasing tempos (m. 20) as he "shows off his new acquisition," and (m. 75) as his school chums "cause quite a commotion." Their departure leads to a return to the quiet opening. Beginning in measure 75 we witness the clearest example here of Copland's folklike melodies. The "commotion" is manifest both tonally and rhythmically. Though Copland employs diatonic material elsewhere in the movement, in measures 90 through 93 and 100 through 107 he juxtaposes two different tonal centers a tritone apart. And a careful study of meter in measures 75 through 123 will reveal a progression from a basic duple meter to the juxtaposition of duple and triple (measures 98 through 107) and finally, at the climax of the section (mm. 118–123), an absence of duple meter, with overlapping patterns of triple meter in which each eighth note is accented. (One might also wish to compare the opening and closing passages from the standpoint of meter.)

Source: © Copyright 1951 by Aaron Copland; Renewed 1951. Reprinted by permission of Aaron Copland, Copyright Owner, and Boosey & Hawkes, Inc., Sole Licensee.

Recordings: Columbia MS 6583, *Copland: The Red Pony;* Odyssey 31016, *Copland: The Red Pony*; Columbia M 33586, *Copland Conducts Copland.*

The Gift   Copland

═127═

BALLET

Igor Stravinsky (1882–1971)
Le Sacre du Printemps: Introduction and Augurs of Spring

Serge Diaghilev (or Dyagilev), best known as the impresario of the Ballet Russe, was a seminal force in the arts in Paris during the early years of our century. In addition to introducing Russian paintings, music, and dance to Parisian audiences, and hence to the West, he was also responsible through his commissions for a whole raft of well-known works, originally intended as ballets, which include Ravel's *Daphnis et Chloé* (1912), Debussy's *Jeux* (1913), Satie's *Parade* (1917), Falla's *Three-Cornered Hat* (1919), Milhaud's *The Blue Train* (1924), and Prokofiev's *Steps of Steel* (1927). (His choreographers included such famous names as Vaclav Nijinsky and George Balanchine, and he also engaged a number of talented young artists to supply the decor, among them Pablo Picasso, Georges Rouault, Juan Gris, Max Ernst, André Derain, and Joan Miró.) Diaghilev also launched the young Stravinsky's career outside Russia, commissioning the three famous ballets by which Stravinsky is best known today: *The Firebird* (1910), *Petrushka* (1911), and *Le Sacre du Printemps* ("The Rite of Spring," 1913). (The two collaborated in seven later works as well.)

All three ballets are examples of Stravinsky's folkloric style, being based on Russian subjects. The style of the first two owed much to Rimsky-Korsakov, Stravinsky's teacher, and were enormously successful. The latter two make use of a number of Russian folk songs or of material clearly derived from them. In the case of the *Rite*, it has recently been determined that those that Stravinsky used as his models were appropriate to spring rites in Russia, and were in use among the peasants in his own day.

The idea for the *Rite*, whose subtitle is *Scenes of Pagan Russia in two parts*, came to Stravinsky, as he said, in "a fleeting vision," in the spring of 1910, while he was finishing *The Firebird*: "I saw in imagination a solemn pagan rite: sage elders, seated in a circle, watched a young girl dance herself to death. They were sacrificing her to propitiate the god of Spring." The two parts of the work are entitled "Adoration of the Earth" and "The

Sacrifice." We give here the opening of part 1, and include the "Introduction," to be played before the curtain rises; "Augurs of Spring," which is subtitled "Dance of the Young Maidens," and is a puberty dance by members of a primitive tribe.

Stravinsky's *Rite* is commonly regarded as one of the most important compositions of the twentieth century. Written in a style that consciously evoked primitive rites, the work was understandably radical in cast and initially proved challenging to both performers and audiences. It was to require 120 rehearsals to prepare, and the initial performance, in Paris, provoked a riot in the theater. The audience apparently reacted as much to Nijinsky's choreography as to Stravinsky's startling music. Its behavior, as described by several witnesses, reminds one more of professional wrestling matches than of a ballet performance:

> A certain part of the audience was thrilled by what it considered to be a blasphemous attempt to destroy music as an art, and, swept away with wrath, began, very soon after the rise of the curtain, to make cat-calls and to offer audible suggestions as to how the performance should proceed. The orchestra played unheard, except occasionally when a slight lull occurred. The young man seated behind me in the box stood up during the course of the ballet to enable himself to see more clearly. The intense excitement under which he was laboring betrayed itself presently when he began to beat rhythmically on the top of my head with his fists. My emotion was so great that I did not feel the blows for some time.
>
> One beautifully dressed lady in an orchestra box stood up and slapped the face of a young man who was hissing in the next box. Her escort arose, and cards were exchanged between the men. (Such an exchange was usually a prelude to a duel.)
>
> Jean Cocteau saw the old Contesse de Pourtalès stand up in her box with face aflame and her tiara awry and heard her cry out, as she brandished her fan, 'This is the first time in sixty years that anyone has dared to make fun of me!' [Eric White, *Stravinsky*, 176—177]

The technical difficulties of the work have long since been mastered; it often appears today on programs of the best university orchestras. In mastering them, however, instrumentalists have created a curious sort of problem. Stravinsky surely expected a strained, perhaps even crude, sound from the bassoonist as he struggled to play his very highest notes at the beginning. But bassoonists, faced with a challenge, have worked hard over the years to make them sound less labored; most have succeeded. As for the audience, with the passage of time most listeners have come to accept Stravinsky's jarring dissonances and pounding rhythms. Nowadays the *Rite* is seldom performed as a ballet, being most frequently heard in the concert hall.

Like his contemporaries, Stravinsky was deeply concerned with finding ways out of the dilemma posed by what was widely viewed as the wearing out of the tonal system—that is, with finding new ways to create a sense of order in music. His solution in this work was to replace the earlier hierarchy of tonal relationships—tonic, dominant, subdominant—by what he called "the polar attraction of sound, of an interval, or even of a complex of tones." We shall see the clearest evidence of this in the *Augurs of Spring*. We shall also examine a number of other aspects of Stravinsky's technique in this piece.

Stravinsky's orchestra for the *Rite* is immense; but it is no larger than those used by such late-Romantic contemporaries as Gustav Mahler and the young Schoenberg. We list the forces below:

> 1 piccolo; 3 flutes (3rd also 2nd piccolo); 1 alto flute in G; 4 oboes (4th also 2nd English horn); 1 English horn; 1 piccolo clarinet in Eb or D; 3 clarinets in A or Bb (3rd also 2nd bass clarinet); 1 bass clarinet in Bb; 4 bassoons (4th also 2nd contrabassoon); 1 contrabassoon; 8 horns (7th & 8th also Wagner tubas); 1 piccolo trumpet in D; 4 trumpets in C (4th also bass trumpet in Eb); 3 trombones; 2 tubas; 5 timpani (2 players); triangle, ancient cymbals, bass drum, tambour de basque, tam tam, cymbals, large gourd; strings (individual sections divided into as many as 5 parts).

The Introduction shows strong evidence of Debussy's influence, even though it is utterly different in expressive intent. (Rimsky-Korsakov was alarmed to find these influences in some of Stravinsky's student compositions). The opening, with a solo instrument playing in a hitherto unexplored register, inevitably brings to mind the *Prelude to the Afternoon of a Faun* (see no. 122), as does Stravinsky's use of a number of short melodic motives that are suggestive because of their fragmentary nature. (Years later Stravinsky was to say that the opening of the ballet "should represent the awakening of nature, the scratching, gnawing, wiggling of birds and beasts.") Five motives in particular, most of them diatonic or pentatonic in character, dominate the Introduction. Three are closely associated with a particular instrument and hence sonority: bassoon (m. 1–3); English horn (m. 10–12); and *clarinet piccolo* (m. 54). The sonority of the other two motives changes: bassoon (m. 14–15), later *clarinet piccolo* (m. 20), and finally A clarinet (m. 57); and oboe (m. 52–53), later D trumpet (m. 61). Stravinsky's method of construction here is to alternate motives, combine them in various ways, and finally, as a climax, combine the last four (mm. 61–65) in an incredibly rich texture of the sort that one encounters on occasion in Debussy's orchestral scores. It is only because of the assertive quality of the D trumpet that one hears its motive dominating the passage. Thus

we have at hand another example of a piece that is non-Germanic since it is nondevelopmental, where the rich orchestral texture often used by earlier Russian composers as an accompaniment has almost become an end in itself. Stravinsky signals the ends of sections, both large and small, by abruptly stopping and turning to something else. But the return of the bassoon in measure 66 ensures the sense of a closed form for the Introduction. The rhythm here, because of Stravinsky's tendency to use elaborate arabesques, is very fluid in character. Even the constant changes of meter, always based on the quarter note as the beat, are not particularly evident. Thus the polymeter he establishes in measures 39 and 57, by the same means as Debussy (no. 122—the grouping of triplet figures by twos— emerges as the strongest regular pulse present.

In the *Augurs of Spring* we find some very different techniques in use, though, as in the Introduction, Stravinsky again builds a climax by means of increasingly complex texture (see mm. 216—247). Here pounding rhythms come to the fore. All the orchestral instruments function at times as percussion instruments—even the strings, whose normal repertory at the time called for beautiful, singing lines. Melodic materials are again short and fragmentary, diatonic in nature, and clearly derived from folk song. One recurring "polar attraction" in the first part of the piece is a complex sonority that combines an F-flat major triad and and E-flat major triad with an added minor seventh. (One could analyze this amalgam by traditional means as the simultaneous sound of V and VI in A-flat minor, but such information tells us nothing about how it is used.) This sonority, which is viewed by some as a forerunner of the sound masses prevalent in recent music (see no. 133), is presented in block chords (m. 76). Three pitches from it are subsequently presented (m. 84) as a four-note ostinato that persists throughout the rest of the dance—except when the block chords recur. Initially identified with the English horn until measure 161, it then moves to other instruments before returning to the English horn in measure 216 but now transposed. The melodic shape of the ostinato is common in Slavic folk song.

In this dance we also find evidence that Stravinsky's dissonant harmonies are less an extension of late-Romantic chromaticism than a juxtaposition of bitonal chords and chords built on intervals other than the third, and are used for their sonority, not in any functional way. In measure 98 we encounter a bass that is clearly anchored in E-flat, above which the violas are playing a C-major triad, with an E natural. Shortly afterward (m. 101) Stravinsky adds on top of this a chord of four superposed fifths in the trumpets, which is followed by a chord of five superposed fourths, again in the trumpets (m. 109). Still later (m. 224), chords of three superposed thirds are introduced in the horns as the dance builds to a climax. The end of the dance is again abruptly signaled by the beginning of the following one.

Fascinating as the sonorities in this dance are, the rhythms are even more so, approaching in complexity those found in the late fourteenth century (see vol. 1, no. 25). Although the written meter remains constant, and much of the piece projects a clear sense of duple meter, there are times when the ear senses a different meter, or meters, in the music. For example, by means of accents the otherwise undifferentiated block chords at the beginning project the following complex metric pattern: 2/8, 3/8, 4/8, 5/8, 6/8 (or is this a rhythmic pattern?). Whichever it is, this pattern functions as a thematic motive that recurs, among other places, in measure 210 in the winds, and in a slightly altered form, in the trumpets at measure 101. A close look at measures 98 through 109 will disclose an example of polymeter. Here there are three simultaneous meters: 2/4 in the ostinato presented by the English horn; 3/4 in the doublebass and cello, which together establish another ostinato through a recurring pitch pattern based on fifths (see also measures 190 through 215); and an effective 6/8 in the violas by means of triplets. Surely Stravinsky's intent was not for the listener to hear each meter individually; rather, it was to use yet another means to contribute to an extremely rich texture of sound.

Source: Kalmus Music Publishers reprint edition.

Recordings: Numerous available.

Le Sacre du Printemps   **Stravinsky**

ВЕСЕННІЯ ГАДАНІЯ.   LES AUGURES PRINTANIERS.
ПЛЯСКИ ЩЕГОЛИХЪ.   DANSES DES ADOLESCENTES.

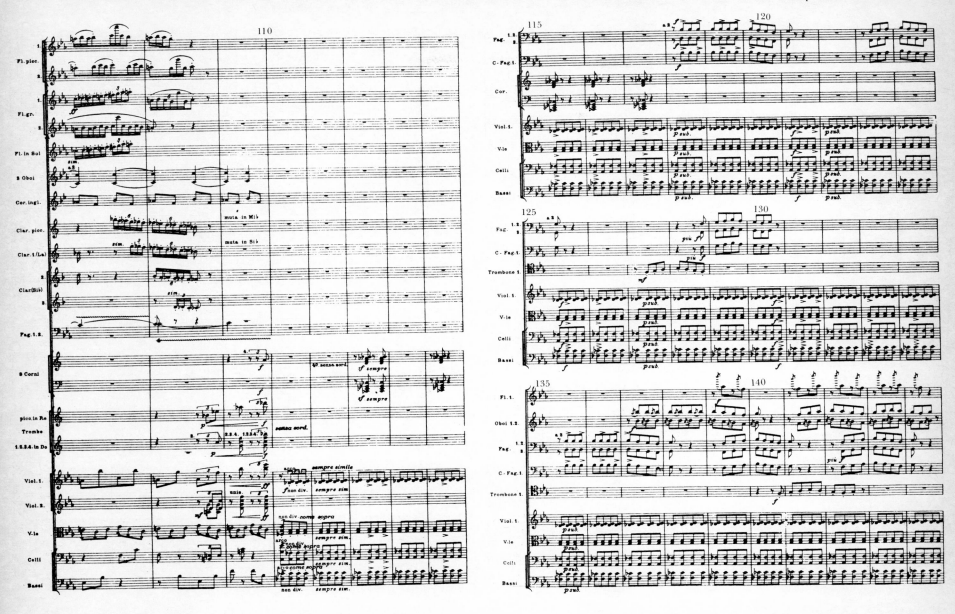

══128══

OPERA

Alban Berg (1885—1935)
Wozzeck, Act III, scenes 1 and 2

One of the most brilliant opera composers of any era, Berg based his *Wozzeck* on an unfinished work by the radical German playwright, Georg Büchner (1813–1837). Büchner's play, focusing on man's inhumanity towards his fellow man, was based on an historical figure, Johann Christian Woyzeck, a barber and soldier who was executed in Leipzig in 1824 for murdering his mistress in a fit of jealousy. Berg was deeply moved by a Viennese performance of Büchner's drama in 1914, and set to work immediately on an opera based on the play. The work occupied him for seven years, with an interruption for service during World War I in the Austro-Hungarian army.

Büchner's play survived as a loosely organized collection of twenty-five scenes. To forge this material into a coherent opera was a major challenge to Berg, and one that he met brilliantly. He achieved coherence on several levels, first by organizing the libretto into three acts, each with five scenes, and by reducing the number of characters. Each act was designed to fulfill a different dramatic function: exposition, dénouement, and catastrophe.

Musical coherence was more difficult to attain. As a disciple of Schoenberg and a leading figure in the Second Viennese School (no. 112), Berg chose not to use such earlier musical techniques as the strong return to a home key at climactic points in the drama. Instead he sought structural unity through employing a combination of old and new formal conventions borrowed mainly from instrumental music, selecting each with a view to its appropriateness to the dramatic situation. Perhaps most unusual is his treatment of the second act, the longest of the three, which is a symphony in five movements. The first act consists of five character sketches (Suite, Rhapsody, Military March and Cradle Song, Passacaglia, and *Andante affetuoso quasi Rondo*). The third contains a set of inventions, one fo r each scene, plus a sixth one for the long interlude that precedes the final scene. As in Wagner's opera, music is continuous throughout each act, short inter-ludes between the scenes permitting both rapid scene changes and changes in musical mood.

Sensitive to criticism of his use of such instrumental forms in an opera, Berg said that

> my aim was musical variety and the avoidance of Wagner's method of 'through-composing' every single one of these many scenes. Therefore I had to give to every scene a different structural basis . . . . the dramatic unity of these scenes demanded a similar unity in the music. This could best be achieved by the employment of closed musical forms.

As yet another means of achieving musical coherence Berg made use of characteristic motives throughout the work. The most striking of these, and one that is most closely related to the social theme of the opera, is first heard in the opening scene. Wozzeck, reacting to the taunts of the Captain, bursts out "Wir arme Leut! Sehn sie, Herr Hauptmann, Geld, Geld! Wer kein Geld hat'. . . ." (We poor people! Don't you see, Captain, money, money! He who has no money. . . .)

Wir ar-me Leut!   Sehn Sie,   Herr Haupt-mann, Geld,   Geld!   Wer kein Geld   hat!

This motive appears several times in the opera, and is last heard at the powerful climax to the long, impassioned interlude that precedes the final scene.

The action preceding our excerpt is as follows:

The five scenes of Act I relate Wozzeck to the other characters in the opera. In scene 1 he is shaving the Captain, who taunts him for having fathered a child out of wedlock. His reply, "Captain, the Good Lord will not ask my poor child whether the Amen was said over it before it was made . . ." climaxes in the first appearance of the "Wir arme Leut" motive. In the next scene Wozzeck has joined another soldier, Andres, to gather firewood in a field at sunset. He is haunted by a fear of the unknown, and talks of the strange sights he imagines he is seeing. Scene 3 introduces Wozzeck's mistress, Marie, in her room playing with their child. She waves to the passing Drum Major. Shortly Wozzeck enters and tells her he has no time to stay; he must return to the barracks. Marie is disturbed by his confused talk. In the following scene we meet the Doctor, who is paying Wozzeck to be a subject for his medical

398

experiments. The Doctor is fascinated by Wozzeck's increasing incoherence. The Drum Major passes by again in Scene 5, and Marie, flattered by his attentions, flings herself into his arms as the two disappear into her house.

Act II opens in Marie's room, where Wozzeck is tormented by suspicions and turns to the sleeping child with a lament that opens with the "Wir arme Leut" motive. In Scene 2 the Captain and Doctor meet Wozzeck in the street and torment him about Marie's infidelity. In the next scene Wozzeck, whose growing psychosis is graphically depicted in the music, meets Marie in front of her house. They argue and she cries "Better a knife in me than a hand on me . . ." He leaves, muttering the same words to himself. Scene 4 takes place in a beer garden where Wozzeck sees Marie dancing with the Drum Major. A small onstage orchestra plays distorted Austrian Ländlers as Wozzeck watches with rising fury. In the final scene, in the barracks, Wozzeck tries to sleep but keeps seeing visions of a knife. The Drum Major swaggers in; soon he and Wozzeck are fighting. Wozzeck is soundly beaten.

Berg's incredible gifts as a dramatic composer are most obvious in the third act. Careful study of the dramatic structure and content of its first two scenes will show how apt has been his choice of musical techniques for each. Moreover, the richness of detail invites study from several points of view. We can merely note certain characteristics and details and invite you to find more on your own.

From the standpoint of musical structure, scene 1 is an invention on a theme presented at the outset by a trio of solo strings. It comprises seven variations and a closing fugue (m. 52). Against this background Marie alternately reads from the Bible and gives vent to her feelings of despair and guilt. Berg's vocal styles underline the difference between these two actions. Marie's emotional outbursts are delivered in a traditional singing style—though her melodic lines would never be mistaken for those in Italian opera. For Marie's readings, however, Berg employs *Sprechstimme*, a half-sung, half-spoken vocal style borrowed from Schoenberg, in which pitch is only approximate. The means of notation can be seen in measure 5. *Sprechstimme* will also be encountered in scene 4. Berg's texture, like Schoenberg's, is often so complex that he felt it necessary to borrow Schoenberg's new set of symbols to identify where the principal line or "melody" lies at any instant. (See no. 123 for a discussion of the terms *Hauptstimme* and *Nebenstimme*.)

Scene 2, the murder scene, is an invention on one note: B. First introduced by the contrabass as the curtain rises (m. 71), this note gradually permeates the entire orchestral fabric, appearing now in the upper register (m. 80), now in the lower (m. 85), and finally throughout (m. 97). The effect borders on the hypnotic and underlines Wozzeck's obsession. The in-

terlude following this scene is remarkable. In it we see only one instance of Berg's overwhelming concern with control. There are two earthshaking crescendos on B, the first achieved by a combination of the addition of instruments and their crescendo, the second by full orchestra employing a crescendo alone. Careful investigation of the first of these crescendos (mm. 109–113) shows that the rhythm that will dominate scene 3, invention on a rhythm, is first projected through the successive entries of the strings, and also of the winds, in effect creating a rhythmic canon, even before it is forcefully performed by the bass drum (m. 114).

The second orchestral crescendo leads directly into scene 3, not included here, which takes place in a badly lit tavern. Wozzeck enters and the revelers notice blood on his arm. Berg employs a technique here that had not been used since the fifteenth century: isorhythm (see vol. I, no. 28). Setting aside all considerations of pitch, almost every rhythm in the scene, whether in vocal lines or in the orchestra, can be related to the rhythm first presented in the preceding interlude. In scene 4 Wozzeck returns to the pond to search for the knife. In an even more psychotic state, he imagines the water is blood and, wading out into the pond as he searches, he drowns. Berg has based this scene on a six-note chord (invention on a chord), that at one point graphically depicts the rings that spread on the water as Wozzeck drowns. A long, impassioned interlude follows, an *in memoriam* Wozzeck, passing in review all the motives employed in the opera and is the one strongly tonal passage in the opera (invention on a key, D). Given the pervasive sense of abnormality in the story, and Berg's apt projection of this state through his music, this tonal passage inevitably gives rise to a strong sense of normality as well as of compassion for Wozzeck. The curtain rises on the short final scene, musically an invention on a persistent rhythm (Perpetuum Mobile), in which Marie's child is seen playing with other children when a youngster rushes in to tell them that Marie's body has been found. Pointing at the child he says, matter of factly, "You, your mother is dead." The children rush off, Marie's child following them on his hobby-horse. The curtain falls on an empty stage. Some have argued that the closing harmony could resolve into the opening chord of the opera, thus suggesting an endless cycle, and that by this means Berg has symbolized the futility of the society he depicts.

Our discussion has of necessity focused on musical techniques. But we must close with Berg's own comment on his techniques.

No one in the audience, no matter how aware he may be of the musical forms contained in the framework of the opera, of the precision and logic with which it has been worked out, no one, from the moment the curtain parts until it closes for the last time, pays any attention to the various figures, inventions, suites, sonata movements, variations, and passacaglias about which so much as been written. No one gives heed to anything but the vast social implications of the work which by far transcend the personal destiny of Wozzeck. This, I believe, is my achievement.

Source:

Recordings: Numerous available.

Translation:

Act Three
Scene One.
Marie's room. It is night. Candle-light. Marie, alone with her child, is sitting at the table, turning the pages of the Bible and reading . . .

MARIE . . . 'And out of His mouth there came forth neither deceit nor falsehood.' . . . Lord God! Lord God! Look not on me! . . . (*She turns the pages and reads further*) . . . Wherefore the Pharisees had taken and brought to Him an adulterous woman. Jesus said to her: "Thus condemned shall you not be. Go forth, go forth in peace, and sin no more." ' . . . Lord God! (*Covers her face with her hands*)
(*The child presses up to Marie*)

MARIE   The boy looks at me and stabs my heart. Be off! (*pushes the child away*) . . . Go proudly in the sunlight! . . . (*Suddenly more gentle*) Ah, no! Come here . . . (*draws him closer*) Come to me. 'And once there was a poor wee child . . . and he had no father, nor any mother . . . for all was dead, there was no one in the world, therefore he did hunger and did weep . . . day and night . . . Since he had no one else left in the world . . .'

. . . But Franz has not come yet . . . yesterday . . . this day . . . (*She hastily turns the leaves of the Bible*) . . . What is written here of Mary Magdalene? . . . (*she reads*) . . . 'And falling on her knees before Him and weeping, she kissed His feet and washed them, and washed them with her tears, anointing them with ointment'. (*Beats her breast*) . . . Saviour! . . . Could I anoint Thy feet with ointment . . . Saviour! . . . as Thou hadst mercy on her, have mercy now on me, Lord!
SLOW CURTAIN.
Scene Two.
Forest Path by a pool. Dusk is falling. Marie enters with Wozzeck, from the right.

MARIE   The town lies over there . . . it's still far . . . let's hurry!

WOZZECK   You must stay awhile, Marie. Come, sit here.

MARIE   But it's getting late . . .

WOZZECK   Come! (*They sit down*) So far you've wandered, Marie. You must not make your feet so sore, walking. . . . It's still, here in the darkness. . . . Tell me, Marie, how long has it been since our first meeting?

MARIE   At Whitsun, three years.

WOZZECK   And how long . . . how long will it still go on?

MARIE   (*jumping up*) I must go!

WOZZECK   Trembling, Marie? . . . But you are good? . . . (*laughing*) and kind? . . . and true? . . . (*He pulls her down again on the seat*) (*He bends over her, in deadly earnest*) Ah! How your lips are sweet to touch, Marie! (*kisses her*) All Heaven I would give, and eternal bliss, if I still could sometimes kiss you so . . . But yet I dare not . . .
You shiver . . .

MARIE   The night dew falls . . .

WOZZECK   (*whispering to himself*) . . . Who cold is . . . you who shiver . . . will freeze no more in cold morning dew . . .

MARIE   What are you saying? . . .

WOZZECK   Nought!
(*A LONG SILENCE*)
(*The moon rises*)

MARIE   How the moon rises red! . . .

WOZZECK   Like a blood-red iron . . . (*He draws a knife*)

MARIE   You shiver? (*She jumps up*) What now?

WOZZECK   No one . . . Marie . . . if not me, then . . . no one . . .

MARIE   Help!! . . .
(*Wozzeck seizes her and plunges the knife into her throat. Marie sinks down. Wozzeck bends over her. She dies.*)

WOZZECK   Dead! . . . (*He rises to his feet anxiously, and then rushes silently away*)
CURTAIN.

Wozzeck

Berg

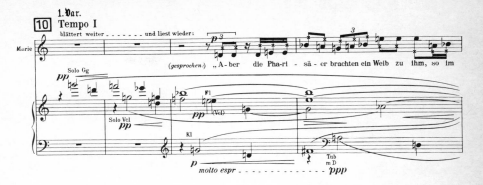

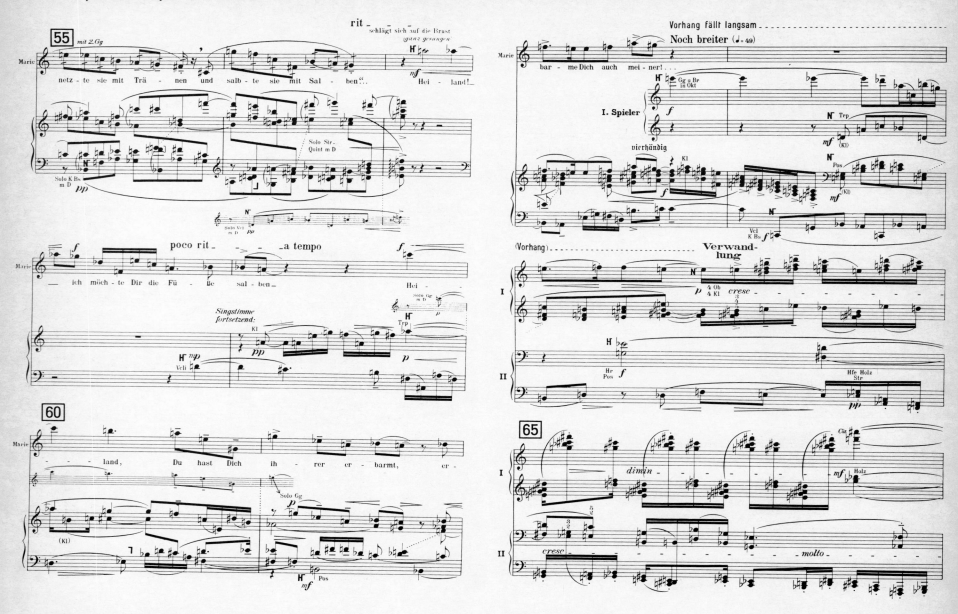

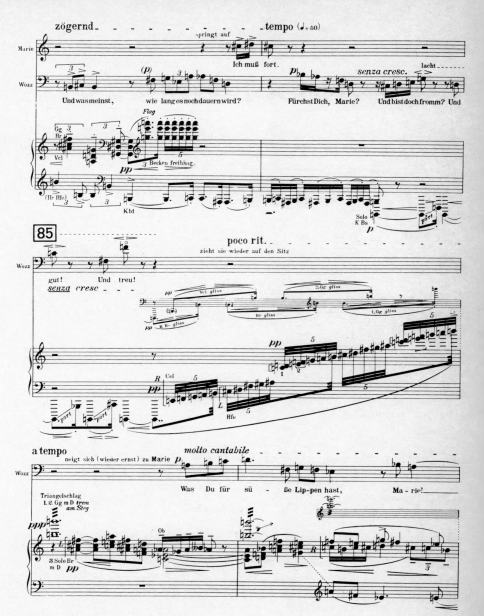

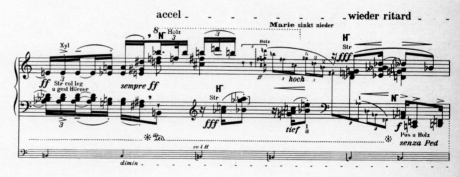

STAGE PLAY WITH MUSIC

Kurt Weill (1900–1950) and Bertold Brecht (1898–1956)
Die Dreigroschenoper "The Threepenny Opera"

The original title of this work can be translated as: *Kurt Weill, the Threepenny Opera, A Piece with music after John Gay's 'The Beggar's Opera" by Elizabeth Hauptmann. German edition by Bert Brecht.* The roles of the various persons mentioned should be clarified. You may already be familiar with Gay's opera (see vol. I, no. 62), which was first performed in London in 1728. The title implies that Elizabeth Hauptmann, assistant to the famous playwright, Bertold Brecht, produced what is called the "book." Other evidence indicates, however, that her main role was to call Brecht's attention to the work, which had achieved great success in a London revival that ran from 1920 to 1924, and to prepare a German translation for him. (Paul Hindemith's publisher had also noted its success and asked him in 1925 if he was interested in preparing a modern musical version. He was not.) Brecht had already sketched six scenes of a German version by the time a young and inexperienced Berlin producer, Ernst Robert Aufricht, early in 1928 offered him the possibility of a production. Brecht invited the composer Kurt Weill to collaborate with him. (The two were then working on a full-length opera, *The Rise and Fall of the City of Mahagonny,* which was to be completed in 1929; five numbers from it had already been performed in 1927 under the title *Mahagonny Songspiel* or *Das kleine Mahagonny.*)

Considerable confusion surrounded the preparation of *The Threepenny Opera,* which many informed people in the Berlin theater fully expected to be a failure. Aufricht, fearing that Weill's music would be inappropriate, secretly asked another musician to prepare a version of Pepusch's original score. On the very afternoon of the opening performance in 1928, when the play was still undergoing revisions, Aufricht is reported to have been asking "where he could find a new play in a hurry." [Lotte Lenya, quoted in Otto Friedrich, *Before the Deluge,* (London, 1974), p. 140]. Nor were matters much better with the actors. One of the catastrophes involved Peter Lorre, who was to have played Peachum, but who fell ill and had to be replaced. Years, later, in 1949, Weill's wife, the singer/actress Lotte Lenya, described the circumstances surrounding the composition of the opening song.

> Paulsen, vain even for an actor, insisted that his entrance as Mackie Messer [Mack the Knife] needed building up: why not a song right there, all about Mackie, getting in mention if possible of the sky-blue tie that he wanted to wear? Brecht made no comment but next morning came in with the verses for the "Moritat" of Mack the Knife and gave them to Kurt to set to music. This currently popular number, often called the most famous tune written in Europe during the past half century, was modeled after the *Moritaten* ("Mord" meaning murder, "tat" meaning deed) sung by singers at street fairs, detailing the hideous crimes of notorious arch-fiends. Kurt not only produced the tune overnight, he knew the name of the hand-organ manufacturer—Zucco Maggio—who could supply the organ on which to grind out the tune for the prologue. [Lotte Lenya, introduction to English language edition of the libretto (New York, 1949). Originally published in *Theatre Arts* as "That was a Time."]

The play was an immediate success throughout Germany, enjoying some 42,000 performances in a single year. Though banned by the Nazis in 1932, it soon enjoyed success in other countries. (The first of several successful postwar productions in New York, off-Broadway in 1954, ran for 2,707 performances.) Because of a number of differences, both political and aesthetic, Weill and Brecht parted ways in 1930. Political realities soon forced them both to leave Germany. Weill, a Jew, moved to New York and to success in the world of the Broadway musical, never again writing art music. Brecht, who had become an ardent Marxist in 1930, also ended up in this country during the Second World War, returning to East Berlin in 1948 to great acclaim as both playwright and director.

Brecht and Weill adopted Gay's format: a play with interpolated songs that interrupt the action from time to time. Weill said of the format, "We deliberately stopped the action during the songs which were written to illustrate the 'philosophy,' the inner meaning of the play." [Ronald Sanders, *The Days Grow Short* (New York, 1980) p. 359] This, of course, is the format of the typical Broadway musical. Brecht transferred the setting of Gay's play to Soho, a district in London, in the early nineteenth century, and bettered Gay's absurdly contrived happy ending, a parody of eighteenth century opera seria, by having MacHeath pardoned, ennobled, and pensioned by the newly crowned Queen Victoria.

Weill's choice for his musical style, towards which he had been moving even before his collaboration with Brecht began, was roughly analogous to Gay's, which was the popular music of his time. In Weill's case this meant the jazz-influenced style then heard in the Berlin cabaret, an institution that had developed in postwar Berlin from French models and which was a center for intellectuals and hence for liberal political and social ideas. The reasons for this choice are not hard to find; at about this time Weill is reported to have said, "I am not struggling for new forms or new theories, I am struggling for a new public." [Hans Heinzheimer, *Fanfare for Two Pigeons* (New York, 1954), p. 177] For a longtime believer in the social purpose of the arts, like many artists in the Weimar Republic, such a choice would seem inevitable. In 1926 Weill further justified his turning to the jazz-based style then employed in dance music.

> Some parts of dance music so completely define the spirit of the age that they could exert a lasting influence over a specific part of 'art music'. . . . Unlike art music, dance music reproduces nothing of the perceptions of the exceptional individual who stands above his times; instead it mirrors the instinct of the masses. And a glance into any of the dance halls of any continent shows that jazz is as precisely the external expression of our time as was the waltz of the nineteenth century. [Kurt Weill, *Ausgewählte Schriften*, ed. David Drew (Frankfurt, 1975), pp. 132–3.]

Three years later he was to say:

> Jazz appears, within a time when artistry is increasing, a piece of nature, as the most healthy and powerful expression of an art which, because of its popular origins, has immediately become an international folk music of the broadest possible consequences. Why should art-music isolate itself from such an influence? [*Ibid*, pp. 132–33.]

It is no surprise, therefore, that Weill wrote for the kind of voice heard in the cabaret, rather than for those heard in the opera house, and that, like many of his works, *The Threepenny Opera* is scored for the kind and size of heterogenous ensemble that passed for a jazz band in the Berlin cabaret or hotel of his time—though he clearly understood the difference between pure jazz and popular music that had adopted some of its mannerisms. He requires eleven players, who were to be placed on the stage, in full view of the audience, rather than in the customary orchestra pit. Most doubled on several of the following instruments: soprano, alto, tenor, and baritone saxophones; flute; clarinet; bassoon; two trumpets; trombone; percussion; piano; harmonium or reed organ; celesta; accordion; cello; bass; banjo; guitar; and Hawaiian guitar (not electrified).

Weill's overture is roughly modeled after the French overture as composed by Pepusch for Gay's play. Though Weill does not differentiate the sections sharply in tempo, there are the customary opening and closing homorhythmic passages, pompous in character, that surround a central fugue.

The "Ballad of Mack the Knife" that follows is a memorable piece of writing whose surface simplicity hides an ingenious and carefully contrived structure. It has a sixteen-measure melody whose range is less than an octave. (Weill, it will be remembered, had the untrained singer in mind.) Weill had the audacity to repeat the melody seven times (though the number of times varies widely on different recordings). Variety is achieved not only through the changing text but, more important musically, through varied accompaniments for most of the repetitions. These comprise changes in rhythm, a dialogue between voice and instruments that begins at measure 49, and chromatic slides from measure 65. (An interesting performance tradition has appeared among small combos that play this piece in clubs or bars. Typically having fewer instruments than Weill's ensemble, and hence less possibilities for the changes in color that he relied on to generate a sense of growing excitement, these combos employ changes in key for the same purpose; successive repetitions of the melody are each performed a half-step higher.) Although Weill indicates "Blues-Tempo" for this song, the harmonic structure of the blues is not present.

The *Morgenchoral des Peachum* ("Peachum's Morning Hymn") that follows contains the only musical quotation from Gay's opera. Since it appears as the first air in the earlier work, "Through all the employments of life," where it is also sung by Peachum, and since, as we have seen, "Mack the Knife" was added at the last minute, it would appear that Weill's initial intention was to show by musical means at the outset the close bonds between the two works. Brecht's text is just as cynical as Gay's. In fact, Brecht's libretto is, on the whole, even more biting and critical of society than Gay's, and reflects the deep despair that lay beneath the surface glitter of Berlin in the 1920s.

The final two numbers here, the "Instead-of Song" and the "Wedding Song for Poor People," further demonstrate Weill's propensity for imaginative accompaniments that serve as a foil for his simple vocal lines, often beginning in a banal manner only to veer off in unexpected ways.

Recordings: Columbia 021 257, Kurt Weill: *Die Dreigroschenoper*; Odyssey Y2 32977, Kurt Weill: *Die Dreigroschenoper*; Telefunken HT 23, *Kurt Weill: Die Dreigroschenoper* (excerpts from the German recording of 1930); Columbia, 798 Kurt Weill: *The Threepenny Opera* (Joseph Papp production of 1976 in New York); MGM SE 31201C, Kurt Weill: *The Threepenny Opera* (Marc Blitzstein adaptation of 1954 for New York).

Translation:

OVERTURE
Streetsinger [*spoken*]:

You are about to hear an opera for beggars.
And since this opera was conceived with so
     much splendor
As only beggars can imagine it—
and since nonetheless it was to be so cheap,
that even beggars can pay for it,
it is called the Threepenny Opera.
First you will hear a penny-dreadful ballad
about the bandit Macheath, called Mack the
Knife.

ACT I

A Fair in Soho. The beggars are begging, the thieves are thieving, the prostitutes are prostituting themselves. A penny-dreadful ballad singer is singing a penny-dreadful ballad.

THE BALLAD OF MACK THE KNIFE

Streetsinger:

And the shark has teeth
And he wears them in his face
And Macheath, he has a knife,
But the knife one does not see.

Oh, the shark's fins appear
Red, when he spills blood.
Mack the Knife, he wears his gloves
On which his crimes leave not a trace.

On a nice, clear-skied Sunday
A dead man lies on the beach
And a man sneaks round the corner
Whom they all call Mack the Knife.

And Schmul Meier disappeared for good
And many a rich man
And Mack the Knife has all his money,
Though you cannot prove a thing.

*Mr. Peachum, together with his wife and daughter, all out for a walk, cross the
    stage from left to right.*

Jenny Towler was found
With a knife stuck in her chest;
At the docks Macheath is walking
Who doesn't know a single thing.

And in Soho, the great fire
Did in seven kids and one old man—
In the crowd's Mack the Knife, who
Isn't quizzed and knows nothing at all.

And the widow, still a minor,
Whose name is known to all
Woke up and got raped;
Mack, what was the price to pay?
Woke up and got raped;
Mack, what was the price to pay?

*There is a burst of laughter among the prostitutes. A man [Mack the Knife]
    detaches himself from their group and quickly crosses the entire length of the
    fair ground.*

Streetsinger [*spoken*]:

Jonathan Jeremiah Peachum has opened a store, in which the most
    miserable of the miserable could assume the type of appearance
    which appealed to the more and more calloused hearts.

The wardrobe room of Jonathan Jeremiah Peachum's beggars' supply store.

MR. PEACHUM'S MORNING HYMN

Peachum:

Wake up, you rotten Christian!
Begin your sinful life!
Show what a rascal you are;
The Lord will settle your score in the end.

Sell out your brother, you rogue!
Auction off your wife, you scoundrel!
The good lord, to you he is nothing but air?
He'll show you on the Last Judgment Day!

Streetsinger [*spoken*]:

Polly Peachum hasn't come home.
Mr. and Mrs. Peachum sing the
INSTEAD-OF SONG

1
[**Peachum, Mrs. Peachum:**]

Instead of,
Instead of
That they stay at home and in their cozy beds,
They must have fun, they must have fun,
Just as though they were something special.

Mrs. Peachum:

That is that moon over Soho
That is that damn "Do-you-feel-my-heart-beating" theme.
That is that "If you go somewhere, I'll go there too, Johnny!"
When love's beginning and the moon still is on the rise.

2
Peachum:

Instead of,
Instead of
That they would do something with some sense and purpose,
They have fun,
They have fun
And then naturally go to pot in the gutter.

Both:

What then is the use of your moon over Soho?
What then happens to their damned "Do-you-feel-my-heart-beating"
    theme?
Where is then that "If you go somewhere, I'll go there too, Johnny!"
When love's beginning and the moon still is on the rise.

Streetsinger [*spoken*]:

Deep in the heart of Soho the bandit Mack the Knife celebrates his
    wedding to Polly Peachum, daughter of the king of the beggars.

*The members of the gang rise and sing hesitatingly, feebly, and unsure of
    themselves:*

WEDDING SONG FOR POOR PEOPLE

Chorus:

Bill Lawgen and Mary Syer
Last Wednesday man and wife became.
Three cheers for them, hurrah, hurrah, hurrah!
When they stood before the registrar,
He did not know where she got her bridal dress

But she was not too sure about his name.
Hurrah!
Do you know what your wife is up to? No!
Have you abandoned your life of vice? No!
Three cheers for them, hurrah, hurrah, hurrah!
Just recently Bill Lawgen said to me:
I'm satisfied with a little part of her!
The swine!
Hurrah!

Die Dreigroschenoper   **Weill and Brecht**

Nr. 1. OVERTURE

Nr. 2. MORITAT VOM MACKIE MESSER
(Ausrufer)

Nr. 3. MORGENCHORAL DES PEACHUM

(Die Melodie dieser Nummer wurde als einzige der alten „Beggar's Opera" entnommen)

*) Von hier ab singt Frau Peachum aus dem Nebenzimmer heraus mit

Nr. 4 ANSTATT DASS-SONG
(Peachum, Frau Peachum)

Nr. 5. HOCHZEITS-LIED
(zuerst a cappella gesungen, verlegen und langweilig.)
(Später eventuell in dieser Fassung.)

130 and 131

SONGS WITH PIANO ACCOMPANIMENT

Charles Ives (1874-1954)
The Cage and *Charlie Rutlage*

Charles Ives is undoubtedly the most fascinating and complex figure in the history of American music. Music historians, cultural historians, and now "psychohistorians" have all taken a stab at explaining the phenomenon of a highly gifted composer who, deliberately isolating himself as a composer, produced music of striking originality that either anticipated or coincided with stylistic advances in European music, while at the same time pursuing a successful career as an insurance executive that was to bring him great wealth. (During his lifetime, few colleagues in the insurance business, where he is remembered even today for a training pamphlet he wrote entitled *The Amount to Carry,* knew of his other career as a composer.)

Ive's music reflects both the complexity of his personality and a fearless delight in sonic experiments that he inherited from his father, a trained musician who was conductor of the town band in Danbury, Connecticut, and who, exhorting his son to "stretch his ears," introduced him to such ideas as singing or playing in two keys at once. Trained as an organist, Ives held church positions as a youngster in Danbury and New Haven, and after he had settled in New York City following his graduation from Yale in 1898 he held a similar position for several years in Bloomfield, New Jersey and in one of the New York City churches. Although he studied composition while at Yale, and wrote over forty compositions as an undergraduate, it is clear that the German-trained professor of composition, Horatio Parker, from whom Ives appears to have received good though coventional training, had as little sympathy with what Ives was about as did his more "musical" classmates. Hence, conforming outwardly to society while fiercely maintaining his musical integrity inwardly, Ives chose a career in business, relegating composition to weekends. In the years between 1906 and 1918 he wrote a prodigious amount of music under such circumstances, all but ceasing to compose in the latter year only because of deteriorating health. Given the originality of Ives's music and the musical climate of the time in this country, it is no surprise that little of his music was published or performed before 1939, when he was sixty-five. Earlier, in 1922, with encouragement and at his own expense, he had privately published a collection of songs, sending copies to many prominent musicians as well as simply giving them to anyone who asked. It is from this published collection, *114 Songs,* that our two examples come.

The *114 Songs* contains an amazing range of songs, among them sacred songs, sentimental songs, and war songs, both youthful and mature. Ives included at the end a Postface that is revelatory of his mixed feeling concerning the publication. A few sentences will give a hint of its flavor and of his characteristically cryptic prose style.

The printing of this collection was undertaken primarily, in order to have a few clear copies that could be sent to friends who, from time to time, have been interested enough to ask for copies of some of the songs; but the job has grown into something different,—it contains plenty of songs which have not been and will not be asked for. It stands now, if it stands for anything, as a kind of "buffer state,"—an opportunity for evading a question, somewhat embarrassing to answer,—"Why do you write so much—,which no one ever sees?"

If a fiddler or poet does nothing all day long but enjoy the luxury and drudgery of fiddling or dreaming, with or without meals, does he or does he not, for this reason, have anything valuable to express? . . .

This is a question which each man must answer for himself. It depends to a great extent, on what a man nails up on his dashboard as "valuable." Does not the sinking back into the soft state of mind (or possible non state of mind) that may accept "art for arts sake," tend to shrink rather than toughen up the hitting muscles,—and incidentally those of the umpire or the grandstand, if there be one? To quote from a book that is not read:—"Is not beauty in music too often confused with something which lets the ears lie back in an easy-chair? . . . Possibly the fondness for personal expression . . . may throw out a skin-deep arrangement, which is readily accepted at first as beautiful—formulae that weaken rather than toughen the musical muscles. If a composer's conception of his art, its functions and ideals, even if sincere, coincide to such an extent with these groove-colored permutations of tried-out progressions in expediency, so that he can arrange then over and over again to his delight—has he or has he not been drugged with an overdose of habit-forming sounds?

That Ives did not wish to "let the ears lie back in an easy chair" is readily apparent in the short song, "The Cage," composed in 1906. Like many of his works, it was adapted from an earlier work, in this case a *Set for Cham-*

ber Orchestra, where it was initially entitled "In the Cage." Ives's recollections in 1931 concerning its origins were as follows:

> [*In the Cage*] is a result of taking a walk one hot summer afternoon in Central Park [New York City] with Bart Yung (one-half Oriental). . . . Sitting on a bench near the menagerie, watching the leopard's cage and a little boy (who had apparently been a long time watching the leopard)—this aroused Bart's Oriental fatalism—hence the text in the score and in the song. Technically this piece is but a study of how chords of 4ths and 5ths may throw melodies from a set tonality.

In adapting this event as a song Ives, as was often the case, wrote his own text. The song contains an imaginative mix of tonal materials. The piano part, as Ives noted, consists of chords built on fourths and fifths, though those on fourths predominate, changing only once to chords on fifths (or to chords on other intervals, but never simply thirds) for the sake of textual emphasis. The vocal line, on the other hand, goes its own way, uncompromisingly, using both forms of the whole-tone scale (see no. 119) as well as the diatonic scale; changes from one to another scale have again been determined by the text. This combination of materials, as Ives suggests, results in a song that lacks any clear tonal center, and anticipates by some three years related developments in the so-called atonal music of Schoenberg (see no. 123). There is also a clear sense of return, which can again be justified on textual grounds. Since the song is essentially unbarred, the usual role on accidental holdings throughout a measure cannot be observed, as Ives makes clear in a footnote.

Though Ives never composed any song cycles, he did on several occasions consider grouping a number of his songs into sets. "Charlie Rutlage" is one of these. The title he had in mind for this particular set was *The Other Side of Pioneering,* the other songs in the set being "The New River, "The Indians," and "Ann Street." Ives took his text, by D. J. "Kid" O'Malley, from a 1920 printing of *Cowboy Songs and other Frontier Ballads,* collected by John Lomax. He finished the song in 1921.

Ives frequently quoted hymn tunes, patriotic songs, and other popular melodies of his time in his music, whether vocal or instrumental. Though often literal, these quotations could become distorted as the occasion warranted, whether for humorous or macabre purposes. One such quote is included in "Charlie Rutlage." Ives's setting of the ballad starts out in a straightforward manner, the only clue of what is to come being the somewhat unusual bass line in the piano and the rhythmic jolt in the voice part at the end of measure 4, obviously introduced for the sake of textual

emphasis. The rustic quality of the text is further enhanced by the occasional "wrong notes" in the bass in measures 7 through 9. Ives's emphasis on the word "tough" involves a brief harmonic excursion outside B-flat, the key then established. The character of the setting changes radically in measure 21 as the ballad begins to describe Charlie's fate. Ives calls for the singer to move from a "half spoken" manner to out-and-out recitation. The piano part, meanwhile, has become much more subtle. The basic meter in the left hand remains 5/8 in measures 21 through 29 while the right hand, initially in the same meter, changes to 4/4 in measure 25, as Ives quotes from a known tune, indicating the text above the part. Though he retains the rhythm of this tune in a subsequent repetition, the tune itself has been markedly changed. As the climax of the tale nears, Ives increases tempo, dynamics, and the dissonance in the piano part, resorting finally to tone clusters that are to be delivered by the fist (m.39). His intent in this passage is clear from the footnote. A return to the opening rounds out the song. It will be noted that Ives does not observe tonal unity here.

It would be a mistake to think that the attention given to Ives today is simply a matter of recognizing one who was "ahead of his time." His music has an expressiveness and genuineness that has gained for the composer the highest respect of audiences and critics alike.

"Charlie Rutlage" was one of seven songs by Ives performed at the First Festival of American Music held at Yaddo in Saratoga Springs, New York, in 1932. Its performance, by baritone Hubert Linscott and pianist Aaron Copland, made such an impression on the audience that it had to be repeated.

The Cage

(1906)

evenly and mechanically,
no ritard., decresc., accel. etc.

(repeat 2 or 3 times)

f A leop-ard went a-round his cage from one side

back to the oth-er side; he stopped on-ly when the keep-er came a-round with meat;

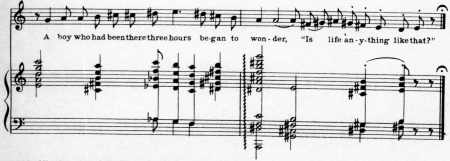

A boy who had been there three hours be-gan to won-der, "Is life an-y-thing like that?"

NOTE:- All notes not marked with sharp or flat are natural.

10
Charlie Rutlage
(from Cowboy Songs)

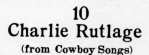

mp

An-oth-er good cow-punch-er has gone to meet his fate, I hope

(In moderate time)

mp

he'll find a rest-ing place, with-in the gol-den gate, the gol-den gate. An-

oth-er place is va-cant on the ranch of the X I T, 'Twill be hard to find an-oth-er that's

liked as well as he. The first that died was Kid White, a man both tough and

mf   *f*

horse the creature spied   and turned and   fell with him,   beneath poor Charlie died,_____ His

*fists
8va lower slower
r.h.
l.h.

as in the beginning

relations in Texas his face never more will see, But I ____ hope he'll meet his loved ones beyond in eterni-ty, in

about the time at the beginning

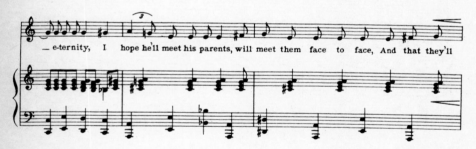

─ e-ternity,   I   hope he'll meet his parents, will meet them face to face, And that they'll

grasp him by the right hand   at   the shining throne, the shin - ing throne, the shining throne of grace.

*In these measures, the notes are indicated only approximately; the time of course, is the main point.

=132=

WORK FOR CHORUS AND ORCHESTRA

Igor Stravinsky (1882–1971)
Symphony of Psalms: movement 2

Stravinsky was one of four composers commissioned in 1929 by Serge Koussevitsky, conductor of the Boston Symphony Orchestra, to write a symphonic work for the orchestra's fiftieth anniversary in 1930. (For another work that owes its existence to a commission from Koussevitsky, see no. 125.) The other three composers, Serge Prokofiev, Arthur Honegger, and Albert Roussel, all produced symphonies. So, too, did Stravinsky, but of a unique sort. His was a work for chorus and orchestra, which he possibly called a symphony merely because of the nature of his commission. Three factors probably played a part in Stravinsky's decision to write such a work. One was his expressed intent at the time to write "a work of considerable scope." Another was his lack of sympathy at the time with the symphonic tradition; it was not until 1939 that he was to return to a form that he had not cultivated since his days as a student of Rimsky-Korsakov, since 1907, in fact. A third was a spiritual crisis that he appears to have undergone in the mid-1920s, which was to result in his return to the Russian Orthodox faith in 1926. This return had already led him to compose three Slavonic sacred choruses by the time he received Koussevitsky's commission. Some years later, Stravinsky was to say that he began to compose the *Symphony of Psalms* in Slavonic, only later shifting to the Latin of the Vulgate that appears in the finished work. (The Vulgate, the bible of the Roman Catholic Church, is the Latin translation prepared by St. Jerome in the fourth century; the term *Vulgate* derives from the Latin *vulgus*, the common people, and indicates Jerome's intent to make biblical texts available to anyone in his time who could read Latin.) Stravinsky's dedication is unique: "This Symphony, composed to the glory of GOD, is dedicated to the Boston Symphony on the occasion of the fiftieth anniversary of its existence."

Stravinsky's later recollections as to the reasons for realizing the commission as he did, and how he proceeded, are also revealing of the man:

The commissioning of the *Symphony of Psalms* began with the publisher's routine suggestion that I write something popular. I took the word, not in the publisher's meaning of "adapting to the understanding of the people," but in the sense of "something universally admired," and I even chose Psalm 150 in part for its popularity, though another and equally compelling reason was my eagerness to counter the many composers who had abused these magisterial verses as pegs for their own lyrico-sentimental "feelings." The Psalms are poems of exaltation, but also of anger and judgment, and even of curses. . . . My publisher had requested an orchestral piece without chorus, but I had had the psalm symphony idea in mind for some time, and that is what I insisted on composing. [Igor Stravinsky & Robert Craft, *Dialogues and a Diary* (Garden City, 1963), p. 76]

My idea was that my symphony should be a work with great contrapuntal development, and for that it was necessary to increase the means at my disposal. I finally decided on a choral and instrumental ensemble in which the two elements should be on an equal footing, neither of them outweighing the other. In this instance my point of view as to the mutual relationship of the vocal and instrumental sections coincided with that of the masters of contrapuntal music, who also treated them as equals, and neither reduced the role of the choruses to that of homophonic chant nor the function of the instrumental ensemble to that of an accompaniment.

I sought for my words, since they were to be sung, among those which had been written for singing. And quite naturally my first idea was to have recourse to the Psalms. [Igor Stravinsky, *An Autobiography,* (New York, 1936) p. 254–5]

The juxtaposition of the three psalms is not fortuitous. The prayer of the sinner for divine pity (prelude), the recognition of grace received (double fugue), and the hymn of praise and glory are the basis of an evolutionary plan. The order of the three movements presupposes a periodic scheme and in this sense realizes a 'symphony.' For a periodic scheme is what distinguished a 'symphony' from a collection of pieces with no scheme but one of succession, as in a suite. [Igor Stravinsky, quoted by Phillip Ramey on Columbia M 34551]

My first sound-image was of an all-male chorus and *orchestre d'harmonie* [i.e., wind instruments alone]. I thought, for a moment, of the organ, but I dislike the organ's *legato sostenuto* and its mess of octaves, as well as the fact that the monster never breathes. The breathing of wind instruments is one of their primary attractions for me. [*Dialogues,* 79]

Though I chose Psalm 150 first, and though my first musical idea was the . . . rhythmic figure in that movement, I could not compose the beginning of it until I had written the second movement. Psalm 40 is a prayer that a new canticle may be put in our mouths. The Allelujah is that canticle. . . . One hopes to worship God with a little art if one has any, and if one hasn't, and cannot recognize it in others, then one can at least burn a little incense. [*Dialogues* p. 78]

As can be seen from Stravinsky's comments, this is a very different work from his *Rite of Spring* (see no. 127), which is the most famous piece from his so-called Russian period. The *Symphony* is an example of what has been called his Neoclassic style in that he sought models, as he said, in earlier music, in this case the contrapuntal composers of the Baroque era.

(He had been employing this manner since 1920, and was to surprise the musical world in 1952 by changing manners again, now adopting serial technique.)

The twenty-three-minute piece, which has been characterized as a work of "austere grandeur and profound religious conviction," comprises settings of three psalms that are to be performed without break. For the first performance, in Brussels, subtitles were attached to the movements— Prelude, Double Fugue, and Allegro symphonique—but these were to be dropped before the work was published.

Stravinsky's abhorrence of what he saw as the excesses of Romantic music crop up several times in his remarks. It is reflected in his insistence that the *Symphony* be performed only in Latin, a "dead" language whose sole overtones were that of ritual, never of personal expression. It is also reflected in his choice of performing resources in the present work. In order to avoid any suggestion of Romantic "expressiveness" he suggests in the score that, if possible, the pure tone of children's voices be used rather than the warmer sound of women's voices for both soprano and alto. A similar concern is evident in his choice of instruments. Violins, violas, and the "modern" clarinet are conspicuously absent. In their stead are what he considered to be the more objective sounds produced by five flutes (one of which doubles on piccolo), four oboes, English horn, three bassoons, contrabassoon, four horns, *tromba piccola* in D, four trumpets, two tenor trombones, bass trombone, tuba, timpani, bass drum, harp, two pianos, cellos, and contrabasses.

We present here the second movement, based on Psalm 40 from the Vulgate. Its textual relationship to the preceding and following movements has already been mentioned, as has the fact that it is a double fugue. Though this term is, unfortunately, used loosely, it always denotes a fugue with two subjects. Here there is one for the instruments (m. 1), another for the voices (m. 29). Stravinsky explains that the source of the first subject is an ostinato figure in the first movement (m. 41) comprising a sequence of interlinked thirds in the order minor-major-minor. Using the principle of octave equivalence (see no. 124), he has transposed the third note up an octave, transforming the last two intervals into sixths, minor followed by major. (A very similar musical idea is encountered in the movement entitled "Eccentric" in his *Four Studies for Orchestra* [1928].) Since the final movement of the *Symphony* contains the same play of major and minor thirds in measures 4 through 8, it is clear that this was Stravinsky's means of binding the three together musically.

We leave it to the reader to examine the structure of the movement, taking into account the roles of both chorus and orchestra. We note only that the instrumental fugue is clearly anchored in C minor (though not by means of functional harmony), that Stravinsky uses a countersubject (mm. 6–9), and that he employs exclusively treble sonorities that contrast with the bass sonorities to be presented in the ensuing choral fugue. Stravinsky commented that it was a challenge to compose a four-voice fugue using only treble sonorities. It is also a challenge, however, to his performers, who must achieve a balance even when the third flute is playing in its lowest and weakest register (mm. 13–17) against the more assertive oboe that is sounding above it. We further note that the ensuing choral fugue is anchored in E-flat minor (again not by eighteenth-century means), and that three other procedures common to the eighteenth-century fugue are also present here: episodes, augmentation, and stretto, the latter in both instrumental and vocal fugues. A closing section (m. 71ff.), in which the chorus declaims in a homorhythmic texture the final verse of the psalm while the instruments present their subject in stretto at the outset, serves not only as an effective climax to the movement but also as a fitting preparation for the final movement, a monumental hymn of praise. It has clearly been patterned on Handel's common manner of ending fugal movements.

Source: © Copyright 1931 by Edition Russe de Musique; Renewed 1958. Copyright and Renewal assigned to Boosey & Hawkes, Inc. Revised Edition Copyright by Boosey & Hawkes, Inc.; Renewed 1975. Reprinted by permission.

Recordings: Numerous available.

Translation:

> I waited patiently for the Lord:
> and He inclined to me and heard my cry.
>
> He brought me up also out of an horrible pit,
> out of the miry clay, and set my feet upon a rock,
> and established my goings.
>
> And He hath put a new song in my mouth,
> even praise unto our God;
> Many shall see it, and fear,
> and shall trust in the Lord.
>
> —Psalm 39, 2–4 (Vulgate)
> —Psalm 40, 1–3 (King James)

Symphony of Psalms   **Stravinsky**

═══133═══

UNACCOMPANIED CHORUS

Krzysztof Penderecki (b. 1933)
Stabat Mater

Since the Second World War Poland has been in the vanguard among Soviet bloc countries in new developments in music. Among Polish composers to achieve international standing have been Witold Lutoslawski, Tadeusz Baird, and Krzysztof Penderecki. Penderecki, who has taught composition at Yale, has thus far produced a wide variety of works including operas and film scores, orchestral and chamber works, and a sizable number of works for chorus, many of them sacred and using texts from the Roman rite. The latter include the *Passion According to St. Luke, Dies Irae, Te Deum*, and *Stabat Mater*. The last, under consideration here, was composed in 1962. It takes as its text the highly emotional thirteenth-century sequence and hymn that describes Mary's grief at her only son's crucifixion and contains a petition for her assistance. This text is used today as the Office Hymn on the Friday after Passion Sunday (the Sunday before Palm Sunday), and for the Feast of the Seven Dolours (Seven Sorrows) of Mary on 15 September, though Penderecki surely had in mind a broader use for the work than simply these two liturgical situations. Penderecki has not set the entire text, however, choosing only six of the hymn's twenty stanzas, as can be seen from the translation included below.

In *Stabat Mater* we encounter our first evidence of the expansion of available sonorities in choral writing, and in the context of spatial sound. Penderecki has written a piece for three choirs that sometimes play off one another and at other times combine for stunning mass effects. Furthermore, he will often employ a rich texture that uses only some of the voice parts in each chorus. And on one occasion (m. 86) the choirs are expected to divide into forty-eight different parts, each with a different pitch. As for the kinds of sounds the singers are to produce in addition to their normal voices, the tenors are called on to use falsetto (m. 29), and the chorus as a whole employs a *quasi recitando* style in which singers half speak and half

sing (m. 37). Penderecki also has the chorus whisper (m. 52)—an effect that comes across better in a live performance than on a recording—and employs two passages of choral recitation (mm. 87 and 89). But perhaps the most unusual new effect is the use of sound masses, a technique that was foreshadowed in the block chords in Stravinsky's *Rite* (see no. 127), and in the later tone clusters of Henry Cowell and Edgard Varèse. On several occasions he builds up blocks of sound that comprise adjacent semitones. For example, the low A in the basses near the beginning is soon reinforced by the altos at the octave (m. 15) and then considerably clouded by one of these clusters in the basses (m. 16) and even further clouded by the tenors shortly thereafter (m. 20). (A similar effect is employed at the end of the piece, from measure 95 on.) Once (m. 85) he uses what is called a **panchromatic** chord since it includes all twelve notes of the chromatic scale.

One more example of Penderecki's skillful use of sonority should be mentioned, the passages for all basses in measures 2 through 13. As is well known, the bass voice is particularly rich in upper partials. By the use of a slow tempo in which successive syllables of the text overlap, Penderecki can focus in turn on each of the vowel sounds in the text. Sometimes the *o* sound dominates, as in the word *dolorosa*, sometimes the *a* as in *Stabat Mater*. And the vowel sounds are mixed, at other times as well, giving a kaleidoscopic effect to the passage as a whole.

Penderecki's comments concerning *Threnody*, a work he composed in 1960, indicate how he conceived of a piece at the time:

> my style of composing at that time was just to draw a piece first and then look for pitch. . . . I just wanted to write music that would have an impact, a density, powerful expression, a different expression . . . I used to see the whole piece in front of me—*Threnody* is very easy to draw. First you have just the high note, then you have this repeating section, then you have this cluster going, coming—different directions from the one note, twelve, and back—using different shapes. Then there is a louder section; then there's another section, . . . Then it goes back to the same cluster technique again and the end of the piece is a big cluster. . . . [David Felder and Mark Schneider, "An Interview with Krzysztof Penderecki," *The Composer* 8, no. 1 (1977), p. 12.]

Although it may not appear so at first glance, the overall pitch plan of the piece is very carefully controlled. We have already noted the prominence of A at the outset—a prominence that is ensured by its being doubled at the octave from measure 15 and being set one dynamic level higher than most other parts. From measure 94 to the end, D is handled in a similar fashion, appearing first in the alto and shortly thereafter (m. 105) at the octave in the bass and again at a slightly higher dynamic level than the other parts. As the clusters produced by the other voices increasingly dominate the passage, this pitch is overwhelmed, but returns triumphantly in the final D-major triad. (Close examination of the voice leading into this final chord will reveal that almost every part has a leading tone, either above or below one of the notes in the final chord.)

Penderecki has created a two-part form that reinforces the text he has chosen. (The reader is invited to examine closely the relationship between text and music at any point in the piece, taking particular note of the prominence of melodic semitone figures traditionally associated with sorrow.) Each part begins with the same material, a short melody that closely resembles plainchant but has not been borrowed from either of the chants used with this text. A sense of return near the end (m. 94) has been produced by reverting to the slow, measured repeated notes of the opening bass part.

In connection with a somewhat later piece, his *Capriccio for violin and orchestra (1967),* Penderecki makes it clear that the matter of tension in a piece can for him be more important than the performance of each and every note, a remark that surely applies to the effects he wants from singers in this piece:

Sometimes when writing a group of notes in a very fast tempo, like in *Capriccio* for example, I know it is impossible to play all of them. But I did it because then I had achieved a tension in the sound. If I would have written only four or five notes, he would just do it, you know, so you would lose all the tension I have in the piece. I know this exactly. Performers ask me all the time: "Please, this is impossible." I reply that it is absolutely possible—"You will do it." Maybe the player will miss two or three of them, but there is a tension there. [*ibid,* p. 14]

In a performance of *Stabat Mater,* it is certain that tension will be present as the singers struggle not only to find their pitches but also to maintain them against the other parts.

Recordings: Wergo, 60 020, [=Muza XL 0260], *Krzysztof Penderecki.*

Translation:

 1. The grieving mother stood weeping by the cross upon which hung her son.
 5. Where is the man who would not weep to see the Mother of Christ in such agony?
 9. O mother, source of love, make me feel the depths of thy sorrow so that I may mourn with thee.
10. Make my heart burn with love for Christ my God, so that I may please him.
19. Christ, when I go hence, may I attain through Thy mother the victor's palm.
20. When my body dies, may my soul receive the glory of Paradise.

Stabat Mater   **Penderecki**

Duration: 8' 30''

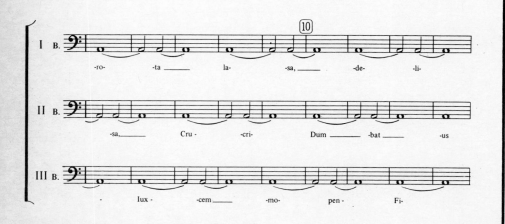

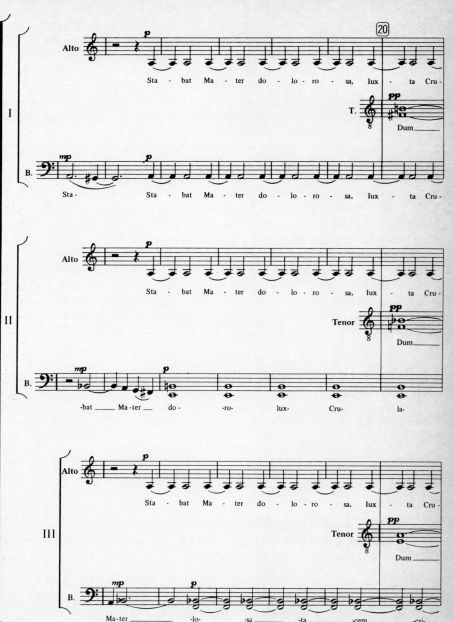

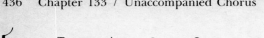

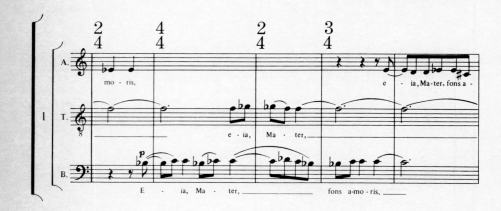

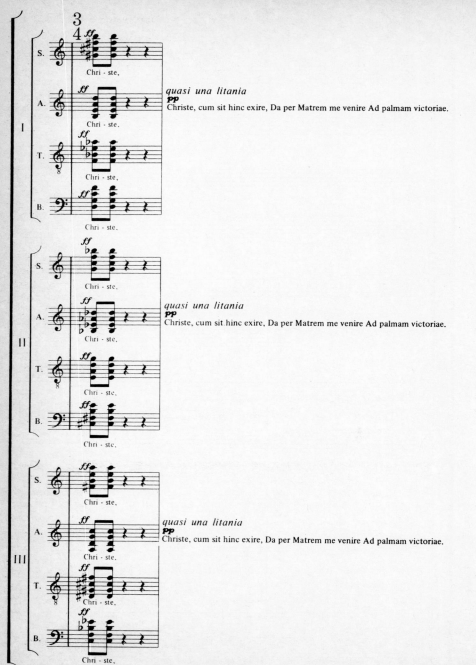

quasi una litania
pp
Christe, cum sit hinc exire, Da per Matrem me venire Ad palmam victoriae.

quasi una litania
pp
Christe, cum sit hinc exire, Da per Matrem me venire Ad palmam victoriae.

quasi una litania
pp
Christe, cum sit hinc exire, Da per Matrem me venire Ad palmam victoriae.

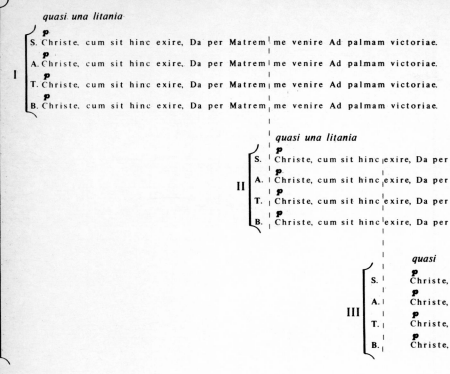

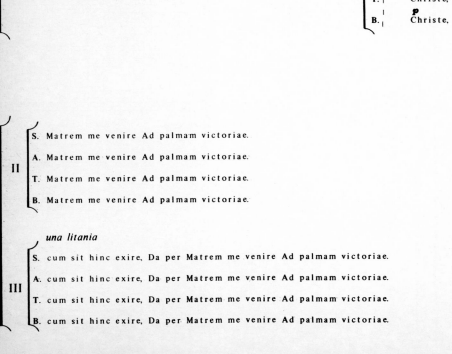

439

=134=

STRING QUARTET

Arnold Schoenberg (1874–1951)
String Quartet no. 3, op. 30: movement 1

In a previous commentary (no. 123) we discussed an earlier work by Schoenberg, noting there his abandonment of triadic harmony as a means of creating a tonic and hence of the use of tonality to create musical structure. We also considered his search for other means of giving coherence to a piece of music, which was to culminate in the years between 1918 and 1923 in the development of the twelve-tone system as he used it. We present here the opening movement of his Third String Quartet, one of his earliest large-scale works to employ the twelve-tone system. It was written in the early months of 1927 and was dedicated to Elizabeth Sprague Coolidge, an American patroness of music who was subsequently to commission Schoenberg's Fourth Quartet following his immigration to the United States in 1934.

It is said that Schoenberg used as a model for this work Schubert's famous Quartet in A minor (D. 804). Such a suggestion is intriguing since the first movement of Schubert's quartet, as of Schoenberg's, is in sonata form. The question inevitably arises: If the sonata form throughout its earlier history was always conceived of as a tonal form, how can one construct an example in which the sense of tonic is specifically negated? We shall return to this question once we have dealt with the use of the twelve-tone technique in this piece.

As we have seen (no. 124), the first step in the analysis of any twelve-tone piece is to identify the tone row. This is not always so easy as it was in the earlier piece. In the present case the row is not stated in its entry in a single instrument at the outset and must be derived from the music. (We leave it to the reader to figure out how we have established the row in the present piece. One might wish to begin by comparing the two passages beginning at measures 1 and 174, respectively.) As before (no. 124), we will again construct a matrix below that shows all possible transpositions of the row in all of its four possible forms.

	I →												
	↓												
	0	9	8	2	5	10	11	4	3	6	1	7	
P→ 0	G	E	D#	A	C	F	F#	B	A#	C#	G#	D	0
3	Bb	G	F#	C	Eb	Ab	A	D	C#	E	B	F	3
4	B	Ab	G	C#	E	A	Bb	Eb	D	F	C	F#	4
10	F	D	C#	G	Bb	Eb	E	A	G#	B	Gb	C	10
7	D	B	Bb	E	G	C	C#	F#	F	Ab	Eb	A	7
2	A	F#	F	B	D	G	G#	C#	C	Eb	Bb	E	2
1	Ab	F	E	Bb	C#	F#	G	C	B	D	A	Eb	1
8	Eb	C	B	F	G#	C#	D	G	F#	A	E	Bb	8
9	E	C#	C	F#	A	D	Eb	Ab	G	Bb	F	B	9
6	C#	A#	A	D#	F#	B	C	F	E	G	D	G#	6
11	F#	D#	D	G#	B	E	F	Bb	A	C	G	C#	11
5	C	A	G#	D	F	Bb	B	E	D#	F#	C#	G	5 ← R
	0	9	8	2	5	10	11	4	3	6	1	7	
												↑	
												RI	

Turning first to the structure of the row and the ways in which Schoenberg uses it in this movement, we note that if one divides it into six separate segments of two notes each, it consists of only three different intervals, arranged as follows: minor third, tritone, perfect fourth, perfect fourth (allowing for octave equivalence, see no. 125), minor third, tritone. It is also clear that this order of intervals will be the same in the inversion, and that both the retrograde and retrograde-inversion rearrange the order only slightly: tritone, minor third, perfect fourth, perfect fourth, tritone, minor third. A study of measures 174 through 180 will show that the cello part, which carries the melody here [it is the *Hauptstimme* (see no. 124)], has

been constructed in such a way, through changes in direction in the line, that these intervals are clearly projected (see also measures 62–68). In measures 207 through 211 all three intervals are also clearly present, while the first two dominate measures 212 through 228. Schoenberg also segments the row in other ways. One of the commonest is the grouping 5 + 2 + 5, which is clearly in evidence in measures 1 through 9, and 19 through 32, where each segment is assigned to a different instrument. Still another segmentation, also into three parts, is 4 + 4 + 4 (see the last two beats of measures 68 and 180). Though the various forms of the row appear in a number of transpositions throughout the movement, Schoenberg stresses two in particular, P-O and I-5. One or the other of these occurs at important structural points in the piece (mm. 1, 62, 94, 174, etc.)

We must now turn to what it is that allows us to define structural points in this piece. Clearly there must be other factors than the rows that determine them. If, as we have suggested, the movement is in sonata form, we are obligated to consider what justifies our use of the term. The key plan does not, although the particular form of row used might. And if Schoenberg avoids triadic harmony, how is he to signal the end of an exposition, where cadential action has always been the clue before? In fact, how can one articulate any part of the form in the absence of the cadence? Turning to the score, we note that there are a number of spots where Schoenberg calls for a ritard that is almost invariably accompanied by a momentary decrescendo and thinning out of the texture. Close examination of these spots will disclose that most are followed by some sort of change in musical action, often a new figure or manner of articulation, or a change in rhythm from long to short notes, or vice versa. Moreover, in much of the movement one senses a hierarchy in materials here that was common in Schubert: a division into melody and accompaniment. The question is, how has Schoenberg created this hierarchy, outside of merely using the term *Hauptstimme* to call attention to one of the voices? And what is it that establishes identity when one comes to thematic materials? A comparison of four passages (mm. 7–26, 62–94, 174–206, and 239–258) will disclose that each of the first two is very closely related to one of the latter two; so closely , in fact, that we can speak about thematic repetition, if one defines the term "theme" very carefully. (Both pairs should be closely examined from the standpoints of the form of the row being employed, rhythm, and texture.)

One begins to sense that rhythm is one of Schoenberg's most important means of creating structure. Several other rhythmic phenomena should be noted before we leave the piece. Though both second violin and viola establish a clear duple meter at the outset, and one senses this to be the dominant meter of the movement, there are a number of disturbances of this meter. Perhaps the most obvious is from the third beat of measure 51 through the third beat of measure 61. Here the meter is clearly five, and the texture is isorhythmic—that is, the rhythm repeats exactly though pitches change (see vol. I, no 28). It will be noted that this takes place in connection with "thematic preparation." (Other examples of isorhythm are encountered in measures 324 through 332, serving here for a closing section, and in one of the two thematic passages we identified above.) We also point out Schoenberg's device for closing the development section, this time involving both rhythm and interval. Beginning at measure 150 there are a series of two-note, six-beat figures, initially identified as *Hauptstimme*, that move through the instruments, one by one. Each successive statement expands the interval, which begins as a semitone and ends as an eighteenth(!).

Finally, one of the more interesting problems arising in connection with twelve-tone technique concerns the matter of intonation. As we have seen, our notational system was initially designed for the diatonic scale, the only scale then known. And it serves this scale well, even though there are two semitones buried in the staff that can give endless trouble to the beginner who quite naturally assumes that successive lines and spaces always indicate the same-size interval. The staff still serves quite well for the chromatic style that came increasingly into favor in the nineteenth century. But it serves not at all for music that by definition uses only the twelve pitches of the equally tempered scale. How does one indicate a note that is neither F-sharp nor G-flat, but somewhere in between? Furthermore, how does an instrumentalist such as a violinist or trumpeter play such a note if all his training has been to play in tune—that is, to make the difference between F-sharp and G-flat that is found in tonal music? (No such problem exists for the pianist, who is unable to affect intonation except by having the entire instrument retuned.)

Source: Used by permission of Belmont Music Publishers, Los Angeles, California 90049, and European American Music Distributors Corporation, agents for Universal Edition, Vienna.

Recordings: Numerous available.

String Quartet no. 3   **Schoenberg**

I

=135=

MINIMAL MUSIC

Terry Riley (b. 1935)
In C (1964)

Much American music composed in the 1950s and 1960s was concerned with pushing out all the previously accepted limits of music. On the one hand there were concerted efforts to find new sonorities, either by using existent instruments in new ways or by adopting new devices, such as the brake drum, as musical instruments. It was also during these decades that the electronic synthesizer and tape recorder emerged as new means for creating music. New ways of organizing musical materials were also sought. Improvisation, hardly new to music, played a more important role in Western music than it had since the end of the eighteenth century. In extreme cases a piece could consist of simply a graph or diagram, bereft of either pitches or rhythms, which the composer supplied the performer as a guide. Or he would supply the performer with a number of modules that could be performed in any number of orders. Indeterminacy could also play a part in the creation of either the pitch or rhythmic content of a piece, the roll of the dice often being the active agent in this case. Some witnesses to these experiments observed that if anything goes, nothing goes—that the failure to make decisions on these matters signaled the end of music as an art form. Others saw such experimentation as healthy since it forced a reexamination of our attitudes towards music and the current institutions for music-making.

Though Terry Riley's *In C* is a product of these times, and has a number of indeterminate elements, it also has clearly defined limits. Under the first heading, Riley has specified nothing about dynamics or the number or kind of instruments that are to be used. Sonority can therefore vary widely in different performances. (In this recording, by means of overdubbing, performers on eleven different instruments have produced twenty-eight parts: three vibraphones, two marimbaphones, three flutes, three oboes, two clarinets, two bassoons, three saxophones, three trumpets, three trombones, three violas, and piano.) Nor has Riley said anything about the length of the piece. This aspect of the piece resembles the music of India, wherein the typical piece has no set length and can last anywhere from sev-

eral minutes to several hours, at the will of the performers. This recording of *In C*—doubtless by design—lasts exactly forty-three minutes so that it fits nicely on two sides of an LP; like an Indian piece, it could just as easily be much shorter or much longer, though it is doubtful that one would capture most of the flavor of the piece in a performance lasting only a few minutes. What Riley has specified is the overall shape of the piece, the pitch content and rhythmic organization of individual figures and how they are to be coordinated with one another, and the order in which they must be played. The overall pitch and rhythmic organization of the piece is thus unchanging from performance to performance.

The piece demonstrates Riley's interest in the effect of organic growth brought about by extensive repetitions of short figures that are coordinated by a regular pulse, and is a seminal work that has served as a model for numerous later pieces. It consists of the fifty-three figures given in the score, each of which is to be repeated an unspecified number of times by each performer. Not notated in the score is the piano part, or Pulse, which comprises the two highest Cs on the instrument, which are repeated as even eighth notes throughout the piece. Each of the fifty-three figures is coordinated with this pulse. Since it is up to the individual performer when to move from one figure to the next, a rich tapestry of sound results as one hears as many as four or five different figures sounding at any instant. The extensive repetition of such simple figures results in a kind of minimal art that is bound to affect our ways of perceiving music. Here the first appearance of a markedly different rhythm or pitch is readily identified and assumes an importance out of all proportion to its content. For example, figures 6 and 7 stand out because of their rhythm, figure 14 because it introduces F-sharp for the first time. Riley has assured variety in a number of ways. Meter, for example, can be duple, as at the outset, or triple, as in figure 11. And since it can exist simultaneously at different levels, as in figures 29 through 31, where successive metric units comprise three half notes, a dotted whole note, and a dotted quarter, a rich rhythmic play results. Riley's choice of pitches project in turn the keys of C major, E minor, C major, and G minor. It is instructive to determine at what point in the piece he has placed the melodic high point, the nature of the figure at that point, and how he creates a sense of return following it.

Riley's purpose is revealed in an interview with Hugh Gardner that was published in *East West Journal* in 1974 and must be viewed against the background laid out in the opening paragraph above: "What I'm trying to do in my music is to fill what I see as a need. Call it a need for unity, centeredness, internal balance, whatever. I just know that I couldn't find it in the musical forms that were handed to me. It has a lot to do with how you concentrate on ideas and how these ideas unfold. My music doesn't jump around full of contrast from one idea to the next . . . but tries to let the thread unwind in the most organic way possible. I think more of that feeling and that way of thinking is what a lot of people need today."

Hearing this work is very much like viewing the earth from a high-flying airplane or space shuttle. At any instant one sees a vast and complex panorama that stretches from horizon to horizon, but as the plane or shuttle moves, the panorama constantly changes as features disappear over one horizon while new ones come into view on the other. The aural effect of Riley's piece is just as fascinating as a visual effect of this sort.

Source: Score, copyright by Terry Riley, 1964. Used by permission.

Recording: Columbia MS 7178, *Terry Riley in C.*

In C   **Riley**

=136=

ELECTRIC STRING QUARTET

George Crumb (b.1929)
Black Angels: Thirteen Images from the Dark Land,
opening three sections

In an earlier commentary (no. 135) we noted the types of experimentation found in American music of the 1950s and 1960s—experimentation that pushed to the limits all earlier notions of what music was. In a work such as *Black Angels* we witness the successful integration of a number of new techniques into what could be called the mainstream of music. What strikes one immediately about Crumb's music is its broad emotional appeal, brought about in large measure by its evocative sonorities, which have been characterized as "haunting, sweet or macabre." Some result from the use of unusual sources of sound, such as the crystal glassware used for "God-music" in *Black Angels*. Others result from new uses of conventional instruments. Among the procedures called for here are the use of contact microphones to amplify the sound to the threshold of pain at the outset, and the use of a contrabass bow on a tam-tam. Crumb often calls on the players to vocalize, in this piece asking them to whisper or shout numbers in different languages at various points. And his expressive purpose is also often served by quotations from earlier pieces. But what is most telling about Crumb's music is his ability to integrate all of these disparate styles and techniques into a cohesive and convincing whole.

Crumb has written of this work as follows:

Black Angels (Thirteen Images from the Dark Land) was conceived as a kind of parable on our troubled contemporary world. The numerous quasi-programmatic allusions in the work are therefore symbolic although the essential polarity—God versus Devil—implies more than a purely metaphysical reality. The image of the "black angel" was a conventional device used by early painters to symbolize the fallen angel.

The underlying structure of *Black Angels* is a huge arch-like design which is suspended from the three "Threnody" pieces. The work portrays a voyage of the soul. The three stages of this voyage are Departure (fall from grace), Absence (spiritual annihilation) and Return (redemption).

The numerological symbolism of *Black Angels*, while perhaps not immediately perceptible to the ear, is nonetheless quite faithfully reflected in the musical structure. These "magical" relationships are variously expressed: e.g., in terms of phrase-length, groupings of single tones, durations, patterns of repetition, etc. An important pitch element in the work—ascending D-sharp, A and E—also symbolizes the fateful numbers 7-1. At certain points in the score there occurs a kind of ritualistic counting in various languages, including German, French, Russian, Hungarian, Japanese and Swahili.

There are several allusions to tonal music in *Black Angels*: a quotation from Schubert's "Death and the Maiden" quartet (in the *Pavana Lachrymae* and also faintly echoed on the last pages of the work); an original *Sarabanda*, which is stylistically synthetic; the sustained B-major tonality of *God-Music*; and several references to the Latin sequence *Dies Irae* ("Day of Wrath"). The work abounds in conventional musical symbolisms such as the *Diabolus in Musica* (the interval of the tritone) and the *Trillo di diavolo* (the "Devil's trill" after Tartini).

The amplification of the stringed instruments in *Black Angels* is intended to produce a highly surrealistic effect. This surrealism is heightened by the use of certain unusual string effects: e.g., pedal tones (the intensely obscene sounds of the *Devil-Music*); bowing on the "wrong" side of the strings (to produce the viol-consort effect); trilling on the strings with thimble-capped fingers. The performers also play maracas, tam-tams and water-tuned crystal glasses, the latter played with the bow for the "glass harmonica" effect in *God-Music*. . . . The score is inscribed: "finished on Friday the Thirteenth, March 1970 (in tempore belli)."

We include here two diagrams that Crumb supplies with the score, one that he calls the Program, another indicates the placement of the performers on stage. We also include his extensive notes on performance, characteristic of many contemporary pieces and necessitated by the unusual sonorities Crumb requires.

It is left to the reader to determine the variety of ways in which number is manifest in this work.

Source: *Black Angels* (New York: C.F. Peters, 1971), pp. 1–4. Copyright 1971 by C.F. Peters Corporation. All rights reserved.

Recording: CRI SD 283.

Black Angels: Thirteen Images from the Dark Land   **Crumb**

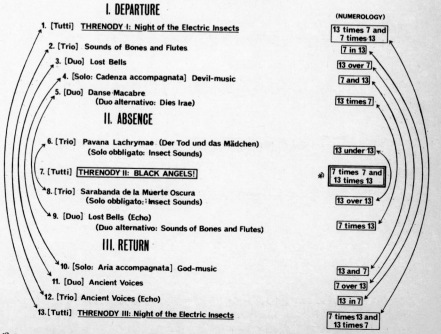

PROGRAM

I. DEPARTURE

(NUMEROLOGY)

1. [Tutti]   THRENODY I: Night of the Electric Insects — 13 times 7 and 7 times 13

2. [Trio]   Sounds of Bones and Flutes — 7 in 13

3. [Duo]   Lost Bells — 13 over 7

4. [Solo: Cadenza accompagnata]   Devil-music — 7 and 13

5. [Duo]   Danse Macabre — 13 times 7
         (Duo alternativo: Dies Irae)

II. ABSENCE

6. [Trio]   Pavana Lachrymae (Der Tod und das Mädchen) — 13 under 13
         (Solo obbligato: Insect Sounds)

7. [Tutti]   THRENODY II: BLACK ANGELS! — 7 times 7 and 13 times 13 *)

8. [Trio]   Sarabanda de la Muerte Oscura — 13 over 13
         (Solo obbligato: Insect Sounds)

9. [Duo]   Lost Bells (Echo) — 7 times 13
         (Duo alternativo: Sounds of Bones and Flutes)

III. RETURN

10. [Solo: Aria accompagnata]   God-music — 13 and 7

11. [Duo]   Ancient Voices — 7 over 13

12. [Trio]   Ancient Voices (Echo) — 13 in 7

13. [Tutti]   THRENODY III: Night of the Electric Insects — 7 times 13 and 13 times 7

*) This central motto is also the numerological basis of the entire work

PERFORMANCE NOTES

1) All players read from score.
2) Each note is preceded by an accidental, except in case(s) of an immediate repetition of a pitch or a pattern of pitches. N.B.: the tonal passages are notated in the traditional manner.
3) The amplification of the instruments is of critical importance in BLACK ANGELS. Ideally, one should use genuine electric instruments (with a built-in pick-up). Otherwise, fine-quality contact microphones can be attached (by rubber bands) to the belly of the instrument. The player should find the best position for the microphone in order to avoid distortion of the tone. If the amplifier is equipped with a reverberation control, this should be set on "high" to create a more surrealistic effect. The dynamic level should also be extremely loud (for the <u>forte</u> passages) and the level should not be adjusted during the performance.
4) The following percussion instruments and special equipment will be needed:

    a) Violin I: maraca
                    7 crystal glasses
                    solid glass rod (about 6 inches in length and 3/16 or 1/4 inch in diameter)
                    2 metal thimbles
                    metal plectrum (<u>e.g.</u> paper clip)

    b) Violin II: tam-tam (suspended), about 15 inches in diameter
                    soft beater for the tam-tam
                    contrabass bow (for bowing tam-tam)
                    7 crystal glasses
                    solid glass rod (about 6 inches in length and 3/16 or 1/4 inch in diameter)
                    2 metal thimbles
                    metal plectrum (<u>e.g.</u> paper clip)

    c) Viola: 6 crystal glasses
                    solid glass rod (about 6 inches in length and 3/16 or 1/4 inch in diameter)
                    2 metal thimbles
                    metal plectrum (<u>e.g.</u> paper clip)

    d) Cello: maraca
                    tam-tam (suspended) about 24 inches in diameter
                    soft beater for the tam-tam
                    very hard beater for the tam-tam (this should produce a percussive, metallic sound)
                    contrabass bow (for bowing tam-tam)

5) The crystal glasses (used for the "glass-harmonica" effect in <u>God-music</u>, on page 7) should be goblet-shaped (like wine glasses, with a stem). A fine grade of crystal will produce a truly beautiful effect. The glasses should be securely mounted on a board (by taping). The glasses can be tuned by adding water, although the tone loses in purity if too much water is used. The following pitches are required (N.B.: the glasses sound one octave higher than written):

6) The tam-tam harmonics are variable in pitch. The player should bow the "lip" of the tam-tam with a well-rosined contrabass bow.
7) All glissandi occupy the total duration of the note to which they are affixed. Use portamento only where indicated in the score.
8) All spoken sounds (whispering, shouting) must project! The whispered passages can be slightly voiced if the acoustics of the hall require this. The tongue clicks (in "Sounds of Bones and Flutes," on page 2) are percussive clicks off the upper palate (<u>not</u> clucking sounds).

9)   = a quarter tone higher than written pitch

            = a quarter tone lower than written pitch

            = three seconds   **5**   = five seconds

            = fermata lunga

            = normal fermata

            = slight pause or "breath"

            = extremely short pause or "breath"

    tr(½)   = trill a half step above principal note

STAGE POSITIONING

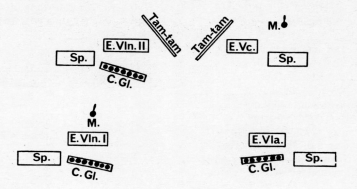

(Sp.= Speaker, C. Gl.= Crystal Glasses, M.=Maraca)

I. DEPARTURE

1. Threnody I: Night of the Electric Insects [Tutti] 13 times 7 and 7 times 13

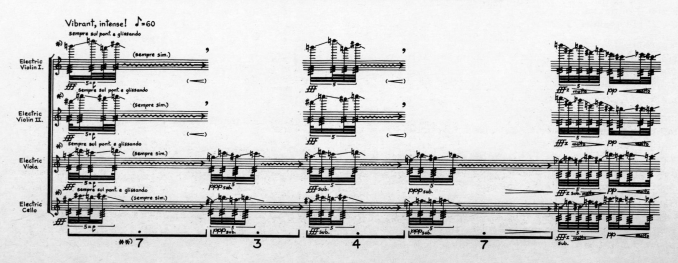

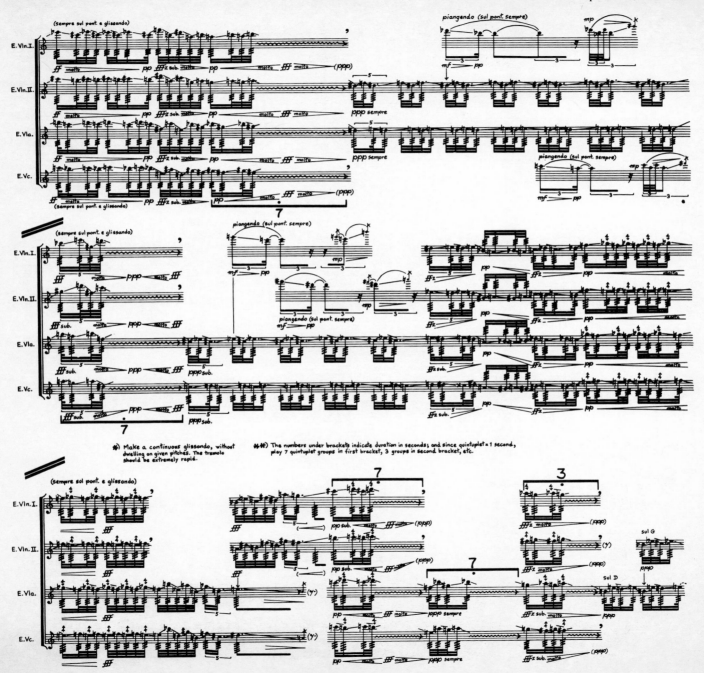

✳) Make a continuous glissando, without dwelling on given pitches. The tremolo should be extremely rapid.

✳✳) The numbers under brackets indicate duration in seconds; and since quintuplet = 1 second, play 7 quintuplet groups in first bracket, 3 groups in second bracket, etc.

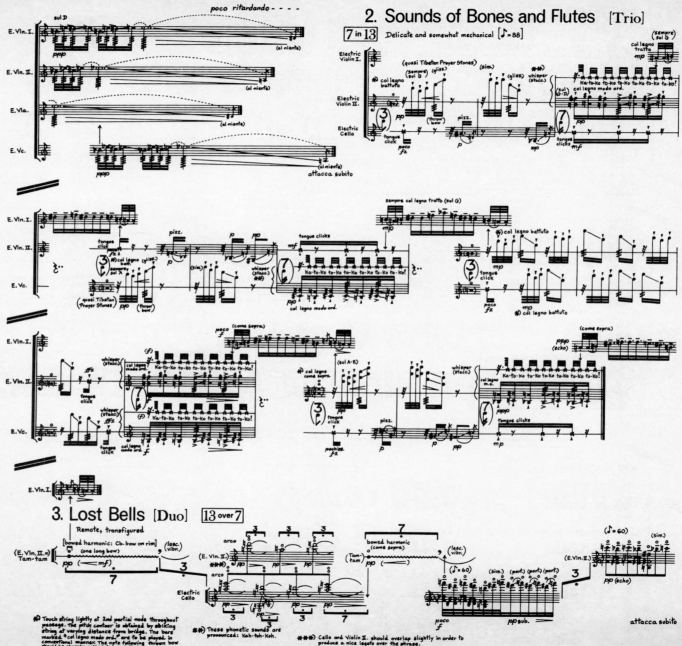

2. Sounds of Bones and Flutes [Trio]

3. Lost Bells [Duo]

INDEX OF COMPOSERS

INDEX OF TITLES AND FIRST LINES

INDEX OF MUSICAL FORMS AND GENRES